DEATH IN CORNWALL

DEATH IN CORNWALL

G.M. Malliet

SEVERN
HOUSE

First world edition published in Great Britain in 2021 and the USA in 2022
by Severn House, an imprint of Canongate Books Ltd,
14 High Street, Edinburgh EH1 1TE.

Trade paperback edition first published in Great Britain and the USA in 2022
by Severn House, an imprint of Canongate Books Ltd.

severnhouse.com

British Library Cataloguing-in-Publication Data
A CIP catalogue record for this title is available from the British Library.

ISBN-13: 978-0-7278-5038-6 (cased)
ISBN-13: 978-1-4483-0631-2 (trade paper)
ISBN-13: 978-1-4483-0630-5 (e-book)

Typeset by Palimpsest Book Production Ltd.,
Falkirk, Stirlingshire, Scotland.

This book is dedicated to John and Shirley.

And to all the frontline workers whose courage saved so many during the coronavirus pandemic. The world is forever in your debt.

ACKNOWLEDGEMENTS

Special thanks to my agent, Mark Gottlieb of Trident Media Group, and my editor, Carl Smith of Canongate/Severn House, for their excellent advice, serene guidance, and remarkable professionalism.

My thanks also to the talented Piers Tilbury, Natasha Bell, and Katherine Laidler of Canongate/Severn House.

And above all, to Bob.

CAST OF CHARACTERS

- Detective Chief Inspector Arthur St. Just of the Cambridge Constabulary.
- Portia De'Ath, specialist in criminology at the University of Cambridge, and St. Just's fiancée.
- Sybil Gosling, uncanny follower of the Wiccan way.
- The Reverend Judith Abernathy, curate at St. Cuthbert's church in Maidsfell.
- Sepia Jones, art gallery owner.
- Morwenna Wells, famous restaurateur. She owns the Michelin-starred Maiden's Arms.
- Callum Page, famous reality TV star. Is he a rival for Portia's affections?
- Clive Banner, Esq., head of the Maidsfell Village Council, tasked with arbitrating a bitter dispute over alterations to the village waterfront.
- Will Ivey, local and vocal fisherman. He wants the village's medieval harbour preserved.
- Cynthia Beck, estate agent and ardent supporter of SOS – Save Our Shore – a local preservation society opposed to the fishermen's cause.
- Lord Titus Bodwally of Revellick House, life peer used to having his way.
- Jake Trotter, proprietor of the Anchor restaurant. Lord Bodwally is his not-so-silent partner.
- Ramona Raven, née Medguistyl Buglehole, writer of romance novels.
- Constable Whitelaw, special constable and keeper of the peace in Maidsfell.
- Detective Chief Inspector Tomas Mousse of the Devon and Cornwall Constabulary. He recruits St. Just to help him solve a crime of murder.

Most arts have produced miracles, while the art of government has produced nothing but monsters

– Saint-Just, 1793

ONE
Scarecrow

Sunday

There were words for women like Sybil Gosling – words like Wiccan or Druid, or basically any spiritual alliance that fell under the pagan umbrella – but 'fey' described her best, particularly since she rejected all organized religion, even the outliers. She believed in harming no one and wishing everyone 'well and happy'. Possibly as a result, she was a bit of an outcast. She was affable for the most part, and thought to be harmless, but she marched to the beat of her own (Shamanic ritual) drum.

Sybil lived alone on the Cornish moors in a small cottage at the edge of the known British world – not far, in fact, from Land's End. She tended a vegetable garden and bartered for whatever else she needed; she knitted woollens which she sold in a shop in nearby Maidsfell to supplement her pensioner's income. When her brother died, she was alone in the world but he left her the house to live in.

She told people she was affiliated with English Heritage, an organization from which she had in fact retired some years before. Actually, it had been quietly suggested she might enjoy an early retirement with more time to spend in her garden.

At the time, the trust for the organization had been in a flurry of pandemic cutbacks anyway and so, quite unsupervised and un-authorized, Sybil had carried on her duties tending the historic Fourteen Maidens on the headland overlooking Maidsfell – duties which included shooing away teenaged (and other) lovers, keeping evergreen spindle trees and hardy shrubs trimmed and nourished so they could thrive despite cold winter winds and salt air, and collecting rubbish left behind by picnicking non-believers who did not know or care they were in a sacred and holy place.

Children laughed at 'Sybil the Scarecrow'. The fear behind this taunting pained her, for she loved children. It was the parents who were so often difficult to love, but Sybil never stopped trying. People just needed to channel their energies better and teach their children to do the same.

Her main worry was vandalism, as had occurred when ruffians spray-painted the Fourteen Maidens all colours of the rainbow. She supposed she should be grateful they'd used a washable paint, but her heart had stopped when she'd walked up the cliff path that day and seen the desecration. It had been their idea of a joke, of course. People were ignorant and lacking the imagination to know there would be repercussions. Horrid repercussions.

Another concern, and really the one that kept Sybil awake at night, was the fragility of the cliff itself. With the next heavy rain there could be a cliff fall – huge chunks of mud and stone and grass might break off, the whole site collapse and take the ancient, precious standing stones with it. That sort of thing happened all the time along the Cornish coast, but few monuments like the Fourteen Maidens had been erected atop the precarious cliffs.

A cliff fall would be a calamity not just for the Maidens but for the entire village. The church and churchyard, built on a promontory above the standing stones, was in particular danger. She had tried to warn the village council but been unable to convince the pearls-and-pumps brigade to take up the cause. Her letter to the council, so painstakingly composed, had been read aloud at the meeting. It had been met with witless mirth but no action.

Still, she could not entirely blame them for their ignorance. No one living knew the truth of the Maidens and what they guarded but Sybil herself.

She had decided it was best for now to keep it that way.

One balmy day in August, as Sybil was weeding round the stone closest to the cliff's edge, her hands froze in their task, hovering as if suspended by ropes above the sacred ground. Without knowing how she knew – Sybil never could divine where the Knowing came from – she knew there was trouble coming to the village of Maidsfell.

A very large, dark-haired man was on the way, a man at the

wheel of an oddly small red conveyance. A woman sat at his left. Sybil knew he was a good man, a just man, but trouble had sent him and his lady on their journey.

Or perhaps they were *bringing* the trouble.

Fleeting, confused images of falling bodies, of blood and fire, passed through Sybil's mind. She sat back on her haunches, trying to steady herself, only gradually able to slow her breathing.

She wouldn't know until she met the pair and took their measure. There was no doubt they were headed to Maidsfell.

But whatever brought them or why, the secrets of the Maidens must be kept at all costs.

It was Sybil's sacred trust.

TWO

On Holiday

It was the height of the summer season in Maidsfell, a village once little known, tucked away as it was on an obscure rocky coast. It had been home to miners, but when the tin mines went into a decline, many men had relocated with their families to the colonies.

The fishers, but fewer of them each year, remained.

All this was changing. Maidsfell's picturesque stone cottages, scattered haphazardly along clifftop paths with dramatic views of the Atlantic, had inspired artists for decades, but only since the Plague Time had the village become a draw for the well-to-do. If one had to shelter in place, the thinking went, one may as well do it in paradise. Even once the crisis faded, the wealthy found they quite liked the idea of somewhere to escape from it all – 'all' generally being London.

For Arthur St. Just and Portia De'Ath, an August holiday offered a rare escape from the pressures of their jobs – she a Cambridge fellow in criminology at St. Michael's College, he a detective chief inspector in the Cambridgeshire police. It was a chance for them finally to celebrate their engagement to be married, which had been delayed by one crime or crisis after another. On impulse, they'd decided against their tentative plans for Italy, lured instead by what an online advertisement described as a 'deliciously private' rental cottage overlooking Maidsfell Harbour in Cornwall.

Their wish was for peace and quiet – blissful nights, late mornings, and days filled with hiking, sunbathing, picnicking, fine dining, and sketching the local scenery (him) or taking notes for a future crime novel (her – Portia moonlighted as a well-known detective novelist). Weather forecasters had promised a few sunny days, interrupted by the usual summer storms that would turn up uninvited but just as suddenly disappear.

They had taken the train from Cambridge and rented a car at Truro station. The mid-size model St. Just had ordered online being mysteriously unavailable, they'd been given a tiny red Fiat that made the large policeman look like a circus clown at the wheel, knees jutting up to meet his elbows, nose mere inches from the windscreen. He successfully navigated them out of the crowded streets of Truro but took a wrong turning at a roundabout on the outskirts. In no time they were lost.

'Looking on the bright side,' said Portia, as he again aimed the car towards what he hoped was Maidsfell, 'a mid-size car would probably never make it through these narrow— *Sheep!*'

He stopped just in time. A flock of sheep had appeared as if dropped from the sky, a rustic-looking shepherd egging them on. St. Just and Portia could have petted the bleating animals as they passed by.

St. Just waited for the shepherd's approach before winding down his window for a word. One of the flock took this as an invitation to hop in and St. Just gently pushed its face back out, rolling up the window to a three-inch gap.

'Excuse me, sir,' said St. Just. 'How much further is it to Maidsfell?'

'From here?'

'Well, yes, I thought I might start from here.'

'Easier to start from Truro.'

'Probably so. But I need to get to Maidsfell from where I am now.'

The shepherd gave this poser some thought, scratching his wiry brown-and-grey beard, which fell nearly to mid-chest.

'Depends. If you took Fourteen Maidens Road, it would take you an hour.'

St. Just and Portia exchanged glances. They had downloaded directions from the rental website to their holiday cottage, which directions indicated they should be very near Maidsfell by now.

'An hour,' repeated St. Just. 'Is that the shortest route?'

'Depends. If you're in a tractor, you can add half an hour.'

Ah, thought St. Just. Now they were getting somewhere. He was quite certain he was not in a tractor. 'And how do I get there?'

'You can't get there from here. You'll need to start in Truro.'

St. Just gave the man his sternest look. Any sensible Cambridge criminal would have quaked at the sight, but this man of the sheep seemed imperturbable. 'We already started in Truro.'

'There you are, then. Just head straight to the end of this road and turn left for, oh, about twenty miles. Be right back. Looks like Maggie's bound for trouble.'

St. Just realized these might be directions back to Truro or onward to Mars. He suspected his leg was being pulled, but also that they were edging nearer the truth, which he might be able to prize out of the man if and when he came back.

Meanwhile, a couple of sheep had seized on the interruption to their day as an opportunity to ramble off, and the shepherd began chasing after them as well as the troublesome Maggie, leaving the others to bleat and poke about the tyres of the little car.

'I'm sorry,' he said, keeping an eye on the sheep in case of an opening to squeeze the car through. 'I should have taken the offer of a satnav to go with the rental.'

'That's all right,' said Portia. 'At least you stopped to ask for directions.'

He turned to look at her, taking in her beautiful wide smile and deep-blue eyes. She wore a white T-shirt over pink shorts that came to just above her knees. They were called pedal pushers in his mother's day; God knew what they were called now. It was clearly Portia's going-to-the-beach outfit, probably bought new for this adventure. He realized he'd mostly seen her around Cambridge dressed in the rather bohemian style she favoured and looking like the esteemed Cambridge don that she was.

'You're laughing at me,' he said.

'I'm laughing with you.'

'We'll never get there at this rate. And I'm famished – aren't you?'

'Yes. But I really think we're close now. Can't you smell the sea air?'

'All I can smell is sheep.'

'I know. Don't they ever wash them?'

'You *are* a city girl, aren't you?'

'You're hardly a shepherd yourself, Arthur. How much do you really know about sheep?'

'Very little; unlike you, though, I have watched many nature documentaries, probably while you were watching reruns of *The Crown*. Sheep are frequently mentioned in *The Blue Planet*.'

'Is that so? It's a jolly good thing we're having this discussion *before* we get married.'

'Remember, I am no stranger to these parts. I know they wash the sheep once a year before they're shorn for their wool. Until then, it's best to stay downwind. Also, I know that after the females are clipped, the offspring can't recognize their own mothers, which quite naturally makes the lambs cry.'

'Well, that's rather sad,' said Portia, looking round her as if for mismatched sheep. 'So what happens? Do the mothers just randomly adopt the nearest lamb?'

'Probably. I don't really know, but I don't think the lambs are bright enough to know the difference; as long as someone feeds them, they're fine. Anyway, I used to come here with my parents every summer and we'd stop on the way home to watch the sheep being shorn.'

'Ah, so you do know more than I do,' she said. 'On this topic, at any rate. Anyway, I'm very glad we decided on Cornwall, even if it's taking a bit longer than we'd planned.'

'Hmm. Yes. Are there any more of those biscuits in the glove box?'

'I finished them off at the last roundabout. Sorry. That sounds like the title for a literary novel – *The Last Roundabout*. What's up with the shepherd, anyway?'

'He's playing with us. We are what some Cornish call Emmets, among other things: Weekenders, Townies, London Blow-ins.'

'Emmet?'

'It's Old English for "ant". We're like ants at their picnic. Anyway, messing with people who come here on holiday probably helps pass the time for this man. Shouldn't he have a border collie to speed things along?'

And so they passed the time, the conversation moving on to whether they should get a dog and, if so, what breed. It was as if the wheels of the car had become embedded in concrete; there was nothing for it but to wait patiently. After all, a slower pace and a bucolic change of scene was what they'd come for, even though this was much like Cambridge in rush-hour traffic.

Portia began poking about the screen of her mobile. 'Still no signal,' she said. 'I wish we could let someone know. Although who would believe us?'

St. Just felt sure their landlady would believe them. When he'd told her on the phone they'd be driving from Truro and planned to arrive in Maidsfell by five p.m., she'd laughed and said, 'Chance would be a fine thing. You'd best build in an hour for incidentals and serendipity. And pure bloody karma, unless you've led a blameless life.' He hadn't understood what she'd meant, assuming it was to do with the train service, which he'd heard could be a game of chance depending on the weather, but now, of course, he could catalogue the many possible hazards on their route. Thus far, they'd been stuck behind one heavy goods vehicle, two wide-load lorries operating in low gear, and a horse-drawn cart of vegetables being taken to market. The windscreen had just escaped damage when a cabbage rolled off the cart, bouncing along the Fiat's bonnet like a football.

Once the sheep cleared off – seemingly on their own initiative, for St. Just and Portia never saw the shepherd again – they reached their destination by following various old-fashioned fingerpost signs for Maidsfell. The signs also marked the way to train stations he knew no longer existed, so St. Just's hopes were low until they breached the village boundaries and saw the *Welcome to Maidsfell* signs for themselves. On the way, they passed two new housing developments with bilingual street signs – Cornish translated into English, or whichever way round.

'That's progress,' St. Just told Portia. 'The Cornish language

– Kernewek – nearly died out in the last century. Now it's being taught in schools.'

'That's very good news,' said Portia, one eye on the map and another on the road. 'There's a sharp right turn ahead, nearly a U-turn.'

St. Just slowed for a group of elderly but exceedingly fit backpackers.

'Left here.'

'During the Tudor era, Cranmer did his best to stamp out every trace of the language in church services.'

'Hmm. One more turn in about a hundred metres and we should be at the lane where she said we could leave the car. Oh, my – will you look at that!'

At the turning, a sweeping panorama of the village and its harbour popped open before them. They'd seen from online photos the setting was like a four-layered cake, but nothing could prepare them for the fairytale 'reality' of the place. An old church and graveyard sat atop the higher of two cliffs that embraced the foamy waves, looking much like a decoration on a wedding cake. There was a centre layer, or filling, where a prehistoric site with standing monuments jutted out over the sea. Several cottages, including one that would prove to be theirs, were strewn further down, clinging to each side of the winding path. The most desirable of these little homes had windows and patios with views directly over the water.

At the base of the cake sprawled the village of Maidsfell with its beach and harbour, the sea an impossible blue-green, twinkling in the fading sun.

They left the car at the foot of the lane as instructed by their landlady and retrieved their luggage from the boot. St. Just carried his ancient Gladstone bag as Portia wheeled her suitcase over the cobblestones. Maidsfell's sandy coves were only about a quarter of a mile from where they left the car. In truth, apart from taking it for day outings to tourist destinations such as St. Ives or Port Isaac, St. Just was certain the car would remain where it was. It was a walkable village.

'Ancient cobblestones are much more attractive in theory than in practice,' Portia commented after her bag caught on a stone and flipped over.

'Here, let me,' said St. Just, grasping the bag by its handle. '*Oof.* What on earth do you have in here?'

'A few books,' she said. 'Travel guides and some research for my next novel. It's set in Cornwall, like the others, but being here is such an opportunity to see and verify things for myself.'

'There's an invention called the internet,' he said. 'Most people would download information that way.'

'I consider that to be cheating, actually. A real researcher has seven books open on a table at once, cross-referencing.'

'If you say so. I'm still just trying to get through *Baudolino.*'

'You did say you couldn't get very far with it – not because it was a bad novel, but because your reading always got interrupted by a murder case.'

'Then I always have to start over from the beginning. At least that won't happen this time – being interrupted, I mean. I should make great headway, just sitting on the beach reading and relaxing.'

'Absolutely. We're on holiday. Besides, I never saw a village less likely to boast a high crime rate.'

'Right you are. Anyway, the *Baudolino* hardback weighs about three stone so I finally downloaded a copy rather than carry the book with me everywhere. I am finding the new ways are good, Portia. Here we are.'

They stopped in front of the rental cottage, St. Just dropping his Gladstone to take in the whitewashed single-storey building with red door and shutters and a Cornish slate roof. A sign by the front door confirmed it was Seaside Cottage; indeed, waves could easily be heard crashing into the shore far below. The outer walls were cushioned in lichen; it was probably a running battle to keep it at bay. Likely a conversion from an old fisherman's cottage, it looked enchanted, built for a children's tale. St. Just supposed there were fewer fishermen and their families in the village needing housing. He would come to learn he had that idea slightly wrong.

Inside, it was spotlessly clean and modern, and while everything about it said *utilitarian holiday let*, it was on the quaint side and lived up to its advertising as *deliciously private*. The neighbouring cottages on either side were thirty feet away.

A sofa rested opposite a mounted TV with an electric fire below, and a separate kitchen had a miniature gas oven and hob, a fridge, and a microwave. A dining table for two overlooked a low-walled patio with a view up the cliffs and down over the bay, where waters sparkled endlessly in the setting sun. A firepit was faced by two rattan patio chairs and a low matching table; hydrangeas bloomed from a built-up flowerbed to one side.

Portia pronounced this 'perfect'. St. Just was pleased, as he'd chosen the place himself.

The bedroom had a king-sized bed and en-suite bathroom. A yellow, black, white, and red plaid was the dominant motif on the windows and bedclothes.

'A bold choice,' murmured Portia. 'I expected something more . . . blue. More nautical.'

'I expect it's what the owners think the tenants will want. I'm certain they don't live here – they have a house somewhere outside the village.'

Theirs was indeed an absentee landlady, Penelope White and her husband having bunked off to their Mediterranean yacht for the season. They left the cottage to be rented out by the week, with the door key left under a flowerpot. The policeman in St. Just was horrified by this but he imagined Maidsfell was that sort of village, with a negligible crime rate, most of it involving the odd dodgy driver and a spot of vandalism by bored teenagers. When he'd gently remonstrated with Penelope about the key's hiding place, she'd said, 'Ah, but there are dozens of pots and rocks and things, and I change it all the time so they don't know which pot to look under. Sometimes I put it under the welcome mat.'

'They'll never think to look there,' said St. Just.

There was a pause while she considered whether he might be mocking her.

'There's no crime in Maidsfell,' she said stoutly. 'None big enough to worry about, any road. A little crime against property, maybe.'

Precisely what they were talking about, but he said nothing more. She swept on: 'This time the key is under the pot of daisies. Oh, and if you wouldn't mind watering them if it doesn't rain.'

Of course he wouldn't mind. But he also knew rain came with the territory in Cornwall, even in summer.

'It's the Cornish national tartan,' he informed Portia as she stood marvelling at the eye-watering colour scheme, 'in case we forget for one moment where we are.'

'The Cornish aren't joking about reclaiming their history.'

'Not joking at all.' Cornwall had in recent decades petitioned Parliament hard to help salvage its heritage, especially its fast-vanishing language. 'They're deadly serious.'

THREE
The Artist's Way

After washing off the dust of their journey, St. Just and Portia set out in search of dinner.

'Several places we saw on the way in looked likely,' said St. Just. 'I think we'll be spoiled for choice.' Walking the cobbled lanes, they passed dozens of shops and restaurants and art galleries, many converted from cottages.

They stopped before a revolving display of postcards. 'Let's try to get to Penzance,' he said, pointing at one. 'It's only a few miles away but Cornwall miles, as we were reminded today, are like dog's years in human terms. Anyway, there's an exhibit of the Newlyn School I'd love to see.'

'Will we have time to get to Tintagel?' she asked.

'Nothing simpler,' he said. 'King Arthur's birthplace is something everyone must visit.'

'You say that as if he weren't a myth.'

He smiled. 'He was real. Merlin, maybe not so much. They just haven't found the evidence for either yet.'

The plain black-and-white flag of Cornwall was on display everywhere, snapping in the light breeze. Also notices in many windows read, *Keep Cornwall for the Cornish.* An outfit calling itself SOS seemed to be behind this demand. Presumably, if you had to ask what SOS stood for, you weren't a local.

They walked the length of the high street, looking through plate glass windows at T-shirts and tea towels stamped *Kernow bys vyken.*

"'Cornwall forever,'" said St. Just.

They stopped at the window of an art gallery called Sepia's Seascapes. The woman behind the counter saw their longing looks – St. Just's in particular – and gave them an encouraging wave, so they stepped over the threshold into the narrow shop. Its long walls were lined on each side with carefully curated paintings of crashing waves and beaches and ferries – the usual holiday scenes, but of good quality. As St. Just strolled past the illuminated artwork mounted against whitewashed stone, he saw nothing costing more than five thousand pounds; most offerings were closer to three hundred. St. Just thought that was about right to capture the impulse buyer wanting a holiday memento that was a bit more than a teacup or T-shirt. He stopped before a painting of unusual power and beauty, drawn in by the artist's coarse but masterful technique.

Portia was admiring a beach scene of sun worshippers and bright umbrellas when Sepia Jones came over and introduced herself to St. Just as the gallery's owner. She was a dark-skinned woman in her middle years with large brown eyes, her hair intricately braided in neat rows tight to her scalp. She wore a black cotton blouse over black slacks, which set her apart from the more hectically garbed people they'd seen so far – the British on holiday were seldom a sight for sore eyes. At her neck and ears Sepia wore large topaz stones set in silver, a perfect choice against the stark black of her outfit.

'You have a good eye,' she told him. 'That's a Matt Quincy Roberts you've been looking at.'

'Thank you,' he said, knowing this was part of a good saleswoman's technique to flatter him into parting with his money. It was working; he was pleased by her praise.

'He's head and shoulders above the best of the lot, I'd say, but don't tell the others if you come across them. They're a competitive bunch, artists.'

'I draw and paint a bit,' St. Just told her, 'so I know the composition of this is unusual. And difficult to pull off.'

'I thought you might dabble – or is it more than that? Cornwall has always attracted artists. It's the light here – like nowhere else on earth.'

St. Just again fought down the easy temptation of flattery, sternly reminding himself he was in all ways an amateur. This Roberts person was a real artist. 'See how he's put the point of view downward from a great height and into the water below, ignoring everything but the rocks on the way down the side of the cliff. It's the point of view of someone falling, I'd say. It's hypnotic.'

Sepia smiled broadly. 'You're not afraid of heights, then? I am, and this one pulls me inside in a most disturbing way. If I'm honest, I don't think I could have it in my home, especially after a glass of wine or two. He painted it from the Fourteen Maidens site – the famous standing stones of Maidsfell, you know. Anyone else would just paint the rocks – they're dramatic enough as they are – but not Matt. He had to turn his back and paint what *they* might see – the Maidens. As if they were alive.'

Portia walked over to join them. She studied the painting a moment, turning her head one way and the other.

'It's rather wonderful, isn't it?' she said. 'I've been reading about the standing stones – the menhirs, as they're called.'

Sepia started nodding her head in an *I know this already* way.

'My pamphlet about them is full of "it was saids" and "archae-ologists believe",' Portia continued, 'but the fact is, they don't seem to know who hauled them up the cliff or why. Or how, for that matter. It must have been a monumental undertaking – forgive the pun. There's also debate as to why the Maidsfell stones are called "Maidens". From the photos, they're difficult to identify as male or female. They're just . . . stones.'

'They've been here since at least the Iron Age,' said Sepia. 'Possibly Neolithic. It all has something to do with stars and the solstice and alignments. That pamphlet you mention is probably the one by our local crackpot. He's made a fortune selling them in the gift shops here.'

'Horace Bude is the author.'

'The very man. But look closely if you go and see them for yourself, which you really must do. Those forms are female – styl-ized and worn away by time, but female. Venus figures, but without the obvious breasts and hips of a Venus of Willendorf. I like to think of them as goddesses or perhaps handmaidens to a goddess, like vestal virgins. Of course, the people who lugged them up there had no written language to tell us what the stones meant to them, but fertility was important in every age, as was survival.'

'Horace mentions human sacrifice. More crackpot theories?'

Sepia folded her arms, turning to look at the Roberts painting with its point of view of a person falling – no doubt the last thing that person would ever see. 'I wouldn't discount Horace's bits about human sacrifice. When crops failed or fish refused to swim into the nets or traps pulled up empty, what were you going to do but sacrifice a few people to get things moving again?'

'Why do I have a feeling they always chose the people they didn't like for the honour?' said Portia, smiling. 'Must have come in handy with a troublesome in-law or two, especially if you were hoping to inherit.' Portia's mind tended to run along such tracks, as her crime novels were filled with murderous heirs knocking people off so they could receive their inheritances ahead of time.

'Nothing changes, does it?' Sepia paused, fingering the stones of her necklace. Her nails were painted to match her necklace and earrings. 'The Maiden Ring does have rather a dark history, as well as a bad reputation in modern days.'

'Oh?' said Portia.

Sepia shook her head. 'Best not dig all that up. You must go and see the Maidens for yourselves and form your own impressions. But if I were you, I'd ignore all Sybil's "Bloodmoon Cave" nonsense – Sybil Gosling, that is. She runs the show up there, if unofficially. She's alone too much, apart from a small group of rather dodgy spiritual friends. "Double, double toil and trouble", we call them.'

'Funny how we all manage to find our tribe,' said Portia. 'With me, it's academics. Talk about dodgy.'

St. Just had returned meanwhile from his full circuit of the gallery. 'We'll certainly stop at the Maiden Ring while we're here,' he said.

'It sounds so mysterious,' said Portia. 'Very much up my alley.'

'To some people, it's just a bunch of rocks, but to others – to those equipped with the right tuning fork – it's a sacred place. Just ask Sybil. At heart she's a Druid sprinkled with Wiccan pixie dust. I don't find much harm in her, but to be honest I'm probably a pagan in my own heart. Established religion is too judgey for me. Look, can I pour you a glass of wine?'

Portia and St. Just both shook their heads, exchanging glances.

'Best not,' said Portia. 'We've been travelling all day on mostly empty stomachs. I would love it if you'd offer what Americans call a raincheck, though.'

'Certainly,' said Sepia. 'You've got it. Any time.'

'And a recommendation for dinner?' Portia added.

'Ooh, that's trickier. So many choices in Maidsfell. Are you wanting upmarket or just fuel?'

'Upmarket,' said St. Just. With a glance at Portia, he said, 'It's rather a special occasion, this holiday. I want to push the boat out.'

'Then I'll send you straight into the Maiden's Arms,' said Sepia. 'The owner – also the chef – will talk your ear off but she's very good . . .' She hesitated, as if struggling to be fair and impartial. 'There's also the Anchor; Jake Trotter owns that. The two restaurants are neck and neck in the ratings, but I'd call the Anchor the winner by a nose.'

'Which restaurant is closer by?' asked St. Just.

'Oh, well.' She seemed relieved by this question. 'Morwenna's place is just at the top of the street. The Anchor is perhaps half a mile.'

'That settles it,' said St. Just. 'I'm too famished to walk another half mile.' Portia nodded her agreement. 'We'll have to try Jake's another evening. We're here all week.'

They left Sepia's with a promise to return for the promised glass of wine.

Continuing up the high street, St. Just said, 'Sepia's collection is superb, isn't it?'

'There seems to be real talent hereabouts,' Portia agreed. 'I wonder where the artists stand on this fishers' issue.' She had stopped before yet another sign, urging people in no uncertain terms to attend an upcoming meeting, because *OUR WAVE OF LIFE DEPENDS ON IT.*

'I would guess they stand firmly against any sort of development, change, or government interference. The village is perfect as it is. A new quay or whatever will spoil the view, and the view is what artists live for.' St. Just felt this was a tribe he could call his own, amateur or no, and so could freely speak for them. 'However, a stone quay might be nice. A true artist could turn that into something, don't you think?'

'It's probably the car park they don't like.'

'Yes. It's hard to romanticize a car park. You'd have to go for stark, dark, moody, and making a statement about how mankind wilfully destroys nature.'

At the end of the high street – where the street proper dribbled into a dirt track – they found the beamed-and-thatched Maiden's Arms. A sign in front promised patio dining overlooking the harbour with *Views to the Cliff of the Fourteen Maidens.*

'And every kind of seafood you can name.' Portia read aloud: '"Crabs, lobsters, oysters, turbot – served with sea beet salad." What is sea beet salad, do you think?'

'It grows on the cliffs round here. It has quite a strong taste as I recall, but it's good if they make it with olive oil and . . . what do you call the little oniony things?'

'Shallots.'

'Shallots. Let's see if we can get a table without a reservation. What do you say to a glass of wine?'

FOUR

Food for Thought

Morwenna Wells was a restaurateur who had 'made it big in London' – her words – before opening a destination place in Maidsfell. The Maiden's Arms had earned a Michelin star, so her success wasn't idle boasting.

On the evening St. Just and Portia arrived for dinner, she wore a long floral sundress, a dress she had made from an antique pattern more suited to her rounded contours than modern designs. She was recognizable in a photo display in the restaurant's hallway as a former Miss Cornwall who had competed in a Miss England contest thirty years earlier. She was a stone heavier now, but it only seemed to enhance her classic beauty.

She eyed the couple as they entered and made a quick assessment before saying, 'Welcome to the Maiden's Arms.'

'Thank you,' said St. Just. 'Might we be seated on the patio? As long as the temperature cooperates, we may as well take advantage.'

'Absolutely,' Morwenna said. 'You're a bit late, missed the usual evening crowd, but I'll get a table set up for you. We have outdoor heaters if the temperature should drop. Now, what would you like to drink while you wait?' She had a deep contralto voice, perhaps coarsened by years of exposure to cigarette smoke.

Portia, introducing herself and St. Just, asked for a wine list as they sat at the polished bar.

'Visiting?' she asked, although it must have been obvious they were.

'Yes,' said St. Just. 'I used to stay in this area with my parents. In some ways, it hasn't changed a bit and in others it's changed far too much.'

'Change,' echoed the woman. 'We don't really like change here. My name is Morwenna Wells, by the way.'

'We noticed a few signs around the village about fishermen and jetties and things,' said Portia. 'I gather there's a bit of a conflict?'

'A bit. The wealthy Townies – you're not Londoners, I gather? Didn't think so; they have a look about them. Anyway, the wealthy Townies who've bought property here want the waterfront left as it is. They oppose the fishermen's plans, adopting a sudden concern for wildlife, which no one believes. Running alongside is a debate about the damage to the economy done by absentee owners – house prices are driving the young and old from their homes.'

'I see. Bound to be bad feeling there,' said Portia.

'There are true conservationists like Friends of the Mackerel and doubtful new preservation societies like SOS or Save Our Shores. What they mean is Save Our Views, but I guess SOV isn't as catchy. Then there's local landed gentry in the form of Lord Bodwally. Everyone's taken a slice in the debate.'

'Ah. And the lord's stance?'

'Opposed, flat out, to the fishers.' Morwenna's full mouth turned down in distaste. 'In it for himself alone, as usual.' It seemed she could say much more but chose not to. Instead, she said, 'A storm is brewing, that's certain. All the fishers want is to build a stone jetty and slipway to help them land their catches. That and maybe a new road and car park. Anything that makes it easier for them to load their vans, you see. Right now they have to transfer fish by dinghy and drag the catch along the beach.'

'Difficult,' agreed St. Just. He tried a sip of the excellent wine Portia had chosen.

'But the authorities are finding everything wrong they can with the planning permissions,' Morwenna continued. 'There have been months – years, really – of fighting and it never seems to get resolved. The SOS bunch are gaining strength. They have tried to force a judicial review of the fishers' plans and they may well succeed. They call themselves a preservation society but really it's all about their expensive views, and too bad about the blokes just trying to make a living.'

St. Just nodded his understanding of both the village politics and the fishermen's plight. His father's people hailed from Cornwall, and those who hadn't been fishermen had been tin miners. Even if he'd never done commercial fishing or mined a day in his life, some feeling of kinship had been passed along to him. But his fishing-and-mining heritage came with advice from both his parents to get an education so he could find a less dangerous way to make a living. He was well aware becoming a policeman was probably not what they had in mind.

Morwenna ran on, polishing the already gleaming bar and pouring them refills they hadn't asked for.

'The weekenders and holiday homeowners – the London blow-ins – want whitewashed cottages and daffodil-dotted hills.' Morwenna recited this last in a sing-song voice, bobbing her head, as if it were something she'd heard a million times from the opposing side. 'They want Portwenn without the day-to-day reality of people barely making a living,' she said, referring to the fictional Cornish village depicted on TV. 'They want *Doc Martin* without the blood. They certainly don't want the day trippers who began mobbing Port Isaac – the stand-in for Portwenn – when the show caught on.'

'Actually, we were planning a visit to Port Isaac,' said St. Just, in an obvious bid to change the tone of the conversation. For DCI Arthur St. Just simply wanted a break from strife, conflict, and, most especially, investigating murder – to escape the burdens and occasional terrors of his working life.

The thought began to run silently in his head like a chyron at the bottom of a BBC newscast (*DCI ONLY WANTED A BREAK FROM MURDER*).

But there wasn't a murder in sight. Why did he feel so on edge listening to Morwenna Wells obsess on this topic?

'The thing is, time is of the essence for the fishers. They bring the fish in mid-afternoon and by the next day restaurants across England have fresh catch on the menu. But it doesn't happen by magic, and the less handling of the fish, the better.'

'But your restaurant is right here,' Portia pointed out.

'I'm not much affected,' Morwenna admitted. 'It's the principle of the thing.' She put away the bar rag she'd been using. 'Now, we'll find you a lovely table with a view that will make you glad you chose the Maiden's Arms.' Looking past them, she said, 'I don't know where the waitress got to.'

She fixed her wide blue eyes on St. Just, sizing him up and liking what she saw. Tall and broad, dark-haired with thick eyebrows over hazel eyes, a high beak of a nose that only added to his attractiveness.

The woman, Portia, was lovely: slender and stylish, with shiny dark hair now being ruffled – stylishly – by the mild breeze coming from a window. Her deep-blue eyes under ravens' wing brows were her most striking feature, suggesting a rather hypnotic, piercing intelligence.

When the waitress came to say their table was ready, Morwenna followed them out. Portia wore black jeans and a white T-shirt with a small scarf knotted at her neck; she carried a black vegan-leather jacket hooked over one shoulder, anticipating the evening chill. Morwenna thought it would have taken her half an hour to tie the scarf just so, let alone achieve the effortless French panache of this simple outfit. The woman wore no jewellery apart from chandelier earrings that emphasized the swan-like length of her neck.

And what looked like a brand-new engagement ring on her finger.

Overall, Morwenna thought it best to give up before she even started.

Too bad. Back in the day, she would definitely have taken a run at St. Just.

When they reached the wooden table on the patio, Morwenna saw their place setting wasn't complete and set about making it right. A wooden hutch stood to one side filled with crockery and bottles of olive oil. She pulled over a stepstool so she could reach the top shelf. Over her shoulder, she said, 'There's a meeting. They're calling it an "extraordinary" meeting, which it likely will be. The councillors finally realized the situation was spinning out of control. You should come.'

'But we don't live here,' said St. Just. 'Can I help you with that?'

'No problem, I'm good.' She grabbed a bottle by the neck and as she clambered back down, said, 'Makes no matter where you're from. We need a show of strength, and Titus Bodwally needs putting in his place. Oh, *excuse* me, *Lord* Bodwally. There's no stopping him now he's a lord.' She set the bottle on the table with perhaps more force than was necessary.

'Being born rich takes no effort,' she said, as if to explain her animosity. 'Making something of yourself once you've arrived – *that's* what makes you special. You'll not see me bowing and scraping to the likes of him.'

It was the classic bitter standoff, the working class against the nobs, but St. Just didn't think it would lighten the moment to say so. Just as he thought he might get another word in, Morwenna continued, 'It's not just him – all the council leaders need taking down a peg. They think if they take a united stand and shout louder than the peasants, we'll tug our forelocks and go away. This is going to make the debates over rat-running look like bun fights.'

'Rat-running?' asked Portia – probably, St. Just thought, to distract the woman. Portia was by nature a peacemaker.

'When people take alternative routes through neighbourhoods to avoid traffic in the city centre,' St. Just told her. 'Cut-through driving. The police get a lot of calls about it but it's difficult to catch people in the act.'

'Oh,' said Portia, who did this all the time in Cambridge's famously clogged streets at rush hour. She supposed now she was engaged to a policeman, she'd be held to a higher standard – like Caesar's wife, she'd have to be above reproach. How tiresome. Still, she'd marry him tomorrow.

'*And*,' Morwenna said, 'a policeman in the audience will bolster our case.'

St. Just sat back in his chair. 'Who says I'm a policeman?' He was sure he'd not mentioned it to their landlady. Somehow announcing his profession on holiday made it less of a holiday.

He also feared his presence in this lovely village might activate crime, like adding yeast to a bread recipe. It had happened so often before.

In fact, he couldn't recall a holiday when it hadn't happened.

Morwenna laughed. 'Just look at you. Of course you're a policeman. Big broad fellow like you?'

St. Just thought there were many occupations that might call for a 'big broad fellow' – an appliance deliveryman, to name one, or a heavyweight boxing champion – but he didn't want to argue. Publicans were known for their ability to read customers. At least, she'd made a good guess and followed it up with certainty. Probably another trick of her trade, like fortune telling.

'I'll warrant you're a detective, too. Hey, that's good! Warrant. Detective. Get it?'

Portia, intrigued, asked, 'What makes you think he's a detective?'

Morwenna shrugged. 'He looks bright and all. They wouldn't waste this one directing traffic, now would they?'

St. Just was torn between annoyance at being stereotyped – *were* the police so easy to spot? – and being flattered by the 'bright and all' analysis. 'We'll try to be there,' he said gruffly, having no intention of doing any such thing, and beseeching Portia with his eyes to play along.

'It sounds lovely,' said Portia. 'It might be a nice way to meet the locals.'

'You'll be in for a treat if some of the Townies show up,' Morwenna assured them. 'You may recognize some from the telly, but they're almost unrecognizable when they're not covered in wigs and makeup or being photographed through a filter. Callum Page is visiting,' she added.

'Really? But he's fantastic!' said Portia.

Who? wondered St. Just.

Morwenna nodded, clearly gratified by Portia's reaction. 'Some are good customers of the restaurant. Makes it tricky, you know. I can't come straight out and tell them to go back home. They'd head over to the competition if I do.'

'Competition?' St. Just asked. But he knew from their earlier conversation with Sepia Jones who it must be.

'Jake Trotter,' said Morwenna. 'He owns the Anchor. He's not from here; came here from London. Parked in Maidsfell to escape the plague and never left, even though he managed to earn himself a right telling off from the Coastguard for travelling all round Cornwall during the lockdown while the rest of us stayed home, bored silly with our jigsaw puzzles.'

'Perhaps he didn't realize?' offered Portia softly.

'He realized. He can read, can't he, and there were warning signs all over the place and in the news. But he's special, you see. Not like us lot, trying to follow the rules and going under all the while.'

'The police were run ragged trying to get everyone to obey the rules during those times,' said St. Just. 'But they were hard to enforce. The rules kept changing for us, too.'

'Oh, I remember. Anyway, the trouble with Jake is he knows nothing about being Cornish, which is not something you learn in any cooking school. It's in your blood, or it's not. He thinks the fishers' scheme will make an eyesore and says it isn't "financially viable" besides.' Morwenna's air quotes were accompanied by a lift of painted eyebrows. 'He talks like that. "Financially viable" and "shift the paradigm" and no end of twaddle. It just means he doesn't care about the fishers. He's lucky they don't boycott selling to him. Truth is, though, none of them can afford to take a stand like that. Only Will Ivey carries on acting like a man with nothing to lose.' She looked up at the ceiling, her plump features buckling momentarily. She seemed to be fighting tears.

'It's just not fair,' she said at last. 'You work and you work, and then, out of the blue . . .' She stopped, shaking her head, visibly pulling herself together. 'Now, have a look at those menus. I'll bring you an *amuse-bouche* to tide you over.'

St. Just and Portia sat drinking their white wine, waiting for their main course – crab and lobster Florentine with sea beet. The dim light from the table's votive candles cast her cheekbones into high relief. St. Just thought there was no place he'd rather be than with Portia De'Ath in this picture-postcard village.

'I do see the problem,' she said.

'Shared, no doubt, by many of the shop owners. On the one hand, the weekenders bring in much-needed cash. On the other, they're seizing the village from locals who have roots going back forever. Morwenna seems to be a local, for all her time in London. Otherwise it's hard to understand her taking the side of the fishers. It's the wealthy incomers who help pay her bills.'

The pair began laying plans for the next day. They'd brought hiking boots and wanted time to walk on the coastal trails, sit on the beach, and drive to Cornwall's various beauty spots.

It was ten before they left the restaurant. Morwenna was nowhere in sight.

'Do you really want to go to this meeting?' St. Just asked Portia as they walked back to the cottage. 'It's not as if we're planning to move here. We're just on holiday.'

'I know,' she said. 'Although I do wish we could stay longer and become one of the tiresome people Morwenna rails about. It's a lovely village. I could telecommute. The department saw the wisdom of that during the Plague Time.'

'You have your students,' he said. 'They like seeing you in person.' A small note of alarm was sounding in his head. He wondered if he could ever adapt to the slow pace of life in a rustic seaside village. What would he do all day without a crime to solve?

'I have books to write,' she said. 'As for my tutorials, I don't need to hang about full-time in Cambridge for that. I can do a lot of that online, as I do now.'

'It sounds as if you've thought this through already.'

Tucking her arm in his, she said, 'It's more a sudden flash of insight or perhaps *longing*. A feeling of connection to the place. But . . . you have your job, and that's an end to it. Maybe one day when you retire, we can . . .'

'I don't know what I'd be if I weren't a copper,' he said.

'You have your drawing and painting, and you're no dabbler; you're very good. As we've already seen, you can't go anywhere in Cornwall without tripping over half a dozen art galleries.'

'Once it ceases to be a hobby, it becomes work,' he said.

'At least you wouldn't need a weapon to do it,' she said.

'I would if I went about it the right way,' he said, hugging her to his side. 'Art thieves might queue up outside our door. It's just that we've built our lives in Cambridge. I don't want to retire until they force me out, or I get too feeble to sign off on a report.'

'"Grow old along with me,"' she quoted, nestling to him. He thought it was the end of the discussion.

They had a nightcap on the patio of Seaside Cottage, staring across a darkened sea in the glow of yellow candlelight. He'd got the outdoor fireplace going, and Portia was reading aloud to him from an article titled *Seventeen Amazing Things To Do in Cornwall.*

'Really, there's nowhere on earth like it, is there?' she said, showing him a photo of the nearby Caves of Colour at Holywell Bay.

He lifted the magazine from her hands.

'I can think of at least one more amazing thing to do in Cornwall,' he said, pulling her from her chair. 'Come along. Our time here is over before we know it.'

FIVE

Fishers of People

Monday

They went to the Lighthouse Café for breakfast, a short walk down the path from their cottage in the foggy chill of a Cornish morning. The cottage's small galley kitchen wasn't up to much beyond making coffee or reheating leftovers in the microwave.

St. Just had pulled himself awake from a dream every bit as hazy as the fog, a mirage that dissolved before he could retrieve it; all he could remember was a frantic cry and a certain knowledge that someone needed his help. He was still trying to collect the elusive threads when they reached the café.

Portia, used to standing by during St. Just's moments of deep introspection, was content with taking deep breaths of the exhilarating sea air. A mist hung in the far distance, promising to burn away in the sun, but for now it blurred the coast of West Cornwall like a white lace curtain. Blue skies were forecast for later that day.

The Lighthouse Café occupied the left side of a semi-detached cottage, the other half of which held Pasco's Butchers and Bakers.

They pulled chairs up to a square gingham-covered table, wooden legs screeching against the stone tiles. Taking advantage of the café's public WiFi, they both checked their email accounts. A young woman in bright fuchsia lipstick and a red apron longer than her jean shorts handed them menus (in both Cornish and English). Food from Pasco's naturally was highlighted. Everything looked tempting.

'It wouldn't be a holiday if I didn't pile on half a stone, would it?' St. Just asked.

'I'll run a bit further in the mornings when I get back home, that's all.'

'Scones,' St. Just breathed. The air carried the scent of scones baking. They would come with clotted cream. And all that sugar. No.

'No, it's too early for me to start with that,' said Portia. 'Eggs, maybe.'

'Quite sensible.'

St. Just's mother had been an enthusiastic amateur cook, in the school holidays rising at four a.m. to bake. From the time he was five, he'd awakened early to keep her company. He wondered now how welcome he was – perhaps she was trying to find time for herself. If so, she never let on.

St. Just ordered the smoked salmon with scrambled eggs, Portia the mushroom and Parmesan omelette. They had picked up a free local newspaper inside the café and they shared its contents as they waited for their food, reading aloud notices of a missing cat named Maddie and a dog named Bongo. According to his owner, Bongo would go with anyone who fed him, so his disappearance was especially worrying. Maddie's eating habits were not documented.

The paper featured a double-page spread with illustrative photos and an editorial decrying the heaps of plastic bags and the food containers left behind by holiday makers.

Cornwall is not your rubbish bin, scolded the editorial, before going on to mention that tourism had increased twenty-five per cent over last year. While a line was not drawn between the two thoughts, the wording seemed to imply that tourists were the major culprits in leaving their rubbish everywhere. St. Just felt unfairly targeted, as both he and Portia were scrupulous about leaving no trace of themselves in parks or at beaches, but he well understood the tendency of people on holiday to hope their sloppiness might go undetected. Given the ubiquity of CCTV cameras in the UK, that was a faint hope, he thought, although he'd not seen a single camera during their stay so far. Their landlady might, after all, be right in believing Maidsfell was a crime-free zone. Or the cameras were cleverly hidden apart from the obvious ones calling attention to themselves in shops.

Portia read aloud from a feature on the opening to visitors of a smugglers' tunnel which ran down from a pub to the cliffs of Sennen.

'I'd love to see that,' she said. 'It would fit right into my book. But we're going to run out of time – a week doesn't seem long enough, does it?'

Their orders arrived. Portia was buttering a slice of toast when a woman wearing a colourful Hawaiian shirt and a clerical collar came in to order a takeaway breakfast. She was perhaps in her late forties, and St. Just took a quick impression of a puckish face and bright blue eyes, with a Peter Pan haircut dyed an unbelievable shade of black. On her feet were a pair of thick leather strap-on sandals of the type a Roman soldier might have worn on manoeuvres. She wore jeans cut off at the knee, and altogether did not resemble any of the clerics of St. Just's youth. He was certain this was one of the trendy new ones who seemed to be everywhere, trying desperately to attract a younger generation to their churches to replace the old and dying. He could easily picture her leading the children's play-group in a manic version of 'This Little Light of Mine'.

The woman noticed Portia studying her guidebook. Having collected her coffee from the café's counter, she walked over to their table.

'Hello, I'm Judith Abernathy,' she said. Her voice was full and melodic, which must have helped in delivering sermons when the PA system cut out. 'I'm the curate at St. Cuthbert's – holding down the fort while the vicar is on an extended "retreat". If you know what I mean.' She astonished them by miming a person tossing a drink down his throat. 'Occupational hazard, I'm afraid. Peder Wolfe is a lovely man but . . . well.'

'Oh,' said Portia. 'He's away being . . . rehabilitated.'

'Let us hope so. As I say, he's a lovely man and it's a shame for him to pickle himself before his time. Anyway, that's why I'm here, to take over for . . . well, for as long as it takes. My husband died right in the Christmas so I was a bit at a loose end and the diocese was kind enough to let me come and help out. Doesn't do not to stay busy, does it? Idle hands! Which reminds me, I'm also the unofficial Maidsfell welcoming committee of one. Lucky for you I'm not armed with a casserole.' She chuckled at her own joke.

'Thank you,' said Portia. 'How kind. I'm very sorry to hear about your husband. I'm Portia and this is my fiancé, Arthur. We're staying at Seaside Cottage for the week.'

St. Just's heart skipped a beat as it always did when Portia referred to him as her fiancé. He wondered how it would hold up once she was able to call him her husband.

After his wife's death, St. Just had resigned himself to living alone, never expecting lightning to strike twice. He had dated a few women, with mixed results. An affair with a professional house organizer had quickly ended, but not before she had alphabetized and colour-coded everything he owned. It had taken him weeks to relocate some of his belongings.

It was tempting fate to question his sudden good luck, but he found it hard to believe Portia was in his life.

'I heard as much – news travels fast here,' Judith said. 'There's little all to do but gossip when you live in Maidsfell. And the less important people are, the more they like to trade in gossip, in my experience. Makes them *feel* important, I daresay, but it's the devil at work. Old Nick himself. One of you is with the police, I hear, and the other is an academic.'

St. Just owned to being a DCI with the Cambridgeshire Constabulary.

'How wonderful! Absolutely super! Although I hope we'll not have need of your services. Here in Maidsfell nothing much ever happens. You have to go a bit further afield to find crime, but even Truro doesn't have much to offer – poverty in the dodgy bits, you know, so a spot of opportunistic thievery.'

'Glad to hear it.' St. Just took a sip of his coffee, dark and perfectly brewed. A cloud of aromatic steam swirled about his face. 'About the crime, I mean.'

He was rather thinking the woman would invite them to attend services and he might need to fashion a dodge to her invitation.

He was on holiday and he wasn't himself clear on whether that included a holiday from all his usual scheduled activities, which in all honesty didn't often include the Church of England.

He rarely had time to attend services, but he liked to visit old village churches when he was travelling, if only to admire the architecture – he was a particular fan of everything medieval. Plus, their notice boards always offered invaluable insight into the life of the town or village where he found himself.

He knew from glancing through Portia's guidebook that parts of St. Cuthbert's dated to the Middle Ages; the place was probably worth a visit based on that alone.

'Doesn't Seaside Cottage have a terrific view?' Judith Abernathy was saying. 'And the décor! Penelope spent a fortune on that tartan, I can tell you.'

He gave rather a thin smile, not daring to meet Portia's eyes.

The curate picked Portia's guidebook off the table and turned it over; pulling a pair of reading glasses from the top of her head, she settled them on her nose.

'Thought so,' she said. 'Horace Bude is a bit of an idiot – if I may be forgiven for saying so – and this is all five years out of date. In some ways, though, nothing much has changed in Maidsfell – not for centuries. Well, the Plague Time did change things, particularly the list in the back of the book of shops and restaurants. A lot of them closed, after a valiant fight.'

'I'm finding as much,' said Portia. 'Such a shame.'

'It is. It is that. Of course, I wasn't here then – I'm from London, but they still talk of that time like it was yesterday. London was hard hit, too, of course, but some of these small villages are still waiting to rip off the plaster and see what's beneath.'

'Cambridge was a ghost town,' Portia told her, 'and it's still recovering in many ways. Without the students, the place was strangely lifeless – I missed them most of all, even their commotion. There was a haunted feel to the place; it was easy to imagine the streets as they once had been, filled with medieval scholars.'

'Oh, but you're a writer – I was forgetting. Of course, you'd see things in a rather otherworldly way. A detached way. You'll have to meet our resident romance author. Anyway, who was it said about detachment, "The ultimate power is the absence of desire"?'

'I don't know but they were quite right. Was it the Buddha?'

Judith shrugged. 'I think we could all look back over our lives and see where they might have been improved by a bit more dispassion. Certainly, when faced with one of the chocolate pastries here' – she looked longingly over one shoulder – 'I would give a lot for less desire.'

'I was just telling Arthur, I will wait to face facts once I'm back in Cambridge.'

'You have nothing to worry about,' said Judith, with a rueful glance down at her Hawaiian shirt, which looked to have been chosen to hide a multitude of pastry sins. 'Anyway, in Maidsfell all you hear is talk of ghost towns – because of people buying second homes that sit empty.'

'Yes, we've heard,' they said simultaneously, hoping to steer her off the topic.

'Naturally, I'm on the side of the fishers.' Judith Abernathy smiled broadly, waiting. 'But then again, I would be, wouldn't I? It's my calling.' Finally, to their blank stares, she said, 'Priest? Fisher of men, as in the Bible?'

Dutifully, they laughed. St. Just was hoping her sermons were better than her jokes. He was looking for a way to end the conversation, but the curate seemed to have no antennae for social cues. In the months following his wife's death, had he too talked too much? Had he pinned perfect strangers to their chairs like this? He hoped not. But he rather feared he may have done so on occasion.

The poor woman. While he could commiserate, he was anxious to get on with the day – this time with Portia was precious, to be measured in minutes.

He was aghast to see Portia smiling, making encouraging noises. Portia could be *too* kind. Every stray dog and cat in the neighbourhood beat a path to her door; every student with a boyfriend or girlfriend or parent problem found a sympathetic ear.

'Of course,' she said. 'That would be in your job description, wouldn't it?'

'Indeed, it is. The church service is at nine on Sunday, by the way. Do come if you're still here.'

'Sorry, we can't; we—'

'We won't be here Sunday,' said Portia. 'But we may pop in for a look.'

'Terrific! I have to run now. There's someone coming to look at a leaky drainpipe – it's always something with these old buildings – and a mutiny is starting among the women of the altar guild. A good name for a horror film, don't you think? *The Women of the Guild*. Their leader has developed allergies to certain flowers and a few of them are looking to seize power.'

'I know how that can go,' said Portia. 'I used to sing soprano in a church choir.'

St. Just turned to her. 'You did?'

'You needn't look so surprised,' said Portia, laughing. 'I wasn't half bad.'

'Enjoy your visit,' said Judith, 'and do let me know if you want to stop in. You might quite like evensong. Here's my card.' She dug around in her shirt pocket, producing a card carrying the logo of the Church of England, her name and mobile number, and the address of St. Cuthbert's.

Handing it to Portia, who dropped it in her purse and offered her own card in return, she said, 'Or better yet – just stop by. As the saying goes, our doors are always open.'

'We may do if there's time,' said Portia. 'But for now, could you point us in the direction of the standing stones? We want to see them before we head to the beach.'

'Nothing simpler,' Judith said. 'Out of the door here, turn right, then go up. And up. Halfway to St. Cuthbert's, you'll see a sign pointing left to the path to the Fourteen Maidens.'

'How far is it?'

'About half a mile, a steep uphill climb. But it's worth the effort. You'll see.'

SIX

Haunted

The path ran through heritage woods to a broad ledge running beneath St. Cuthbert's.

As promised, it was worth the trek.

Catching their breath, they counted thirteen standing stones.

One of the Maidens had apparently gone missing over the years.

They looked to have been undisturbed for centuries, quiet sentinels, witnesses to history. There was something wild, otherworldly about the space. It was like a Stonehenge in miniature, but with no lintels hinging the upright stones.

'There's a legend that when the missing maiden "returneth", the village will enjoy a long period of prosperity,' Portia told him.

'Predictably vague, as predications go. How long is "long", do you think?'

'With all the wealthy new incomers? Not long,' said St. Just. 'But no worries for now. She hath yet to return.'

'That almost sounds like a line from a poem by Edgar Allan Poe,' said Portia, putting her hand on one stone that seemed slightly larger than the others – a stark, ragged shape outlined against a blue sky. '"And this maiden she lived with no other thought / Than to love and be loved by me." I swear, this thing vibrates.'

'It's the sea rumbling below,' he said. 'There's been a retreat of the cliff face. The missing maiden – let's call her Alice – probably fell in a long time ago from soil erosion.'

The remaining stones stood in a horseshoe shape overlooking the sea. The entire protrusion of rock was clearly losing ground to the waves undermining it daily.

'I don't think so.' Portia pointed to a gap like a missing tooth, furthest from the cliff's edge. Behind it grew a large tree, bedecked with ornaments, amidst a tangled mass of gorse bush. 'That must be where the fourteenth maiden stood. The rest are all more or less equidistant apart. Some conquering vandals may have rolled her off the cliff; she didn't just fall.'

St. Just looked round at the remains of the monument, allowing the magic of the place to seep in. No one could guess at what had driven people to labour so intensely to create this tribute over such prolonged periods. No more could anyone explain why people spent decades and centuries building cathedrals.

'Let's come back tomorrow with a picnic,' suggested Portia. 'It's so peaceful here.'

Indeed it was. The fresh air of Cornwall was somehow amplified in the space within the horseshoe; it seemed to carry an electric charge.

'Yes, let's do that,' said St. Just. 'We'll buy some Cornish pasties and a few things to go with them. A good bottle of wine.'

As they headed back towards the downhill path, he quietly asked, 'Did you see the woman hiding behind that tree, watching us?'

'What woman?'

'I think we interrupted whatever she was doing.'

'There's no picnicking allowed here.' A voice rang out and they spun to face the source. The woman stood blocking the sun; an imposing figure, outlined like an icon in radiance. St. Just thought at first it was Morwenna from the restaurant, but then he noticed the cane and realized this was an older, taller, more elongated figure. He knew he was being unduly influenced by the setting but there was something wild and unearthly about her. This had to be the Sybil mentioned by Sepia. A white woollen shawl in a spiderweb pattern hung loose from her thin shoulders; frizzled white hair escaped a hairband woven of some hemp-like material. A sea-blue kaftan fell to her feet, which were shod in sandals of an intricately woven fabric with (undoubtedly) vegan-leather soles.

'It's not safe, you see. All the rain we've been getting this year, it weakens the ground. You weren't thinking of tombstoning, were you?'

'What, jumping off? No, of course not. We were thinking of picnicking.'

She eyed him head to toe. 'No, I can see you're past the age where jumping off cliffs would appeal. Unless you were thinking of doing yourself in.'

'Thank you. I wasn't.'

'Today's young are as foolish as they come. And some *are* attempting suicide. It works sometimes – you can see what a long drop it is.'

'How horrible,' said Portia. 'There are no warnings posted, are there?'

'None needed if you've common sense enough to stay away from the edge.'

This struck St. Just as a rational observation. But then she added, 'The place is haunted, of course.'

'Hmm,' said St. Just.

'I do feel something,' said Portia.

His eyes on her said clearly: *Mustn't encourage this.*

'But I do,' Portia insisted. 'Some places are just holier than others and they don't necessarily have a purpose beyond just *being*. Of drawing people to them.'

The woman nodded approvingly. 'Your husband is the one who looks Cornish to me. He should feel its history as you clearly do.'

'We're not married,' said Portia. With a playful smile, she looked up at St. Just. 'Yet.'

Sybil ignored this affectionate exchange. 'In past days, sacrifices were held here. The Celts in particular were fond of beheading their enemies.'

'Really,' said Portia. 'Of course, they'd choose a spot like this.' She looked down at her feet. Was this the very spot, she wondered, where they brought their victims, already soaked in blood? She shifted awkwardly.

'When prosperity seemed elusive,' the woman explained, 'they had to jumpstart the economy. A fair maiden or two was a small price to pay.'

'They sacrificed girls, you mean? Young women?'

'That's the story behind the name Fourteen Maidens, but I don't think anyone knows. The way these things usually go, they would offer what they thought the gods most coveted. Something young and beautiful generally fit the bill. Boy or girl or lamb – who can say? They probably tried a few things and then one day the fishing boats came back with a big catch and they thought, "Ah, that's it then, it's the maiden sacrificed at the full moon that worked."'

As the woman had moved nearer, St. Just could better guess her age, which still could have been anywhere between a weather-beaten fifty and a well-preserved seventy. Her deeply tanned skin made her blue eyes shine like crystals in their sockets.

Portia smiled. 'I'm sure you're right. I'm grateful to you for helping preserve this spot.'

'We have to keep the old ways. Well, except for the human sacrifice, of course. There are laws against that now. But if we don't preserve what we have, we'll become just another county in England, and no one wants that but the English.'

No need to ask where she stood on tourism, thought St. Just.

As if reading his mind (and he had the uncanny feeling she might be able to), Sybil said, 'We must keep tourism at manage-able levels. We need visitors. We just don't need them by the busload. The property is too fragile and there's little enough funding already to keep it shored up. Even when the Fourteen Maidens are in the news for their pixie lights and folk debate whether this is a place of alien landings, it doesn't increase membership in English Heritage. It only brings more gawkers tromping about, destroying any evidence of aliens that might be there.'

St. Just noticed she didn't rule out the chance of such findings. As she stooped to retrieve the basket at her feet, her long hands, freckled and gnarled, emerged from the sleeves of the kaftan. He revised his estimate of her age as closer to seventy. He noticed she had matching tattoos on her wrists, bracelets of a knotted Celtic design.

'We do gather the influx creates some tension,' he said mildly. 'The weekenders and such.'

'Tension! I should say it does create tension when folk don't even try to understand. It's not all pirates and pasties, you know. It's a deeply felt culture that's endured for aeons, since before recorded time. The tourists treat Cornwall like an amusement park at their risk.'

'Risk?' asked St. Just.

'These are ancient gods and goddesses. They don't like to be ridiculed or ignored.'

Well, and who does?

'I understand you want to preserve—' St. Just began.

But she had reached the podium now. 'That's why there's no picnicking here. You wouldn't bring a picnic into a church, now, would you?'

'No,' said Portia. 'No, of course not. And I can see why they made the rule if people are careless with their litter. It's such a beauty spot. Who would do that?'

'We certainly would never litter,' said St. Just, offended, adding, 'I'm a policeman.' As soon the words escaped him, he realized how ridiculous he must have sounded. Was he showing off for Portia, flexing his official muscles? Probably. *Love makes fools of us all.*

'Careless! *Careless!* You've never seen the like, no matter where you're from. It's vile, what people leave behind. Disgusting. Humans can be disgusting.'

'I'm afraid that's true.' His eyes drifted over to the oak tree in the gap of the dolmans.

'Of course, *that* isn't littering,' the woman said. Tied to the tree rooted in the shelf of land were multicoloured pieces of rag. Here and there beaded necklaces or bracelets had been draped over the branches. The bits of cloth floated and danced in the breeze; the beads made a soft clicking sound.

St. Just knew exactly what all this was but it had been so many years that he could not call the word to mind.

'Clouties, they're called,' said the woman.

'Right,' he said. 'Clouties. For making a wish.'

She scowled. Apparently, 'wishing' was for children. 'Wishing' did not begin to approach the deeper meaning behind the tattered shreds of cloth.

St. Just turned to Portia. 'This custom of tying rags to trees is usually found at holy wells. They've been torn from clothing at the part of the body that hurts or is injured. As the cloth rots away, the wound heals.' To the woman he said jokingly, 'I don't suppose a broken heart could be healed that way, could it?' He realized his sceptical presence upset her and he was trying to lighten the mood.

'Of course it could. Melor Toll's heart was instantly healed when his wife came here to pray and tie on a cloutie. He never had to go back to the doctor. Why, is there something wrong with your heart?'

'No,' said St. Just with a glance at Portia. 'My heart's healed now, thanks to this excellent woman here.'

'I meant serious heart trouble.'

'So did I,' said St. Just.

'Hmph. I tell people never to use polyester, or plastic beads, or any of that rubbish – they'll never get what they want that way.'

'Plus, it's bad for the environment,' said Portia.

This earned her a craggy smile, Sybil's eyes nearly disappearing behind the wrinkles.

'Yes. And Mother Earth is the province of the Goddess. She does not reward such carelessness. Rather, she . . .'

'She punishes?' supplied St. Just.

'If need be,' the woman agreed, nodding. 'She punishes.'

And on that happy note—

'I thought I recognized you,' she said, peering at him. 'Policeman, did you say? Then you'll be at the meeting tomorrow night.'

St. Just wondered why it seemed to follow in everyone's mind, as night follows day, that a policeman would naturally want to spend his holiday sitting in some boring civic meeting – a meeting in which, moreover, he had no horse in the race. He could do that at home when the result might directly impact his council tax, or when inveigled into making a presentation on why the state of lawlessness in Cambridge was not nearly so bad as it seemed to the casual reader of *CambridgeshireLive*.

'How would you recognize me?' he asked.

To that she gave a *duh* look.

'I know you don't live here, but there are Universal Principles at stake.' The capitalized words could be inferred from her tone, the raised index finger of her right hand. 'The very sanctity of the Fourteen Maidens is at risk.'

'Thirteen,' murmured St. Just.

'Their survival, even. They've stood unsullied for aeons and they must be safeguarded now. It would be a sacrilege not to stand up for what's right. You will be there – of course you will. They're showing their true colours, the villagers. And their true colour is the colour of money.'

'Well, I—'

'You'll want to watch out most particularly for the estate agent woman. Cynthia Beck. She reads the *Financial Times* like it's the Bible, which to her I'm sure it is. Completely soulless. Once married to a commodities broker.' She nodded significantly, adding, 'Made a packet out of the divorce, she did, for all she cries poor now. And Lord Bodwally may deign to appear. He doesn't normally mingle with the peasants, but if he doesn't show in person, he's sure to send his partner in crime to speak to his interests. Jake Trotter. There's a dark horse . . .'

'I'll see,' murmured St. Just diplomatically, thinking she'd probably never know whether he was in the audience.

'I'll know,' she said. 'And now I'll take my leave of you. Remember: no picnics.'

With that, she plodded away on her vegan sandals, down the

path to the entrance to the Fourteen Maidens. The only other way in was if an incredibly fit person scaled the cliff. St. Just was certain some athlete or other had given it a try in the past. He could picture Sybil staving them off with her cane.

St. Just and Portia made their way back to the village, stopping at Seaside Cottage to pick up waterproof jackets. They planned a day on the beach but were following local advice to be ready for sun or storm.

Portia closed the door behind them, standing with her back to it. 'Well, that was strange,' she said.

'I did try to warn you.'

'You did not try to warn me.'

'I did. Using my eyebrows, I very clearly warned you. I said, "Don't encourage this woman."'

'I thought you were just expressing surprise. As if to say, "Haunted? Wow! No kidding!" Really, Arthur. You're going to have to be much less subtle in future. What else did your eyebrows say?'

'Simply that, speaking of picnics, I thought she might be a sandwich or two short of one. I've met enough of these peculiar village women to know appearances can be deceiving. One minute they're trading recipes, and the next minute they've got a carving knife in hand.'

'I thought she was rather sweet. A bit eccentric, of course. But she was protecting her turf.'

'You think everyone's sweet. You are far too softhearted for your own good.'

'I take that as a compliment. There are enough hardhearted people in the world.'

'Too true. Don't ever change, please.'

'I imagine she's just no good around people. With any event requiring more than two in the room, she'd run a mile.'

'Still, she plans to be at that meeting. She didn't bother introducing herself but it had to be Sybil.'

'Sybil Gosling.'

'Sybil Gosling,' he repeated. 'Right. Not that it matters. I doubt we'll be seeing her or her Maidens again while we're here.'

But in that St. Just was to be proved entirely wrong.

SEVEN
This Meeting Is Called to Order

They lingered over dinner that night, tired from splashing about in the barely warm sea and walking the rugged cliff paths.

They had chosen a little Greek restaurant just outside Maidsfell. It perched, lonely as a cloud, atop yet another of the area's stony outcrops, with sea views to rival anything on the French Riviera.

They chatted about the guest list for their wedding, and whether Portia might get her college's Master, an ordained Church of England priest, to officiate in the college chapel. Before their dessert had arrived, the windows of the restaurant framed a ghostly blue twilight.

'Let's go to the meeting,' said Portia. 'I'm a bit intrigued by all the drama. Maybe I could make it a scene in a future book?'

'All right,' said St. Just, signalling the waiter. 'For you, anything.'

They rushed to get back to the cottage in time to wash and change for the meeting, but at the village hall they found a crowd still queuing to get in. Everyone seemed in surprisingly good spirits. A stop at the public room of the Maidsfell Arms had probably helped.

The hall was typical of its type, built circa the Second World War to withstand air raids and musicians of doubtful talent. It seemed designed not for comfort, but rather to discourage long speeches and never-ending plays or pageants.

St. Just managed to fit his large frame into a spindly red plastic chair. He folded his hands and pasted a happy expression on his face as if eagerly anticipating the events about to unfold. The crowd flickered with palpable excitement as neighbour greeted neighbour, encouraging allies to stiffen their resolve.

Clearly, he thought, more was riding on the outcome than the petty squabbles of self-interested people. The shape and future of the village was to be determined, councillors tasked with preserving what was beautiful about the place while simultaneously finding the funds to keep it beautiful.

A difficult balance. And their chances of pleasing both sides? None, thought St. Just. He had enough experience of how people operate in groups to know the day would be won by whichever firebrand rose to power and could, by sheer force of charisma or veiled threat, persuade others to his or her side.

He looked for such a one among the five councillors ranged before the audience. Sitting at a long table on a stage that had no doubt hosted countless dramas were two women and three men. The man at the centre, to judge by his stern demeanour, was to lead the evening's events. Another, to go by his dungarees over a Cornwall plaid shirt, was a farmer, and indeed was introduced for the record as Farmer John of Pendennick Farm. The third, a precise man wearing pince-nez glasses, looked as if he might be an accountant. The women were harder to classify, although they exuded the sort of good sense that had doubtless carried the village through wars and pandemics and landed it safely, so far, on the opposite shore.

A small village such as Maidsfell would not have a proper parish council but would make do with whoever could be talked into the unpaid and thankless role of maintaining order and keeping an eye on parking and garden allotments. Planning matters like the fishermen's proposal would fall under their purview, and this was, of course, what had brought everyone out tonight. These volunteers would listen – impartially, one would hope – to all sides of the debate, then meet to decide a vote. Dissenters would be forced to carry the matter to the district authority.

The head councillor introduced himself as Clive Banner, Esq., and after some preliminary business began explaining that he would call first on those people who had signed up in advance to present their arguments. Speakers would not be chosen according to their point of view or the side they'd taken but all were encouraged to speak from the heart. St. Just felt this was a recipe for disaster if ever he heard one. He exchanged matching concerned looks with Portia. Speakers were limited to five minutes.

Councillor Banner went on to explain the situation prompting the meeting.

'The fishermen of this village—'

He got no further. A woman's voice from the crowd rang out, 'And fisherwomen!'

'Right you are,' he replied smoothly. Patrician in aspect, he was clearly a man born to rule unruly mobs. 'The *fishers* of this village have asked for approval of development plans they claim would make their lives easier and more prosperous. There is opposition to this – not just to details of the plan they propose, but to any plan that might permanently alter the seafront. The picturesqueness of Maidsfell is not to be tampered with, say the opposition to the development. Damage to local businesses caused by a reduction in tourism would be ruinous. It is claimed, furthermore, the fishers' plans will curtail property development by making the area less desirable overall.

'In between these two stances so at odds we hope to find a safe middle ground, but as is usual with compromise, we anticipate both sides may come away feeling unhappy. First speaker, please.'

A woman's name was announced – Cynthia Beck. Again, St. Just and Portia exchanged glances: Sybil had warned them about Cynthia.

She stood and introduced herself as a local estate agent. For the occasion, she had shellacked her hair into a multicoloured helmet, and she wore a tailored power suit of cherry red with a white blouse tied at the neck with a bow. Annette Bening's line from *American Beauty*, repeated as she scoured one of her dodgier listings, played in St. Just's head: *I will sell this house today.* She looked completely out of place in a group of farmers, fishers, and leisure clothing-wearing locals.

'They bring in good money, these people we so rudely call Emmets,' she said in a voice clipped and businesslike. 'I need hardly remind you they generate much-needed income for everyone since the Plague Time brought us all to our knees.' She swept round to face the villagers ranged in chairs behind her. 'Or had you all forgotten what it was like?' Heads shook sombrely, practically in unison; no one had forgotten.

'Going forward with these plans would spoil the village and cost us in tourism jobs. Do we really need gangs of unemployed youths hanging about again, looking for something to do – looking for trouble?'

No one seemed to think unemployment was a good idea.

'But the jobs are temporary,' said a woman in a caftan embroidered in blue and gold. In ignoring the council leaders by speaking out of turn, she was setting the tenor for the rest of the meeting. She wore sunglasses on top of her head to hold back her red curls; indeed, she looked as if she had just come from the beach. Her face still gleamed with a whitish sun cream. 'Selling ice cream and pasties to rich Americans looking for their roots doesn't lead to much of anything. And then, come winter, there's naught for kids to do and no money coming in. I have to retrain the helpers in my shop every spring; they've forgotten how to give change by then. All they do is grumble about how Maidsfell is so *boring* and there's nothing for them here at the back end of nowhere. The ones with an ounce of spirit have long since upped sticks and left.'

'That's *precisely* why we need incomers,' shot back Cynthia Beck. 'People spending on removals, furniture, window replacement, and decoration for their new homes. *Educated* people.'

A shuffle of feet as the crowd attempted to parse whether or not they were being called uneducated. Overall, since most of them disliked Cynthia Beck, they decided they were. Arms were crossed and scowls appeared on formerly placid faces.

A woman of perhaps sixty stood. Plump as a laying hen, she had been perhaps a bit lavish in trying out some new cosmetics; her cheeks shone bright red down to her chin, a look that would have appeared natural only on a five-year-old. Permed grey hair tightly coiled suggested a recent perm. St. Just imagined he could smell the ammonia from where he sat.

She identified herself as Beatrice Smith and said, 'Don't anyone' – here a look aimed straight at Cynthia, who never flinched – 'try pretending this is in aid of supporting the local economy. Don't you *dare*. It's a hollowing out of our economy, is what it is. Them builders with their new housing were to blame for schools closing in this area. And the knitting shop and the café – all that was torn down to make room, because builders knew full well the owners wouldn't be around often enough to keep those places going. London, with its posh stores and restaurants – that's where they'd be spending their money.

'And their kids! Their kids would be in boarding schools. I guess schools in Cornwall aren't good enough for the likes of them *educated* folk.' Again, a dart whizzed past Cynthia Beck's head. 'I'm in favour of progress but we don't want Maidsfell turning into another Kensington by the Sea.' Lowering her curly head, she pursed her lips and narrowed her eyes to suggest the builders' actions remained an incomprehensible mystery that would be spoken of for years to come.

Finally, she said, 'My sister owned The Knit Wit for years, as you know. And when she went and had some choice words with the construction overlord, he laughed and told her to stick to her knitting. That man had friends in high places and could do as he wished. And he did.' Her gaze swept the room, searching in vain for the overlord. 'I see that person dared not show his face tonight,' she continued.

Others nodded as she spoke. It was clear hers was an oft-told tale but the sympathy of her friends was still on tap.

'My sister died of a broken heart. I'll never think otherwise.'

There was a long pause as she felt blindly for her seat, to be comforted by the men and women on either side of her, all offering tissues. She soon vanished into a sea of consoling arms, her quiet sobs muffled against the shoulder of one of her friends.

After a decent interval, a portly man of military bearing cleared his throat. Standing ramrod straight, he said, 'What worries me most is the breakdown of law and order. The litter visitors leave behind isn't the half of it – rubbish strewn across the beach, cans and bottles and wrappers and – God help us – used nappies. There is such a thing as making a destination *too* popular, you know. That's the sort of thing that will drive down property values.'

'Too right,' shouted someone from the back.

'Order,' intoned Councillor Banner. 'We'll have order *now*.'

But his voice was overridden by a tall, elderly man with shoulders bowed in a pronounced stoop. Perhaps out of respect for his fragility – it had taken an age for the man to haul himself upright and it seemed a cruelty to tell him to sit – the councillor permitted him to speak, thus throwing all rules of order out of the window for the rest of the night.

'Remember when ruffians targeted the new construction last year?' he asked in a high, querulous voice. 'When those houses being built near the lighthouse were vandalized? "Go Back Where U Came From." And, "U R Not Wanted." All misspelled, of course. And a version of "Go Away", but they didn't say "Go Away"; they said something else. They used language I won't repeat with ladies present.' He shook his head, setting his myriad chins wobbling. Judging by his close-cropped white hair and his general bearing, he – like his portly, slightly younger companion – was ex-military of some stripe, retired to his dream village only to find the demons of war had followed him there.

'It's a clear enough message even if we still don't know who was responsible,' the elderly man added. 'Vandalism is wrong, even if you happen to agree with what's being written. Mind, I might throttle them with my own hands if I could catch them at it. But decency says I can't.' It seemed an idle threat, given his frailty, but he had captured the general mood of many in the crowd.

'I don't see why not,' tweeted an elderly lady at the back, to general laughter. 'I'd help you.'

The old man turned – slowly, mindful of the risk of falling over – and winked at her.

The portly, upright military man (St. Just assigned him the rank of Major) stood, his bald head gleaming in the overhead fluorescent light. He said, 'And then there's the comments on the village Facebook page, speaking of language. The Colonel here is right. It's a scandal. Isn't someone supposed to be monitoring that page?'

Heads swivelled expectantly in the direction of the meeting's leader. He allowed a moment to pass while he collected himself. This seemed to be a subject he'd been dreading but since it was inextricably tied up with the topic at hand, he likely felt he had to address it.

'I'll have it looked into,' he said, sighing. 'Again. It's become a full-time job now the village has something like six thousand followers.'

There were gasps of astonishment at this. St. Just noticed a young man nearby scribbling madly in a reporter's notebook. He had everything but a press pass sticking out of a fedora to mark him as a likely contributor to the local newspaper St. Just and Portia had read just that morning. *At last*, his excited body language seemed to say, *a real story!* Six thousand followers could surely be converted into six thousand readers of his newspaper.

St. Just and Portia tried to read the faces in the crowd; the reactions seemed split down the middle. There would be those who wanted Maidsfell kept to near-anonymity, while others would welcome anything that drew the tourist pound.

'In fact, I've been planning to propose we take the page down,' the councillor continued. 'And the Maidsfell Twitter feed – who authorized that? The exchanges are libellous at times, and there's no way I'm spending my time or the council's policing that. People should have their heads looked at.'

'Too late,' someone shouted. 'They've gone Bodmin already.' This common Cornwall expression was met with general laughter.

'Order,' the councillor said automatically. 'Besides, there's more than one Facebook page. The "How Bloody Dare They?" page has taken off, in particular. I don't know who's behind them all. I only know there are some pages I wouldn't touch with a barge pole.'

The portly Major basked in his moment of vindication, moustaches waggling.

'It's not just us,' a young woman said softly, with a glance at her husband. She might never have spoken up in a public meeting before. 'Folk like my aunt and uncle in the Lake District can't afford to live in the village they grew up in.'

'It's the same all over,' said another. 'The Suffolk coast, the Peak District, Devon – all along the south coast.'

Those who stood to speak had long since stopped introducing themselves, since everyone but St. Just and Portia seemed to know who they were. 'It's funny how the closer the second home is to the sea,' said one, 'the more the homeowners carry on about spoiling the view. When they're not even around to enjoy the ruddy view.'

'They're lucky a road can't be run along the foreshore. Other villages have been forced into that and it's a disaster.'

'That won't stop some from trying to build a road,' said the woman who had offered to help the Colonel throttle the vandals. 'Never say "can't". Look at the Romans.'

No one seemed to know what the Romans had to do with anything but the crowd fell into a respectful silence. Everything the woman wore apart from her sensible shoes looked hand-knitted with soft pastel yarns. With her grey hair wound in a topknot and glasses perched low on her nose, she had the look of a former teacher. She'd probably taught many in the room.

'I thought the government outlawed second-home ownership?' said a middle-aged woman with complicated hair suggesting a standing appointment at the beauty salon.

'Not this lot. People can buy what they damned well please. And they please to buy up everything in Maidsfell but not actually live here.'

'Unless there's another pandemic, of course. *That* brought them all running.'

'Like the Black Death.'

Solemn head-shaking at this.

'I thought some second-home owners said they'd build a jetty elsewhere for the fishermen? What happened to that?' Amid hums of support, a rough-and-ready sort of man stood, barrel-chested and with a brown, weather-beaten face. 'It was an empty promise to start with.' St. Just took him to be a fisher, perhaps sixty years old. He stood with his feet apart, as if expecting a swell of wave to knock him over.

Heads nodded in agreement, accompanied by the occasional 'Hear, hear!' and 'Too right you are, Will!'

A man out of St. Just's sightline said, 'Lord Bodwally could solve this if he'd let the fishers use his Smuggler's Beach. He just can't be arsed to do it.'

Estate Agent Cynthia said, 'The fishing industry is such a small part of the gross domestic product. I don't see what all the fuss is about.' Cynthia appeared to be bulletproof, thought St. Just. Perhaps it was the hairspray. A wiser woman might not have spoken.

'It goes to the heart of who we are!' said the Major.

'I thought you were from Manchester.'

'We're speaking of what is in the *blood*. We're talking of *spirit*, woman. *Heart!* Not that you would know anything about that, you heartless, money-grubbing—'

'Now, just a minute, Major. There's no call for—'

'No, there isn't,' said the council head. 'We'll keep it civil. Will Ivey, I will recognize your right to continue speaking, since as a fisherman – sorry, fisher – you are most concerned with the outcome here.'

Will Ivey nodded. 'Didn't we see clearly during the Plague Time what it could be like for us fishermen forever? What with the British not wanting good British fish but wanting exotic rubbish like tiger prawns?'

'I quite like tiger prawns,' a woman said to her friend.

'Stuff your prawns!' Ivey cried. 'We're dying here, woman!'

St. Just would later come to revisit his assessment of the situation as minor, but hindsight is always twenty-twenty. The Major launched into a flag-waving speech, losing the attention he'd had at the outset. Looking about him, St. Just saw signs the audience was yearning to break away for a drink in the pub.

'If we take down Facebook, how will the tourists find us?' demanded a woman from the audience, bridging the Napoleonic flow. She looked the type to have a dog in every fight, broad-shouldered and wide in the hips, with a pugnacious expression on her deeply sun-damaged face. A small man St. Just took to be her husband sat alertly at her side.

'I think I speak for us all when I say, "Fuck the tourists,"' said Will Ivey evenly.

A collective gasp, then: 'You most certainly do not speak for us all,' said Cynthia Beck.

'Watch the language,' said the head of the council.

'I'll not be silenced,' the seaman continued. 'Me, I've taken to sleeping on my boat to protect it from vandals and pirates. It's come to that.'

St. Just stole a look at Portia, who was avidly following the arguments. He imagined that to a writer it was quite like watching a play.

He told himself he had no stake in the proceedings. And yet he sensed undercurrents and was uneasy in his mind.

It was at that moment he spotted their hostess from the night before. Morwenna stood as if she wanted to say something but quickly thought better of it. Indeed, for someone who had been so much on the side of the fishers, her silence had been conspicuous. She resumed her seat, tightly crossing her arms as if to contain whatever words might otherwise escape, letting the meeting wash over her.

St. Just wondered at the sudden climbdown. Her pro-fisher motives had come across as pure – apart from her obvious dislike of Bodwally and his crony, her rival in the restaurant game, Jake Trotter. What happened? Was she being threatened?

'What about the Duke and Duchess of Cornwall? They've honoured us many times with a visit. Were they tourists, too?' the Major demanded.

'What, Will and Kate?' a man asked with a grin, suggesting he was having the older man on.

'Their *Royal Highnesses* the Duke and Duchess,' corrected the Major. 'Show some respect, man.'

'Oh, *excuse* me, but what do you want next, ruddy cruise ships anchored off the coast? That would make a proper job of destroying the place. As it is, you can barely squeeze your car down the lanes, let alone dream of finding a place to park. Which reminds me, whatever happened to the car park that was supposed to be built *outside* the village?'

Now the cries rose up with renewed energy. Parking problems, thought St. Just, did have a way of uniting people. 'Yes!' 'Car park!' 'More empty promises!'

'You know, you can't have it both ways,' said the council leader wearily. 'And it's past time you made your minds up what it is you *do* want. Otherwise, we'll be having the same argument and fighting the same planning war year after year, getting nowhere. You want tourists, but not too many tourists because they clog up the alleyways and block the roads with their four-by-fours and they make noise and they drink and they run people down with their bicycles. You want more income, but not at the expense of letting rich folk come and buy property – not unless you're wanting to sell your house to them at a nice profit, that is. You want taxes kept low, but at the same time you want to raise taxes to discourage people wanting to buy.'

The teacher said, 'In the end, the question is, are we to let Maidsfell become a protected playground for the rich? Do we really want to go the way of other towns and villages? Do we want to become a ghost village in winter – with all the fancy houses shuttered and the villagers forced out – and a Disney theme park in summer?'

The Colonel, clearly enlivened by a short nap, cried, 'They're all ruining the village! I say, get rid of the rich incomers, and the vandals will slink back to whatever hole they crawled out of.'

More generalized hubbub, then, 'Our MP is on the fisher's side.'

'Well, he would be, wouldn't he? He doesn't live here. No skin off his nose and it makes him look a man of the people.'

'And I say' – the steely Cynthia Beck again, still unruffled but shouting to be heard over the hubbub – 'we need to take the long view. The holiday-home people come here to spend money enjoying themselves and they do – spend and enjoy.'

'I don't want their money,' said a woman who looked as if she might head the Women's Institute. 'I want them gone.'

'But you take their money.'

''Course I do. I'm not daft. It's the least they can do after all the harm they've done.'

Morwenna Wells stood at last, having seemingly found her courage. St. Just recalled she had been famous in London and had brought fame to the village. He wondered if her support of the fishers wasn't a way to assuage her guilt. She, after all, had with her notoriety helped heap all this on the villagers' heads.

Since she was herself from Cornwall – a Miss Cornwall, no less – the guilt might be twice over.

'I'll tell you this much,' she said. 'I cannot rely only on the people who come here during the summer to keep my pub and restaurant afloat. We need people who don't just pretend to be locals, but who *are* locals. Who stay put year-round. Who care because they actually live here. That's not happening. People like shop owners, nurses, teachers, bin men – where are they meant to live once the place is only fit for millionaires?'

She stilled the crowd's response with a lift of one hand.

'I struggle all year to keep the restaurant going,' she continued. 'If I have to close, it will not be the fault of the noisy Townies. It will be the fault of the money-grubbing landlords who let their places to the noisy Townies.'

A louder cheer broke out at this. Another minute and he thought Morwenna might be carried out on the shoulders of the villagers.

'Renting out their cottages to people from out of town and then themselves turning up twice a year does not make them local,' she added. 'But the real problem is, they don't care who they rent to. They only care that their rent gets paid.'

This, too, was greeted with applause. St. Just wondered how their own landlady would take this. He knew he and Portia didn't fall into the noisy demographic, but he suspected Penelope White with her luxury yacht would fit into Morwenna's description of someone who only pretended to be local when it suited.

'But here's the last straw,' Morwenna continued. 'Do you want to hear what the last straw is?'

They assured her they did. 'You tell 'em, Wenna!'

'The last straw is once they've driven me out of business, they'll be the first to complain there are no good restaurants in Maidsfell.'

Another roar went up. St. Just felt they might be wandering a bit from the topic of the fishers' plans, but somehow the issues all seemed to be knitted – or rather, knotted – together. People struggling to make a living were being exploited, or felt they were being exploited, by the non-local wealthy who simply scraped the place bare before sailing off in their yachts.

Morwenna's colour was high. As she paused for breath, a voice from behind her boomed, 'If the ruddy fishermen would drop this idea of the jetty and parking, people might stick around. No one likes all this fighting.'

She rounded on the young man who had said this. 'That's two separate issues, Stefan. The *real* locals care what happens to the fishermen. That's the entire point.' She pointed an index finger for emphasis. 'They will do what's right, which is to keep the fishermen's livelihoods alive. And if it's good for business, for the restaurants, what—'

Abruptly, she stopped speaking. The colour drained from her face, and after standing stock-still for a long moment, she fumbled to regain her seat. Later, St. Just would try to reconstruct that moment. Who might suddenly have come into her line of sight? With such an animated crowd, it was impossible to say. Perhaps it was someone newly arrived. Someone whose presence she took as a threat, implied or otherwise.

The Reverend Judith Abernathy, the local curate they'd met at their morning coffee, rose from her seat. 'It all depends on the rent they ask. If the rich only let to their rich friends, it's not a problem solved for the working man or woman, is it? It's the view they're paying for. But it is God's view and it belongs to all, I say.' St. Just couldn't decide how well this blended with her earlier pro-fisher stance.

'They despoil the work of the Goddess.' This was Sybil Gosling, appearing for the occasion in what St. Just supposed was full

Wiccan regalia. She wore a veiled crown on her head and her black dress looked as if the hem had been run through a shredder. 'They cut down trees and all. Remember that big oak that disappeared? They said it was dying. It wasn't dying. They pretend to be "green" and, behind our backs, everything good and born of the Goddess disappears. That tree stood in the way of development, is what. If you can call such a desecration "development". I will personally tie myself to the next tree they try to remove.' She raised a fist to the heavens. 'Let them all hang for murder!'

The villagers may have been expecting drama but clearly not on this scale. Several settled deeper into their deeply uncomfortable chairs to see what might happen next. The next meeting of the men's group would have *much* to discuss.

Another woman, gloriously middle-aged, swept into the moment, gathering a brocaded cape round her shoulders, stopping only to push a fall of bright red hair from her eyes and adjust the brooch at her heart. She wore eyeglasses with pink frames and lipstick to match and at a guess was not the wallflower type. Portia whispered to St. Just, 'I know her! From her publicity photo. Mind, it's probably ten years out of date, but that's Ramona Raven. She writes romance novels.'

'She certainly came to the right place for writers,' St. Just whispered back. 'Daphne du Maurier and Rosamunde Pilcher, to name two.'

But St. Just felt a frisson of something like nervous apprehension. It had been at a writers' conference held in a Scottish castle that he had first met Portia. Sadly, the castle soon became a setting for crime. He could only hope history wouldn't repeat itself here in Cornwall.

But why, he chided himself, *would it?* Just because one romance writer happened to live in Maidsfell, and a rather unhinged elderly woman was taking a stand for her pagan beliefs, there was no reason . . . He tuned in intently to what Ramona Raven (that *had* to be a pen name) was saying.

In a clear voice, possibly theatrically trained, she picked up the flag Morwenna had so suddenly dropped. 'If they were *affordable* houses, it would be one thing. Houses the young could afford to buy. Or writers, for that matter.' There was general laughter and she beamed in appreciation, batting her fake eyelashes. 'But that's never the plan, is it? To help the struggling writers and artists – who are part of the reason people are drawn here, by the way. There's no one *living* here can afford what's on offer in these new developments. And those houses, mind, are quite small, unless the couple able to buy is getting along very well indeed.' Some further laughter at that. 'But in the end, the young couples – and the struggling artists – go else-where. Even though many of them were born and bred in Maidsfell.'

A general buzz suggested the crowd was in agreement. Only the estate agent and a few others greeted the writer's logic with stony-faced silence. St. Just was reminded of the inscrutable stares of the Maidens that brooded over the village.

'What young person has five hundred thousand pounds at the ready?'

The replies came:

'Brokers!'

'Solicitors!'

'Prince Harry!'

A balding, middle-aged man stood and said, 'I resent that. I'm a solicitor and, as most of you know, a local. Or as local as one can be after ten years living here. I can tell you not all solicitors are rich. But the hiring of London solicitors and outside consult-ants and planners – that's what has added fuel to this flame, which should have remained a small local matter. I feel that with a bit of compromise, everyone can be, if not happy, then satisfied that both sides are being heard. It shouldn't be the them-versus-us situation that's evolved.'

St. Just thought this quite the most reasonable thing he'd heard but, to judge by the sulky faces, no one seemed in the mood for compromise. They were still in the mood for getting their own way.

The meeting continued in the same vein for half an hour more. St. Just and Portia, seated dead centre of the room, realized too late they were trapped; they would have to crawl over nearly a dozen people to make their escape.

But the council chair brought the proceedings to a close at last, thanking people for their input, and St. Just and Portia joined the general exodus. A mistake, since it left them trapped again, this time in a dark alleyway, unable to reach the high street.

It was then they overheard a most remarkable argument.

EIGHT
Some Enchanted Evening

Late that night as he lay beneath the downy duvet, Portia asleep in his arms, St. Just thought he heard the sound of a pan flute coming from up the lane, the gentle notes drifting above the roof and down the chimney of their little cottage. This was accompanied by a percussion instrument, a beating drum, a steady but muffled *thump, thump, thump.* And the occasional metallic rattling of something like a tambourine.

All this was underlaid with a soft chanting of incantations, summoning who knew what. He judged the little concert to be coming from the site of the Fourteen Maidens.

Perhaps Sybil Gosling had gathered a few like-minded friends to observe some pagan ritual or other by the light of the full moon, dressed in druidic robes and waving smudge sticks about. He wondered if *they* had been allowed to bring a picnic. Strangely, he found the tuneless tune comforting, both haunting and soothing, not loud enough to disturb. It was as if the sound had travelled to him from across the millennia.

Through half-opened eyes he thought he saw a small light pass by their bedroom window, shining between the slats of the shutters, but it was soon gone in a swirl of fog. He was thinking he might go and investigate – he really should take a look (was he dreaming it?) – but very soon, the insistent rhythm had lulled him to sleep.

The next morning, his mind groped for the memory of that non-tune. Of course, it was gone, more elusive the more he reached for it, gone along with the sublime sense of peace, a certain knowledge and deep resolve that all would be well – just one or two more hurdles to jump.

What hurdles he could not say. *You're on holiday*, he reminded himself sternly. *You must have fun. It's what people who are not policemen do with their lives.*

Daylight shone between the slats of the window shutters, again triggering some shapeless memory from the night before. He almost felt as if he'd been drugged. He pushed his dark, thick hair back from his brow.

Careful not to disturb Portia, he pulled back the covers and eased his feet into his slippers. His eyes took in the garish décor, so at odds with anything to do with rest and relaxation and lovemaking. The top of a bureau against one wall of the room already held a collection of brochures and little keepsakes from their stay. Today they'd go to the beach, no doubt returning with shells to carry back home to Cambridge, even though Sybil would almost certainly disapprove of the 'theft'.

Memories of Cornwall summers had long held a singular place in his heart, tied as they were to his parents. To celebrate the launch of his new life with Portia, he had wanted to show her the rock-strewn coast carved out by stormy seas; for her to see the land of tin mines and fishing villages that had been home to his ancestors. He had chosen Maidsfell for its central location among the beauty spots, with their beaches and palm trees and tropical plants which were a gift to the area from the Gulf Stream.

He crept into the little kitchen to make coffee. Waiting for the first cup to brew, he called up what he could remember of the conversation he and Portia had overheard the night before.

It had been raining as they left the village hall, a typically sudden summer squall, with water coming down in insistent beats, tiny pellets turning into streams that ran off their jackets and Portia's scarf and made a watercourse of his hat brim.

Waiting for the crowd to disperse was like being held in a dank, dark cave. He had always hated being in a crush of people; it seemed like a vestige of another life, some prior existence when he might have been trampled by a throng fleeing a burning building. He and Portia had pulled back, allowing the alleyway to clear of people, letting friends chatter with friends. As outsiders, they didn't want to push their way into private conversations.

It was from this position they heard quite a different conversation. A woman's voice, high and angry – out of place in an otherwise peaceful scene. Many, in fact, seemed to be rehashing the meeting, but if there was any ill will, he could not detect it. Then came the sounds of discord.

'You're selfish, that's what. Selfish, like all your lot.'

'And you're creating problems where there aren't any.'

'This is a *huge* problem already – what are you saying? I'm not *creating* anything.'

'It'll be the first time, then.'

'You shut up. I'm so tired of having you—'

'We'll keep our secret – full stop. Deny everything, if it comes to that. Everything will be fine.'

'Fine! Only if—'

Just then a motorbike roared by, going much too fast for the narrow, wet cobblestones and drowning out the reply. He and Portia unabashedly leaned in, straining to hear.

'. . . best. You have to trust me.'

'Hah! Trust you? Let me write that down. I keep forgetting.'

'Not this again. You—'

'Don't you fucking dare try to make this about me.'

'Well, it would make a welcome change. Isn't it always all about you?'

'*You're* the narcissist!'

'Me? Look, like it or not, we must stand firm – together. I'll see it's taken care of.'

A burst of raucous laughter from the crowd drowned out some of her reply.

'. . . wrong.' Her voice was an odd mixture of pain and anger. 'I know desperate, what people will do when they have no recourse.'

'When they *think* they have no recourse.'

St. Just dared a peek round the corner but could see only the outlines of a tall male figure looming over a woman eclipsed by shadow. The man's face had moved in very close to hers. They might have been about to kiss.

'Just keep your head,' he hissed. 'I could try talking to—'

'With *your* diplomatic skills?'

A crowd walked by the front of the village hall, laughing and talking at the top of their voices, and again eclipsing the words of the quarrelling couple.

'. . . and be damned.'

'Easy for you to say.'

'Yes, it is, rather. Because at the end of the day, this only seems to matter to *you*.'

There was a sudden hush. The woman may have gone back into the building to wait out the storm. St. Just and Portia exchanged glances.

'Lovers' quarrel?' she murmured. The cold had brought colour to her cheeks; her eyes beneath her scarf gleamed in the darkness, as if a cameraman had shone a keylight.

'Ex-lovers, perhaps.'

They realized the conversation had resumed – or, rather, a new conversation had begun. A substitute player had been sent in, as it were, for a different woman's voice broke the silence.

'I couldn't help but overhear,' she said. 'Forgive me if I'm meddling.'

An inarticulate grunt met this speech. Same man, St. Just thought, different woman. It sounded like Judith Abernathy, their friend of the morning. She had that carrying voice designed for sermons. But now the voice was soft, coaxing.

'Forgiveness makes us twice blessed, you know.' Surely only a priest would talk like this, confirming his impression. The ambient noise of the crowd made it difficult to be certain. 'It blesses him who forgives and—'

'Forgive me. That sort of platitude isn't helpful in this case.'

'You shake your head but you know I'm right,' she said.

'I'll bid goodnight to you. Take care how you go in this rain. I'll see you soon.'

Someone switched on an electric lantern at the entrance to the alley, so at last they could get their bearings. Leaping shapes of the villagers were thrown against the ancient walls like shadow puppets.

There should be three people missing, thought St. Just. Those three involved in the conversations he'd just overheard. But he could not puzzle it out in the sea of bodies.

Slowly, he and Portia made their way back to the cottage. The rain was tapering off but still blurred the landmarks that could guide them home. It was dark with no moon or stars visible, but reflections in the shop windows seemed to follow them. Portia's hair was plastered to her face, proving his theory that nothing made her less beautiful.

They decided against the pub visit they'd planned in favour of a nightcap beside their borrowed hearth.

NINE

By the Sea

Tuesday

The day edged into the morning self-consciously, with bleak grey streaks of cloud stippling a dark grey horizon. But St. Just and Portia had decided on the beach and to the beach they would go.

Having collected all the requisite gear, they trundled downhill and past the harbour. St. Just spotted the fisher of last night's meeting – Will Ivey, the one who especially didn't like tourists. He was doing something seamanlike with his trawler, his hands so calloused and rough he apparently didn't require gloves.

Cliffs rose at each side of Maidsfell Beach like arms embracing the sea; tumbled heaps of rocks lay at the foot of the cliffs, sheared off centuries before into the roiling waters. Sandy coves beyond each of these piles could be reached only by those willing to chance the tide.

Aeons of boulder falls had gouged deep holes beneath the water, creating an unseen, uneven sea floor that could drop into nothingness unexpectedly. A swimmer caught in the resulting rip currents would not soon forget the experience – always assuming he survived. He might wade out from the shore, distracted by the beauty of it all, and with his next step simply disappear beneath the waves.

Still nothing could stop the surfers along Cornwall's north coast, nor the weekend sailors and paddle boarders along its south, nor the kayakers, nor the tourists wanting only to snap photos of the picture-book harbour from the safety of a pub terrace.

St. Cuthbert's crouched over the beach like an ageing lifeguard, surrounded by tombstones in varying stages of decay. Tucked beneath the squat medieval church on a jutting lip of land stood the broken circle of the Fourteen Maidens, their rounded tops just visible from below.

St. Just watched Portia navigate her graceful way round the rock stacks lining the beach. She wore beige trousers and a long-sleeved white linen shirt over her swimsuit; a wide straw hat with a black band covered her hair.

The weather was just cool enough that going in the water might be inadvisable, but Portia had said she wanted to brave it. Indeed, the sun now looked as if it might be open for business as usual, golden rays striking stone and water and reflecting onto their faces. But the next raft of clouds brought a chill, dispelling the illusion.

A small plane flew past, trailing a banner that read, *Happy Birthday Monica*. St. Just smiled, pausing to take in the sight of the crumpled sea, constantly in motion with its shifting layers of white and turquoise and navy. Portia jumped from a low rock into the sand and turned to him, laughing, her cheeks pink with exertion, her eyes a match for the sparkling blue water flecked with sunlight. St. Just again marvelled at his temerity in asking such an exceptional human being to marry him and marvelled even more at her acceptance. He had in fact asked her several times in different settings, to give her every chance to change her mind – hoping against hope, of course, that she would not. It looked as if his luck was holding.

He had warned her that tying herself to a policeman was committing to a life of uncertainty and early-morning awakenings and hours of creeping dread if he failed to return home – it wasn't like writing about crime, he'd foolishly said; it was the real down and dirty of crime every day. It was the closest they'd ever come to having an argument.

'What do you mean?' she'd asked. They'd just been heading out to dinner after a long day. Hunger and tiredness were never precursors to a good conversation. 'There's nothing easy about writing crime novels, you know. You want to talk about early mornings? Uncertainty and creeping dread?'

'No, no, of course not. I mean, of course it's not easy.'

'It's ruddy hard work, is what it is. You wake up at three a.m., you have a deadline, your back is aching from too much sitting, and you've just realized your plot has a hole in it you could drive a lorry through.'

'Yes! Yes. Incredibly difficult, it must be. So difficult. All those hours at the desk and fretting over Oxford commas and dangling participles and so on. Not to mention the eternal colon versus semi-colon debate. And, of course, the impossible deadlines . . .'

'Now you're making fun of me.'

'No, I assure you, I'm just trying to let you know I know it's not as simple as it looks. I meant to say, well . . . I meant to say *real* police work—'

'Perhaps, Arthur, you meant to say *actual* police work. "Actual" would be a better choice of word than "real".' Her voice was several degrees colder than normal. 'I know something about words, you know.'

'Yes! Quite. *Actual* police work is filled with unhappy endings and loose ends and far too often with rank injustices. It's rare that a case can be neatly tied up with a ribbon at the end as in a novel. The lawyers see to that.'

'You feel my novels are unrealistic.' It was not a question.

'No! I feel . . .' – *like an idiot*. Portia's attachment to her writing was no different from his attachment to being a detective. Their callings defined who they were. His was the most frustrating job in the world and the most rewarding, and he would never brook some fool implying that what he did each day was trivial, unimportant. 'I know for a fact, having read all your books with such enjoyment, they are wonderful, absolutely top-drawer, first-rate entertainment, smart and well written and—'

'And wholly unrealistic. But entertaining. Well, that's nice, at least. I am the literary equivalent of the organ grinder's monkey.'

'Um.' Not daring to say another word, St. Just began breathing quietly, rapidly, through his nose, a meditation technique he'd read about somewhere and generally got wrong. Was it in through the nose for four counts and out through the mouth for eight, or the other way round?

'Well, perhaps the books are as you say,' said Portia. 'But entertainment is important in this world, too. And I do go to a lot of trouble with the research.'

'And it shows!' he cried. 'My God, I have never felt so transported as I was in that book you set in Tuscany. It was like being there. The olive oil, the statues, the tomatoes—'

'You can stop now, Arthur. I knew what you meant.'

She smiled. A smile that to him was like the heavens opening. 'As it happens, I agree with you. The dead body on page one and the clever villain captured by page three hundred, sent down in the final "reel" to his just reward – it can only happen in novels. Most villains in real life are quite ordinary and not very bright, as you know. Which is why they get caught.'

'I—'

'I should quit while you're ahead, though, Arthur. Come on, I'm starving. Let's get something to eat.'

TEN
Lifesaver

As Portia and St. Just set about claiming their spot on the beach, they became aware of a distant commotion. St. Just, kneeling to weigh down the corners of their blanket, stood to see what was happening. What he saw was a youngish blond man, and heads turning to look as he passed.

The man was fit, no doubt about it. Not fit in the way that made one wonder at the obsession behind all those hours in the gym, but healthy and strong, the way a man naturally would look if he spent a great deal of time outdoors climbing and hiking and running and jumping about. St. Just, in his early forties, considered himself relatively fit, not yet ready for middle age, and often bristled at being forced into that category by an online form.

This specimen striding towards them was in his thirties – about the same age as Portia, at a guess – and . . . Well. The English language needed a new word for handsome, for he was absurdly good-looking. He wore distressed cutoff jeans and a T-shirt that showed off his muscles, which seemed to flex of their own volition as if attached to electrodes.

A young woman in a tank top practically threw herself into his path. She seemed to have asked him for directions yet she ignored the young god's pointing finger and muscular arm-waving as he replied, instead gazing into his eyes. If a bomb had gone off just then, St. Just doubted she'd notice. She obviously wanted to prolong the conversation, and the man obliged by spinning a long anecdote – quite an amusing one to judge by her hysterical reaction.

Finally, the man managed to tear himself away from his admirer and carry on walking in their direction.

St. Just was a couple of inches taller and broader in the shoulders, but he felt the comparisons could pretty much stop there. He was suddenly acutely aware of the smear of zinc oxide sunblock across his pale nose and began surreptitiously wiping it off.

He felt he knew the man. Something in the way he carried himself. That confident swagger . . .

'Why, that's – oh, what is his name?' St. Just turned to Portia. 'From that show on the telly.' This was maddening. Not only was he in poor physical health, at least in comparison with this bronze vision of all things manly, but his memory was going as well.

'Callum Page,' she said. 'He's the star of *Wild!* It's a reality show on Channel Four.'

'Of course, that's it. Callum Page. Morwenna mentioned him as one of the celebrities we might see in the village. I don't watch reality shows but somehow popular culture manages to seep through the cracks in my armour.'

'I don't watch them either, but you must have seen the promos. They're everywhere lately, promoting his second season. "*Wildly* popular" is the tagline.'

Of course. Whatever the show was about, and St. Just didn't pretend to know a lot about it, it involved dropping the hero, Callum Page, into a life-or-death situation, giving him a few tools of survival – tools little better than a rock and a few sticks and a rubber band – and leaving him to get on with it. Sink or swim.

Of course, they couldn't actually have left him alone in the jungle or the Antarctic or a cave in Thailand or wherever, as there appeared to be cameras following his every move, and wherever there were cameras, there were bound to be camerapersons to operate them. Somehow people bought into the illusion and worried themselves silly over whether Callum would escape his latest adventure unscathed. St. Just wondered idly how Callum managed to maintain that tan at the South Pole.

'Right,' said St. Just. 'I don't know who has time to watch that sort of piffle.' After a moment's brood, he added, 'I'm too busy fighting crime, myself.'

'I was going to give the show a look once it's on,' said Portia. 'These things can be good fun, you know. All my students seem to watch him and I do try to keep up.'

'I don't see the attraction.'

'He's . . . let's see, he must be about my age. Perhaps mid-thirties. Isn't he in amazing condition? He rows, he paddleboards, he runs marathons, he climbs Kilimanjaro.'

'Goes without saying he would climb Kilimanjaro.'

Portia breezed on. 'He's from Yorkshire originally, I believe, and served in the army a few years before he found his calling. His upcoming show is set in Siberia.'

St. Just thought Siberia sounded promisingly far away.

'Good, yes. Good for him.'

'He does a lot of charity work and fundraising, visiting schools – he even helps build schools. His causes are disadvantaged youth, youth in trouble, youth with disabilities – he's trying to set a good example.'

'Yes. Wonderful.' *Does the Pope know about this?* St. Just wondered. Perhaps Callum Page could be put forward as the patron saint of dogsledders or something.

'The police do a great deal of work for charity, you know,' he said. 'They prefer to keep it low key, however.'

Finally, Portia took her eyes from Callum Page and looked at him. 'Yes. Of course, they do. Are you all right, Arthur?'

'I think he's headed our way. You don't want to talk with him, do you? He looks awfully busy.'

Callum Page was in the process of pushing one hand through his thick blond hair – probably peroxided to achieve that state of near-whiteness – and grinning at Portia. Surely he possessed twice the number of hair follicles nature allowed? St. Just might have been invisible standing next to Portia – not that he wasn't used to the reaction she often evoked from men. 'Poleaxed' was the word to describe it. But as St. Just watched, the massive, tanned hand – definitely a rower's hands, a climber's hands – stopped in midair. The long-lashed eyes widened.

Portia turned in the direction of his stare, her own eyes growing wide. 'Arthur, someone's in trouble out there.'

The water was full of people and at first he couldn't spot any trouble.

Then he heard it, a faint cry for help, the sound quickly swallowed by a wave. Another cry as whoever it was re-emerged, only to be cut off again. The high-pitched cry of a female in distress. It wasn't a particularly vicious sea that day but St. Just knew these waters were treacherous, deadly with flash rip currents beneath the surface.

Callum Page tore past them, pulling off his shirt as he ran. Reaching the edge of the shore, he stripped to his swim trunks.

St. Just turned towards the lifeguard perch – which was empty. He'd forgotten the beach was not guarded on weekdays – cutbacks made during the Plague Time had not been fully restored. The spot was instead posted with hazard signage telling people it might not be safe to swim; the tide could rise without notice. *FLOAT TO LIVE*, read one sign in high, red letters, illustrated by a cartoon character thrashing about the waves in panic.

People not from Cornwall could never imagine how dangerous the place was. They came for the dolphins and porpoises, the whale-spotting on wildlife tours.

Not for the deadly tides. Not for being swept into the sea by gale-force winds.

St. Just began pulling his own shirt over his head and kicking off his sandals as he, too, headed for the water. He passed his wallet and mobile to Portia, shouting, 'Ring for help.' As he ran, he paused only to take a beach ball out of the hands of a startled toddler, who shrieked at the outrage.

'Wait a minute, you!' yelled the child's mother. 'You give that back!'

A half dozen people were waist-deep in the waves already, having caught wind of the crisis. St. Just knew they would only add to the problem, risking their own lives if they didn't know how to swim out of the currents or to respect their erratic power, the sandbars like moving sculptures, their ridges changing with each tide.

The instinct of a panicked swimmer is to try to swim straight back to shore, the worst possible choice, leading to exhaustion which leads to drowning. The only way out of the almighty, invisible pull of the water is to swim parallel to the shore, out of the side of the current.

St. Just saw Callum Page was doing a crawl stroke through the waves, headed more or less in the direction of the distressed swimmer, who was suddenly nowhere in sight.

Why in God's name is there no lifeguard?

He placed the beach ball into the rip current, hoping it would be pulled to within the victim's reach. Then he plunged into the water, avoiding the current, for it was visible as a dark, relatively quiet river of water compared with the waves on either side of it.

Callum was by now only a few metres ahead of him. From somewhere he'd acquired a fluorescent pink foam noodle which he'd tucked under his left arm. It was slowing his progress but it would be needed by the victim – if he could reach her in time. St. Just, unimpeded, surged ahead, shouting to the victim, her head now visible but her body being tugged about by the current.

'Don't try to swim!' he shouted. 'Float! On your back!'

The swimmer, now revealed to be a girl of perhaps twelve, screamed. In fact, her screaming only stopped during what seemed unending moments when she went under. When her head re-emerged, she would gasp loudly for air.

'*Float!*' St. Just commanded. 'Float! Don't try to swim!'

It wasn't clear if she could even hear him; in any event, she continued to thrash about, making as if to swim for shore and being inexorably pulled away from the beach and from her would-be rescuers.

Callum now appeared at his side, still clutching the noodle. The beach ball floated by on the current, headed straight for the girl.

'Grab the ball!' he and Callum shouted. 'Grab the ball!'

Breathing heavily, regretting the extra nightcap and lack of sleep of the night before, St. Just saw Callum was holding up far better than he was. No question but that he would get to the girl first. 'Grab her from behind and pull her head back by her jaw,' shouted St. Just. 'Don't let her turn or she'll fight and pull you down, too.'

Callum continued his steady one-armed crawl with the foam noodle. It wasn't clear if he'd heard St. Just. But the ball had reached the girl and she grabbed it like a life raft.

A teenaged boy on a surfboard appeared to the left of St. Just.

'Steady on where you are; we'll need that board to take her in,' he said.

* * *

Twenty agonizing minutes later, they all emerged from the water. The girl clung sobbing to the surfboard and the two men and the boy held on to the sides, propelling it to shore.

Portia ran to greet them, throwing a large towel over the shoulders of the shivering girl.

'Thank God, thank God!' she said.

Callum, like St. Just bent over double and breathing heavily, said, 'Where in hell . . . was . . . the lifeguard?'

'Cutbacks,' Portia told him. 'The lifeguards were stretched too thin and had to focus on the beaches known to be dangerous.'

'Well, that needs to change,' said St. Just. 'They're *all* dangerous.'

Scrubbing the water from his face, he looked up towards the sky in gratitude. It was then he saw a figure standing on the cliff opposite the Church Cliff, as St. Just had begun to think of it. A tall, imposing figure taking a Master of the Universe stance, hands on hips. He lifted one hand in salute; St. Just waved back uncertainly.

The figure turned and walked away. It vanished into the silhouette of a large manor house, all gables and chimneys outlined against the grey sky.

St. Just thought he may just have seen Bodwally, the lord of the manor.

ELEVEN

To the Manor

Deciding that was enough of the beach for one day, St. Just and Portia returned to their cottage to shower and change. The landline phone was ringing as they entered.

'Is this Ms De'Ath? Portia De'Ath?' asked a deep male voice. Portia agreed it was.

'This is Lord Bodwally's personal assistant. He asks that you stop by Revellick House this afternoon, if you would be so kind. He would like to meet with you on a matter of some urgency. Of course, your friend is invited to accompany you.'

Portia relayed the invitation to her 'friend', who shrugged. *Why not?*

Why Portia specifically? How did he know she was here? What did he want? All this they discussed an hour later on the five-mile drive to Revellick House, the weather perversely offering the sunshine earlier withheld. They guessed Bodwally's invitation might have something to do with her books.

'Perhaps he's a fan,' said St. Just. Or it might have something to do with that morning's rescue. He was more certain than ever the figure watching from the top of the cliff had been Bodwally.

'He is probably looking for a way into publishing through a side door,' Portia said. 'As so many are. I hate to be the one to tell him, but there is no side door, only ramparts, over which they pour boiling oil on authors with a first manuscript. Even lords.'

They passed a moonscape of moors dotted with wild gorse. It wasn't Yorkshire but somehow in its starkness it suggested Heathcliff and Cathy might suddenly appear in the distance.

'Revellick House is used as a setting in more than one of Ramona Raven's books,' Portia said.

'You've actually read her?' St. Just was surprised, even though he knew Portia's reading was wide-ranging and eclectic. *Great.* First the competition from Adventure Guy and now from imaginary heroes with long hair and massive pectorals.

St. Just had dropped Callum's name into the conversation once or twice on the way over to gauge Portia's reaction. She was satisfyingly indifferent.

'That girl was lucky you were both there,' was all she said.

I really must stop this, he told himself. He'd never been a jealous sort, but Portia seemed to have turned his head completely.

'Ramona is a genius at PR,' she told him. 'Keynote speaker at dozens of book conferences, all over the internet being photo-graphed with adoring fans, huge online following as she blogs about the weather and what she had for breakfast. Colossal book signings with each book launch.' Portia grimaced. 'My first book signing, ten people came. It's better now, of course, but the scars from that sort of thing never heal.'

'We shall hire you a publicist,' he said. 'I'll give you one as a wedding present. Male or female? They all seem to be females named Mandy or Trixie.'

'I love you, but no. I wouldn't know what to do with one. I seem to have misplaced the one I had. She may have moved on to another publisher, or left on maternity leave, and the publisher forgot to mention it.'

A discreet sign directed him to turn off the road for Revellick House.

'Oh, look!' Portia exclaimed.

It was a lovely manor house of manageable size – manageable given a small staff of cooks, cleaners, and other daily help. Their labour was particularly on show in the vast gardens. The place had the Tudor architectural touches St. Just felt had never been improved on – the good strong bones of a medieval house with masonry chimneys, dark timbering, and overhanging floors lending a distinctively cozy charm. It had been added on to here and there but the newer additions of granite and slate had been blended in so the main structure retained its proportions. To one side sat the lichen-covered ruins of what might have been a small family chapel, possibly a relic of the Reformation.

The building sat proudly at the end of a winding shaded drive, cosseted by stately trees and garlanded with glorious flowers. The trees along the drive looked as if they had withstood a storm or two, and gaps in coverage marked where a tree had fallen to the storm gods.

'Ooh,' said Portia on first catching the full view of terraced gardens framing the back of the house. 'Wow.'

'Precisely the reaction the owner was hoping for, I'm certain,' said St. Just.

'It's so *beautiful*. It's all a bit Manderley, isn't it?'

'And even larger inside than it looks, I suspect. I had no idea.'

'It seems a lonely place for a bachelor,' said Portia. 'It definitely has that *Rebecca* Gothic vibe.'

'Let's hope there's no Mrs Danvers sidling about,' said St. Just, turning off the ignition. 'You're right: the place does look lonely. Those gardens – they should have children playing in them. And lots of people invited over for tennis and tea parties.'

'But not fancy-dress parties.'

'What? Oh, Mrs Danvers.'

'Maybe he's just not got round to it yet.'

'The children or the parties?'

'Both, I suppose. Maybe he's planning to host the village gymkhana. Give him time to settle in.'

Suddenly, an oak door swung open and Bodwally appeared; he seemed to have been waiting for them.

'Hello, and welcome,' he said, beaming with the pride of possession, outfitted in suitably expensive if well-worn outdoor gear. 'I hope you had no trouble finding your way.'

He *was* rather a Heathcliff figure, St. Just decided, with dark, hooded eyes and an angular face. He seemed to be aware of his advantages, styling his black hair in a massive swoosh back from his high forehead. His olive skin had probably been made more olive by time spent outdoors hunting, on a yacht, or in other lordly pursuits. He was shorter than St. Just but then most men were.

He looked unwell, however. Had ill feelings from the previous night's quarrel after the village meeting lingered? For St. Just had no doubt, on hearing him speak today, Bodwally had been the male participant in those conversations.

They might have interrupted him in some outdoor pursuit requiring a gun – St. Just detected the scent of gunpowder in the air around him. The hunting jacket was a giveaway, besides.

'It's an enchanting house,' said St. Just, craning to look up at the timber-framed roof. Windows, high in the walls, were filled with heraldic emblems he couldn't quite make out.

'Isn't it, though? Revellick is one of the finest houses of its kind in England.'

'Not what you'd expect to find in Cornwall, really,' said St. Just. 'Not at all.' He returned his attention to Bodwally. 'How did it come to be here?'

'It was gifted to Sir Charles Trellwykken by the king for turning up at the Battle of Bosworth and galloping about with complete disregard for his own safety. It became in essence a holiday home for Sir Charles's family, whose primary residence was in Kent. Luckily, since the house was so little lived in, it retained much of its original flavour and many of its original lines.'

Bodwally waved them inside and led them through the panelled hallway, all alcoves and soaring ceilings and medieval warrior bling, and into a large room dominated by an enormous stone hearth. He strode ahead, his gait long and confident, as if he were leading them into an easy victory over revolting peasants.

But he said, 'Do forgive me if I sit down a moment,' stopping at a seating arrangement before the fire. 'I'm a bit wobbly today.'

'The meeting last night, yes,' said St. Just. 'Rather stressful.'

'What? Oh, I suppose. I try to stay out of local politics.'

St. Just, sure it had been Bodwally in the alleyway, thought he may have been speaking the literal truth: he was not *at* the meeting but outside it.

'I'm not in a position universally venerated,' said Bodwally, 'but I do try to earn my privileges. The vicar, Judith Abernathy, is always wanting donations for bits of the church that keep falling off and I'm not able to help right now. Revellick House's private chapel – you will have seen it on your approach – was destroyed during the Reformation and the family didn't bother to rebuild it. The cost of its upkeep, as I have explained to Judith many times, is still high, even though there technically is no *there* there. It's a shame, really. From early drawings, it had a barrel-vaulted ceiling – quite unusual. But the owners at the time felt it might be wiser not to rebuild and to keep their religion, such as it was, to themselves.'

'Somehow it's more evocative as it is,' said Portia.

'It's a haunting place, isn't it?' said Bodwally, smiling at her appreciatively. 'The family graveyard is just at the back. That stark beauty by moonlight is impossible to describe.'

'I can imagine.'

'What remains nearly untouched of the house proper are this room and the kitchen. Perhaps you'd like to see the kitchen later if you've time? It's virtually a museum piece. Of course, the real kitchen in daily use is in another part of the house. I'm not much given to roasting entire pigs these days when it's generally just me and the telly in the evenings.'

Portia answered for both of them. 'We'd love to see it.'

They were still standing, taking in the room. Bodwally waved them into chairs flanking the fireplace, a polite, rather pained smile creasing his tanned face. Prince Charles's face often held such an expression, especially when he was clearly desperate to escape an old-age pensioner who had grabbed the royal hand and wasn't about to let it go, not before he'd had his say. St. Just didn't often stop to pity the members of the royal family but he supposed, much like police work, their duties consisted of vast swathes of stultifying boredom.

On a wall near the fireplace hung a painting, darkened by time and smoke, of a severe-looking man in a vast chair, one hand grasping the handle of an ornate walking cane. His unyielding expression was of someone who had many heirs and cared for none of them.

'Your grandfather?' St. Just hazarded. 'Great-grandfather?' Although he could see no family resemblance, he recalled Morwenna's grousing about Bodwally's having been born rich.

'A distant relative,' said the lord smoothly. Why did St. Just get the feeling the painting came fitted with the house along with most of the furnishings? If so, why not say so? St. Just supposed insecurity took more than grand honours to erase.

Seated, the lord straightened one of his legs, as if it troubled him. He said, 'I hear you've dined at the Maiden's Arms. Oh, you needn't look surprised. Word travels fast here at the ends of the earth.' He paused before adding, 'I suppose old Wenna has given you an earful about me.'

'Morwenna was rather upset,' St. Just replied mildly. 'In general.'

'She and I have loathed each other in rather a loaded silence for some time.'

St. Just nearly laughed. 'Because of the fishermen and their jetty? Surely that's not a topic to stir such deep animosity.'

'Of course not. Oh, feelings have run high, especially since it affects people's livelihoods. There's also tradition and history to consider. But I'm not sure she gives two figs about the fishermen, for all she pretends. After all, more tourists mean more cash flowing through her till, so I wouldn't trust a word she says on the topic. She just wants to look as if she's on the side of the angels in case the media decides to turn a spotlight on the issue, which of course they're doing already. She doesn't want the day trippers coming to Cornwall and shunning her place – knowing nothing of the issues, they *will* side with the fisherman every time. Trust me, I know this.'

'I see,' murmured St. Just, thinking, *I'm not sure I do trust you, actually.*

'It's more that she opposes *me*,' Lord Bodwally went on. 'In some twisted way, I've come to stand in for . . . oh, who knows what. She thinks I was born with the proverbial silver spoon and she's jealous, I suppose. It could be as simple as that. Her father was in trade, and I'm sure she finds it unfair she's had to work for everything she has – which she will tell you about endlessly if you're not careful.'

St. Just understood Morwenna's rancour, the grudge as old as time held by those who had to scrape a living against those who, like the lilies, toiled not. But part of him, the part that struggled always to be fair, acknowledged Bodwally's lucky parentage was hardly the man's fault. We none of us choose our families. Besides, materially speaking, Bodwally had made rather a success of life.

'Don't mention the cookery classes she taught to make ends meet during the Plague Time unless your sanity means nothing to you. I do wish people who are business managers at heart would not attempt to cook. She nearly took out the entire village with her treacle tart at the Harvest Fayre. Calls herself a gourmet – those are the worst, the deluded ones who always open restaurants.'

St. Just and Portia glanced at each other. They had sampled Morwenna's excellent cooking for themselves.

'You're in the restaurant business also, am I right?' asked St. Just.

'No, no. Not really. I'm a silent partner in Jake Trotter's place.'

And hardly impartial, thought St. Just.

Portia said, 'I'm intrigued. Your assistant said you had something rather urgent to discuss.'

'Did he? Well, I wouldn't call it urgent. It's about some research I've been doing that you might find interesting for one of your books. I do very much enjoy your books, by the way.'

'Oh,' said Portia, pleased. 'I hadn't realized you were one of my readers.'

'Of course I am, dear lady. Especially here in Cornwall, you're quite well known. The local bookshop has a big window display whenever you have a new book out.'

As Bodwally and Portia fell to chatting about books and settings, St. Just stole the moment to saunter over to the window and take in the fantastic view. In full flower, the garden was immaculate, not a petal out of place; the lawn might have been painted on. By the time he returned his attention to the room, Portia was saying, 'That would be the Book Cove? I'll have to stop in.'

'That's right. I've also seen your paperbacks on the rack at the

Post Office store. Listen . . .' He pulled back his sleeve to see the face of his Rolex. 'I'm afraid I rather misjudged the time today. I'm meeting someone later – a last-minute thing. Let's do a quick cook's tour now and arrange a time for coffee tomorrow to discuss my research at leisure, shall we? You won't mind, old man, will you? If I borrow Portia for an hour?'

Whether he minded or not, the old man could see Portia was curious.

'Certainly, he won't mind,' she said. 'And I'd be delighted. Arthur came here in part to capture the scenery – he's quite a good artist, you know – and here's his chance.'

'Let's meet here at the house. Around ten? I'll have coffee and pastries to make up for today. Sorry, I'm not quite myself at the moment.'

'That will be fine,' said Portia. 'I'm sure Arthur won't mind driving me over. Since it's scenery he's after, there's none finer than the grounds surrounding Revellick House.'

St. Just did not imagine the disappointment in Bodwally's expression. Still, he managed to say with some grace, 'Lovely idea. Ten tomorrow morning, then.'

Despite what Bodwally had said, they decided to return to Morwenna's that night for dinner. The food was excellent, and after his trials in the sea earlier in the day, St. Just was past climbing uphill to try out Jake Trotter's place in the interests of fairness.

They found Morwenna at the bar, polishing the burled wood to a sheen. When she raised a hand in greeting, her sleeve fell back, exposing a small tattoo on her wrist. It consisted of two capital letters inked in an elaborate Gothic script and entwined with flowers: *GM*. Morwenna saw them looking and quickly pulled down her sleeve.

'Wine?' she asked. 'Or an aperitif?'

They asked for a dry red. Portia said, 'That's a pretty tattoo.'

'My daughter,' Morwenna said. 'Do you two have children?'

'Not yet,' said St. Just and Portia in unison. They exchanged glances and smiled. 'We want to get the wedding done first.'

'The old-fashioned way of doing things,' said Morwenna. 'That's the way to go. Good for you.' A film of sadness crossed her handsome features.

'Your daughter—' Portia began.

But Morwenna, pasting on a smile, said, 'Still. At the end of the day, it's only a piece of paper, isn't it? But you should come back to Maidsfell for the wedding if you're determined to do it properly. There are several venues round here specializing in weddings. The only place off limits is the Fourteen Maidens. Sybil Gosling sees to that. A wedding procession trampling her precious site might send her right off the—' She broke off. 'Never mind. She's barking, of course.

'Now. Some dinner, am I right? I heard about your exploits today. You must be famished.'

Once she'd seated them with menus, she returned to the bar, which was filling fast with customers. Soon a waitress danced over to take their orders, beaming a welcome. She gathered their menus and danced away with a promise to bring water.

She didn't look to be sixteen. Her mobile rang as she left the patio and she gave a tiny whoop of happiness when she saw who it was. 'Jason!' she cried. St. Just sighed. He hoped she remembered to put in their order with the kitchen.

'So we must wait to see what urgent thing Lord Bodwally wanted to discuss with you,' said St. Just. 'It can't have been that important.' It rankled that Bodwally had talked around him as if he wasn't standing there in the room, making plans for a meeting with his fiancée. 'By the way,' he said, 'you managed him beautifully.'

'Managed?'

'I meant—'

'I know what you meant. I was teasing. I go nowhere without you, Arthur. Especially not into that roué's den.'

'Ah! You thought his intentions may have been dishonourable? So did I.'

'He did everything but twirl his moustaches. Only his being clean-shaven prevented it.'

'I wonder if the whole thing wasn't just a ruse to get you over to the manor house. He didn't even mention the rescue of this morning, and I know he saw it.'

'It put you in a bright shining light; of course he wouldn't mention it.'

As they were leaving the restaurant an hour or so later they passed the bar. The Adventure Man of that morning's rescue happened to be there, so deep in conversation with Morwenna he didn't notice them. Morwenna, behind the bar, gave a friendly wave and resumed listening to whatever riveting thing Callum Page had to say.

Although Morwenna was perhaps twenty years his senior, her face held that vacant, rapt look women seemed to get in his presence.

Portia was flipping through websites on her laptop as St. Just got under the snowy duvet, hidden by day beneath the garish plaid.

Thunder rumbled nearby, and wind whistled through shutters shaken loose by one of the frequent storms. He burrowed deeper under the covers.

'For once they don't exaggerate,' said Portia. 'Maidsfell really is one of the most historic places in Cornwall. Listen to this: "Smuggling was rife in the area, particularly during the eighteenth century, when taxes on some items were so high smuggling seemed worth the risk." I wonder if that doesn't still go on.'

'Of course it does. Luxury items and drugs. Nothing changes. Are you coming to bed soon?'

'Be with you in a minute. I was just going to look at the SOS Facebook site. The "Save Our Shores" people. Look, there's a picture of Morwenna. And that looks like one of the fishers from the meeting.'

'Surely that can wait. Bodwally's ten a.m. invitation, while much appreciated, I'm sure, means we have to delay our plans for Port Isaac by several hours.'

'It'll be fine – it's not that far.'

'What if we run into another shepherd?'

'Factor in an hour for flocks of sheep, sure. And let's take along some cereal bars in case of emergency. But we're on holiday, remember? No timetables. We get there when we get there and enjoy the view on the way.'

'I could get used to this.' St. Just folded his hands underneath his head, looking at the ceiling. A spider had staked out one corner with her web. 'No crime, no investigating, no pieces of the puzzle to put together, nothing to worry about.'

'*No Crime Like the Present.*'

'Well, if we're going in for puns – must we?'

'It's the working title of my current book. Do you simply hate it?'

'Actually, no. It's quite catchy.'

'Good. I wasn't sure.'

'I especially like the "no crime" part.'

TWELVE
Vile Body

Wednesday

They drove to the manor house the next morning under brooding skies that threatened to dampen their plans for Port Isaac. Portia had phoned ahead to Revellick House but no one answered, and no answerphone asked her to record a message. St. Just rather hoped this meant the meeting with the lord had been cancelled.

'No matter,' Portia said. 'I'll leave the book with one of the staff. He's not expecting it to be returned but I'll just scribble a thank you note and tuck it inside.'

'What book?'

'He insisted on giving me a book on local history as we were leaving – you were already headed to the car. I'll never have time to read it so I feel I should return it before I forget.'

St. Just, thinking he should never have left her alone, even for a second, said, 'Shouldn't one of his staff answer the phone if he's not there?'

'I don't know. Overall, I don't think so. He mentioned he had day help, gardeners and such – they wouldn't live at the house. His assistant might have the day off and probably doesn't live here, anyway.'

'Maybe the ringing woke Bodwally up and he chose to ignore it.'

'That's odd.'

'Why? It's what I would do if someone—'

'No, I mean the door is standing open.'

And indeed it was.

Not just standing open, but admitting the Cornish weather, which in the last few minutes of their drive had kicked up considerably.

As St. Just peered inside the manor house, he could see wind ruffling a heavy cloth on a table in the main entrance hall. It was strong enough also to disturb the wall tapestries.

Surely the door had been left open by accident, one of Bodwally's staff being careless – or the man himself?

St. Just could not account for his growing sense of unease. It was, after all, merely a door left open. But, despite an inner voice suggesting he should leave, the policeman in him knew the situation should be explored.

Since they were here at the man's invitation, it didn't seem like intruding to walk in and give a shout.

He signalled to Portia to hang back. The house was filled with treasures, and if there had been an intruder . . .

'Lord Bodwally?' he called. No answer. He turned back to Portia.

'Wait here,' he said, and stepped fully into the hallway, the carpet muffling his footsteps.

'Lord Bodwally' he tried again. Then, 'Is anyone at home?'

He turned instinctively to the room where he had last seen Bodwally, almost in some primitive belief the man must still be where he'd left him. But the cavernous room with its ornate furnishings and fireplace was empty, unless for some inexplicable reason Bodwally had chosen to hide behind the curtains or the massive sofa.

St. Just went back into the main hall. Turning to the main door, he opened his mouth to tell Portia he'd had no luck finding anyone, but she was no longer standing in the doorway.

As he scanned the vast space, trying to decide where she may have got to, he heard a cry coming from a hallway that led deeper into the house.

Then, 'Arthur, come here! The library!'

Portia emerged into the hallway, three doors down from where he stood.

'I think he's dead,' she said. 'Do come quickly.'

Anyone would think her perfectly composed, until they

noticed all the colour had drained from her cheeks. 'There's blood, Arthur. So much blood.'

Once outside the manor house with Portia, St. Just put in an emergency call to the Devon and Cornwall Police, from whom he requested immediate assistance and, further, asked to be transferred to their homicide division. This request caused no little stir at the other end, but after repeatedly identifying himself and offering his warrant card information, St. Just was transferred to a line which may or may not have had to do with murder. There he was put on hold to listen to 'life-saving tips' and urged to visit the website for more information.

The man who finally picked up clearly believed, along with the woman running the emergency line, this might be some sort of hoax. He identified himself as Constable Jones-Heskith. He sounded quite young.

St. Just briefed him quickly, concluding, 'I don't like the look of this. It's no accident.' Portia, able to hear only one side of the conversation, waited out the pause as St. Just listened to the rather high voice on the other end. 'I'm quite sure he's dead, yes.' A longer pause, then, 'Yes, as it happens, I've had rather a lot of experience with dead bodies . . . What? No, I'm not a mortician. Would you please get a homicide team out here?' He put the mobile against his chest, sighing in exasperation. 'No, of course, I won't touch anything until you get here,' he said, a touch of annoyance heightening the pitch of his voice. 'I am familiar with how to secure a crime scene, thank you. How soon can you get here? What? Oh, surely not that long. Very well, we'll wait. What choice do we have? But please, hurry.'

St. Just rang off and stared in frustration at the phone, as if willing it to speed help on its way. He supposed he might put in a direct call to the local Maidsfell constable – Constable Whitelaw, whom he had seen at the fisher meeting. His was a volunteer position at best; St. Just didn't trust him on his own not to bugger up the crime scene. Bigger guns were needed for this.

'Did he really not know who you were?'

'He must not have seen a recent edition of *Who's Who*,' St. Just replied. 'No, of course he doesn't know; I wouldn't expect him to. This is his turf, not mine. In fact, I hope he's on the phone right now to the Cambridge Constabulary, verifying my existence. It wouldn't do to have just anyone running around Cornwall claiming to be a detective who has found a body.'

'He can't be much of a detective if he doesn't recognize the name of the best detective currently active in Great Britain,' said Portia stoutly, willing to overlook the fact it was she, technically, who had found the body. 'Your solution to the case at St. Michael's College alone was nothing short of uncanny.'

'I'll be blushing next,' he said. 'Anyway, he said it would take him an hour to get a team here but he'd send someone quickly to help the local constable secure the scene.'

'Surely they're not sending Constable Whitelaw?'

'He is what they have, yes. Let's just hope he's clever enough to realize he's out of his depth and he's only being sent along in case crowd control is needed. I doubt this village has seen a murder case for decades, perhaps for hundreds of years.'

His mobile phone rang, startling them both. Coverage in the area was spotty enough that you never knew when someone might break through the digital haze.

He didn't recognize the number but he answered, identifying himself. After listening to the caller, he said, 'Yes, atop the south cliff. Not the one with the church, the cliff opposite. If it has a name, I don't know it.' Then, 'No, I don't think that will be necessary. He's dead.'

He rang off. 'Constable Whitelaw is on his way. He asked if he should wear body armour.'

She met his hazel gaze. He had said, repeatedly, that in coming to Cornwall he wanted a break from fighting crime.

They could do nothing but wait for professional assistance with all the gear needed to deal with an unexplained and unexpected death.

Villages like Maidsfell, thought St. Just, were where England kept its secrets, hidden away in coves and caves, concealed behind the friendly smiles or stares of its villagers. They liked it that way. There was no need for outsiders with special equipment and knowledge.

Until now.

He said, 'I want to have a walk round the back. Then I'm going inside, to the library. Are you all right to stay here and greet the constable?'

She nodded, making a vague *Go on* motion with her hand.

'Whoever killed Bodwally is long gone, or I wouldn't leave you.'

'I know,' she said. 'The blood . . . was dried.'

'Bring the constable to me when he gets here. It may take a while even for that much help.' He paused. 'He'll likely show up in full riot gear. You can't miss him.'

She gave him a weak smile and a solemn thumbs-up signal.

'Arthur? Arthur St. Just?'

St. Just looked up from where he squatted on his haunches, making a mental survey of the position of the body of Lord Bodwally.

DCI Tomas Mousse was balding, shorter and rounder than St. Just remembered, but still recognizable as his comrade of years before. A case of art theft, it had been – art stolen from the Fitzwilliam which had ended up in Cornwall. It looked as if Mousse had taken to dyeing what was left of his dark curly hair.

St. Just had been expecting Whitelaw and was prepared to shoo him away from the crime scene. He rose, careful of his knees. Thinking of fingerprints, he didn't dare lean on the nearby chair for assistance.

This was getting to be a job for a young man.

'Arthur St. Just! As I live and breathe.' Mousse's deep voice boomed in the large, book-lined room. 'How are you, my old comrade? When they told me it was you on the phone, I thought it was a joke. Someone pulling my leg, even though it's a serious business we're in. Very little room for anything but the occasional gallows humour. So, what do we have here?'

'We found him like this – my fiancée and I. We haven't touched a thing. It looks a clear case of death by stabbing but the why of it I can't guess.' He shook his head. 'It's quite a vicious attack, as you can see. Half a dozen wounds at least.'

'You can confirm who it is?'

'Oh, I can, indeed. It's Lord Bodwally.'

'Thought it must be. That will be a right mess.'

'Right. A lord's murder shouldn't matter more, but it does, to the media.'

'Of course,' said Mousse, 'given the address, I thought it might be him, but I was rather hoping it would turn out to be – oh, I don't know. The butler or someone like that. Although a butler would be as bad, wouldn't it? A passerby, then; someone trying to break in. Lord Bodwally himself being murdered, well. As you say, the media will get hold of it and we'll be off and running, near as dammit.'

'Yes. Can't be helped.'

'That his body was found inside the house might mean something – do you think, Arthur?'

'That he may have been killed by a friend or acquaintance, someone he'd automatically let inside – yes, perhaps.'

'Otherwise, he'd let someone on his staff handle visitors.'

'When we were here yesterday,' said St. Just, after a pause, 'he greeted us himself. The staff, by the way, don't seem to be around anywhere today, either.'

'It might have been a distraction burglar,' said Mousse. 'They're brilliant at keeping the owner occupied at the front door while another person enters at the back of the property.'

'Doorstep crime.' St. Just nodded. 'Burglars are also good at luring people outside to look at some "problem" or other that needs fixing, or claiming they need to turn off the water to the house. Meanwhile, their comrade goes inside and grabs whatever valuables can be found. Still, this isn't the sort of house a person wanders by. You have to deliberately drive or walk up to the front door; it's a good distance from the road.'

'Quite right. He'd know the visitor.' Mousse paused, looking at the ravaged body, and shook his head. 'Surely the lord wouldn't be the one to deal with someone reading the meter?'

'As I understand it, there are no live-in servants, only day help. Servants haven't existed as an occupation since – I don't know, since the Second World War, except for the tremendously wealthy. Anyway, I sincerely hope we're not looking for two people working in tandem. That can be a right mess – at least, until they turn on each other.'

'As they so often do. So, how did you come to know him, Arthur? I mean, was he a friend?'

They both turned at the sound of a commotion outside the library. Devon and Cornwall Police had arrived *en masse* and were

busy unpacking equipment and cordoning off the area. The two
DCIs moved to the hall to leave room for them to manoeuvre in
the library. They stood at the foot of the great staircase, surrounded
by magnificent linenfold panelling.

'He invited us over to the house yesterday,' St. Just replied.
'My fiancée, Portia, is a writer and he seemed to think she might
want to help him publish his memoirs. Well, that was our assump-
tion, as it happens all the time with her. It's very difficult to make
people understand that her connections in the publishing world
have everything to do with crime writing, and very little to do
with family memoirs or bison meat cookbooks or whatever it is
people want help with. She has trouble saying no to anyone, so
it does get us into some awkward situations.'

'Your fiancée, you said? Congratulations.'

'Yes, thank you. I'm a lucky fellow. Anyway, there was something odd happened. It only seems important now this has
occurred. As we were leaving yesterday, I could overhear her
trying to explain to Lord Bodwally all the ways she doubted
she could help him. But he said, "Oh, but it's a crime I'm talking
about! It will be right up your publisher's alley, I do assure you.
And the public will eat it up." Words to that effect. We'll have
to ask her exactly what was said. About that point I went to
wait for her by the car.'

'Well, that's interesting. He has a crime story to tell and the
next thing he knows, he's the victim of a crime. So, what was
the crime?'

'That's the maddening thing. He never said anything specific.
I think he wanted to be mysterious so she'd be sure to come
back. He arranged to have coffee with Portia today and I offered
– was told – to take my sketchbook and make myself scarce. I
didn't mind, really. Portia seemed intrigued by whatever story
he had to tell and thought she might be able to help, when generally she knows to run a mile from anyone waving sheaves of
handwritten memoirs in spidery old-fashioned script.'

'*Was* it a family history? Some crime in the past?'

'You'll have to ask her – and I will, too, first chance I get. I've
really no idea. He told us he was feeling unwell, gave us an
abbreviated tour of the house and gardens, and promised more for
today. He talked a great deal about the history of the house. I did

gather it wasn't his, in the usual lord-of-the-manor sense. He bought it rather than inherited it. He didn't seem to like talking about that.'

'Bodwally is a life peer for services to something or other. Well, I suppose that's all past tense now his life is over.'

'How exactly did he earn the peerage?'

Mousse shrugged. 'He made a pile of money in the City is all I know. I'm going to guess it was for "financial services". I wonder what that is when it's at home. Now, "banker" – there's an old-fashioned word you can sink your teeth into.'

'So, *not* to the manor born?'

Mousse shook his head. 'He is a living example of British cronyism at its finest.'

'Yes, I'd love to be in the room when the honours list is being discussed, wouldn't you?'

Mousse nodded. 'I do know he bought Revellick House from an outfit that ran it for years as a wedding venue. Unfortunately, the wedding venue people were running in the red from the beginning and went heavily into debt. The directors poured in more money, as loans, but to no avail.'

'I see. Then one day along comes Lord Bodwally to the rescue, clutching his life peerage certificate, or whatever it is they give you. He did mention many times his restoration efforts.'

'To the rescue – precisely. He was able to purchase the property for a song. He redid the whole thing, practically top to bottom, returning it to its original state. All well and good, but his purchase of the place, turning it into a private residence, left about fifty future brides and grooms in the lurch – not one of them could get their wedding deposits returned. Some were many thousands of pounds out of pocket and were told to claim the money from their credit card companies. But those who paid cash for their deposits were completely out of luck.'

'I see. How awful for them.'

'It was an emotional thing, you understand. Most could not really afford the spend, but they had sent out invitations, and had grannies all lined up to attend with new hairdos, and had persuaded bridesmaids to purchase weird-looking fluffy dresses. Then the whole thing just collapsed round their heads. On top of everything, many of their guests also lost their money, since they'd booked to stay at the then-hotel for the wedding weekend. It was a complete fiasco. It dominated the news round here, I can tell you.'

'I see,' said St. Just again, thinking he and Portia might scale back plans for their already small wedding, just to be safe. 'That is bad.'

'It was a combination of disasters, like dominoes falling. In lockdown, weddings had to be put on hold. No wedding receptions or parties either, for obvious reasons. And even when they eased restrictions, guests were limited to small groups. Well, you remember how bad it was. Many people had rescheduled far into the future rather than risk another disaster. Then Bodwally pulled the rug out from under them. Again.'

'Would the brides or grooms really want to take revenge against him, do you think? With a knife? Strictly speaking, it wasn't his fault.'

'You've not dealt often with brides just before a wedding, have you?' asked Mousse. 'And mothers-in-law – don't get me started. Fathers-in-law might have wanted to stab him, also. But the couples were angry with the lord most of all because he refused to let the weddings go ahead, as he could have done. *Noblesse oblige* and all that. It wouldn't have cost him much – he could have delayed his own move-in date by a couple of months to accommodate these couples. He was also asked – they pleaded with him – if they provided their own catering and such, whether they could just use the grounds for the actual wedding day. Not use the rooms but have the ceremony outdoors and a meal brought in to be served under a marquee. No, they could not, they were told. Renovations were due to start and he refused to push back the date.'

'I see. He was within his rights, of course, but it would have cost him little to make so many people happy.'

'That's it precisely.' DCI Mousse pointed at St. Just's chest to emphasize how spot-on the observation was. 'I gather he wasn't in the least sympathetic or what you'd call gracious about it. It was more like, "Rotten luck, poor you, but why should I care? Why didn't you take out cancellation insurance? It's my place now and I'll do as I please."'

'Sounds like the life peerage went straight to his head.'

'He might have been a target anyway, wedding venue debacle aside.'

'How so?'

'He made matters worse just by being who he was.'

'Yes?' St. Just started to lean against the balustrade and remembered just in time: fingerprints.

'Because he's from the City. The people who lost the hotel, who sank beneath a sea of debt, were locals. It was hard for couples who were from the area to blame them. They might run into them in the shops and so on; some of them were probably related, for heaven's sake. So they looked for someone easier to blame. It's the usual outsider thing – I suppose it's human nature, which seldom seems to have a good day. It's much easier to blame the outsider, isn't it? And he was an outsider in so many ways.'

'I do see,' said St. Just. 'It's still an unusual motive but not outside the realms of possibility. The police will need to talk with all . . . what was it, fifty couples?'

Mousse nodded.

'All fifty couples. *And* their relatives. That will be a nearly impossible job.' He paused, considering. 'The few weddings I've been to just missed being bloodbaths. Funerals, too. It's all the drinking that goes on, I suppose.'

'Don't get me started on funerals. More families have been torn apart, and it only takes one bloody-minded aunt or sister-in-law to stir the pot.'

'Or uncle.'

'Certainly. It's an equal opportunity occasion for giving offence to all branches of the family tree. And mark my words, nine times out of ten, the spite is about money or property. Keep the relatives at arm's length so they don't start wondering where the collectibles went to.'

'We'll have to look into his business dealings. Disgruntled employees, deals that went pear-shaped – all the usual.'

If DCI Mousse even noticed this 'we' – this appropriation of a murder case on his turf – he hid it well. He leaned towards his fellow policeman and said, 'It would be easier to track down two hundred crazed bridesmaids and unpaid caterers than sort out the other connections. Lord Bodwally had a way of getting up people's noses that would make our hypothetical aunts or uncles look like saints by comparison.'

'I did gather as much.'

'He also ran into trouble with his grand plans for remodelling his mansion. It's a Grade Two listed property, you know. One can't just go in there and start knocking down walls. Most specifically, he wanted to expand a wine cellar and – wait for it – an underground escape tunnel.'

'OK. Fine. A bit paranoid, but OK. Lots of millionaires go in for that, along with safe rooms.'

'Not OK with the preservationists, I assure you. And since his land abuts National Trust property, he immediately ran up against a mob of people like Sybil Gosling.'

'The Wiccan lady? Yes, we met her. Seems harmless.'

'On the surface, it's all rainbows and daffodils in Sybil's world, yes. But she acts like she owns the place and is said to have had a run-in or two with the lord. His tunnel plans would have run right up against her "ownership" of the Fourteen Maidens.'

'Couldn't she just put a spell on him to do her bidding?'

'You say that in jest but there are people here who are deadly serious about that sort of thing. Anyway, the elevation to being a lord having gone straight, as you say, to his head, Bodwally wasn't going to be told what he could and could not do by a bunch of daft tree huggers.'

'An irritating quality, yes. That arrogance. But not a lethal one, surely.'

'You'd be surprised. And then there were the ladies,' Mousse continued.

'Uh-oh.'

'Yes, always trouble there. The man gave off every signal he wasn't interested in anything long-term in the romance department but that didn't discourage many from trying.'

'For example?'

'Oh, I doubt you'd know them. Local women might include Sepia Jones and Jackie Hollow – headmistress at the local kiddies' school. And Cynthia Beck, the estate agent for the purchase of his stately home. But he wasn't that long moved here from London. The Thames may still run black with the bodies of women he'd seduced and abandoned.'

'I've met Sepia Jones at her gallery. I must say she struck me as a more sensible woman.'

'I'd agree with you, but the list of available men in these parts is short. She and Bodwally were said to be dating, but soon were at loggerheads. I'd say with Lord Bodwally, *cherchez la femme* would be a good place to start.'

Remembering the man's evident interest in Portia, St. Just was not surprised. 'Women must have known he was a philandering rogue. Why didn't they run a mile?'

'You're asking me? I will never understand the biological imperative. None of us will.'

St. Just folded his arms across his chest. 'So. We must look where there's light.'

'Beg your pardon?'

'Oh, it's that old joke. No use searching for clues in the dark, even if that's where the clues are. Look where the light is good. I'd say the light is good wherever Bodwally cast his roving eye.'

'Right,' said Mousse. 'Got it.' Then, 'Funny, now I come to think of it. Bodwally was the last man on earth to care about those couples losing their deposit money for a wedding. He would barely have understood what they were on about. Probably he thought they'd had a lucky escape – cheap at half the price, cheaper than divorce.'

'A view that definitely would not sit well. Yes, someone will have to speak with all those couples. Try to sort which were angry enough to kill over a few dozen wilted flower arrangements, all bought and paid for.'

Mousse sighed. 'The manpower. They will never give me what I need to sort this properly.'

'They never do.'

'Do you know, I've been granted a transfer and I was hoping to leave this area on a high note. Crime numbers down – even property crime down. And now this.'

'Where are you headed?'

'Exeter. My wife longs for the excitement of the city and, besides, we've a grandchild there we rarely get to see.'

'Nothing is competition for a grandchild. Congratulations, by the way. So, what have we got to work with? What do we know about his last movements?'

If Mousse by now objected to the 'we' statements, he still didn't show it. Quite the opposite. It was an all-hands-on-deck situation.

'I've got some people looking into it. My sergeant rang not

long ago to say Bodwally had been seen at a bar near the harbour last night.'

'Alone?'

'Talking with people; cranking on about the new weir, like people do around here. But he was alone when he left.'

'And do we know what time that was?' asked St. Just.

'Well before closing is all we know. The village meeting got them riled so it was a large crowd.'

'Nine? Nine thirty?'

'I'll try to get it nailed down.'

'So we're agreed, we'll start by looking for the ladies?'

Mousse nodded. 'I'll get the preliminaries set in motion – I don't see formally interviewing anyone before the pathologist has had a chance to weigh in on time of death, at least. But I'll get my people busy checking whereabouts last night. Maybe someone saw Bodwally leave the pub.'

'Or left with him. What do you say we meet at nine tomorrow morning at the Lighthouse Café?'

'Not inside – too many flapping ears,' said Mousse. 'But yes, let's rendezvous outside. We can start by having a word with Sepia Jones. She works all hours and lives above the shop but morning will be her slow time.

'Besides, she knows where a lot of the bodies are buried round here.'

THIRTEEN
Going Bodmin

Thursday

The next morning, St. Just showered and dressed quickly, wanting to take in the sea air before meeting DCI Mousse. Late the night before, Mousse had rung him with the names of people known to be in Bodwally's circle in Maidsfell. He called it 'The Rogue's Progress'.

'We won't have time to speak with everyone, but we have to start somewhere,' he'd said. 'I've put in a call to the Yard to see what they can learn about Bodwally's life at the London end.'

Portia was planning to take the rental car to Bodmin for the day. St. Just had suggested the excursion – stage-managed it. He didn't want her entire holiday ruined; beyond that, though, he wanted her out of the village as much as possible for her own safety.

He'd picked up a brochure about the famous Bodmin Jail and read parts of it aloud, talking up the high points. He knew no criminologist would be able to resist. 'Did you know during the First World War they used the prison to hide the Domesday Book and the Crown Jewels?'

Portia played along, realizing he'd be able to concentrate more fully on the case without having to worry she was either bored or in mortal danger.

'I did know that. Also that they've refurbished Bodmin top to bottom – although I'm not sure "refurbished" is the word to use when talking about a prison. If there's time and tickets available, I'm going to tour the exhibits. They've done something called the Dark Walk, one of those immersive, interactive things.'

'Are you sure you're all right with this change of plan? I'm frightfully sorry – this is not what we planned at all.'

'Murder is like that – it does not take reservations. Look, I'll be fine. Up the A30 and back, an easy drive. And if there's time, the Truro museum has an exhibit of Peter Lanyon.'

She didn't mention she was also thinking of popping into Sepia's later that afternoon or the next for the promised wine and chat.

Naturally, St. Just was torn. He would much rather be with Portia but he couldn't justify abandoning a murder inquiry over a museum visit.

'You do know Bodmin is famous as a place of execution?'

'Of course. That's why I'm going. It will probably turn up in the book I'm writing.' She held up two dresses on hangers, one in each hand. 'I suppose black would be appropriate?'

'Wear the green – more cheerful. It's been more than a century since the last hanging, but the place is said to be haunted because of all the executions. If I believed the dead come back to haunt the living, Bodmin and the surrounding moor would be the place.'

She slipped the green dress over her head. Emerging from the folds, she said, 'When you're done with your case, we'll go to St. Ives and see everything. Promise. Hepworth, Nicholson, Frost. And Penzance is quite near – the Newlyn artists and that lot. I know you don't like missing out on today.'

He sighed softly. He was particularly fond of the Newlyn School artists, famous for painting outdoors in the other-earthly light of Cornwall, but also known for their intimate scenes of the home lives of the Cornish people. The Bodwally case, just beginning, might never be resolved, certainly not according to any fixed timetable. Furthermore, it wasn't even his case; he had rather invited himself in.

'We'll just have to come back to the area,' Portia added. 'I wouldn't mind a bit.'

He glanced at his watch. 'I'll have to leave in a minute. Tell me: Bodwally wanted to discuss with you his idea or research for a book, I know, but what exactly did he say? I should pass along what you know to Mousse. And I'm sure he'll want to talk with you himself.'

'I've been trying to remember, Arthur. He just skimmed the surface of topics, thinking, of course, we'd be meeting today to go into more detail. And having no idea he wouldn't be around today, poor man. I wish you'd been in on the conversation, but you were gazing out of the French doors into the garden at the time. When you go into artist mode, I'm not sure how much you hear.'

St. Just knew it was true. He had only the faintest recollection of the murmur of their voices behind him. He'd been wondering how he might capture the Cornish sky – whether to let it take over two-thirds of a canvas, or just the top third, letting the viewer's eye dwell on the rolling landscape.

'It was local history, generally,' said Portia. 'The tin mines, the Fourteen Maidens, and – further north – Tintagel, Merlin. The usual. Oh, and fairy lights and fogous – don't ask.'

'What's a fogou?'

'It's like an underground stone tunnel. Nothing he was talking about would have anything to do with the way he died – at least, not as far as I can see. He did mention a cave. He seemed excited by that.'

'Merlin's cave?'

She shook her head. 'Just a regular cave. He thought it might have been used as a smuggler's hiding place. I did get the idea the book was at least partly a memoir or family history but, to be honest, he didn't seem to have thought it through. That's where I came in, presumably.'

'Perhaps he was descended from smugglers. That would fit his "robber baron" reputation. So he was from here originally?'

She shrugged. 'Maybe. It would explain what drew him here. Roots.'

'That's likely.' St. Just considered. 'The cliff walls round here are like Swiss cheese, riddled with caves, which is why they often collapse. I can't imagine why he thought there was a book in it.'

'He believed there was buried treasure involved – the usual boy's adventure type of thing.'

'Hmm. It was good of you to hear him out. I know you get a lot of that.'

'I do, and ninety-nine per cent of the time I can't do a thing to help. Not via a recommendation, not through a referral. They're usually miles from any topic I know anything about, let alone anything my agent would know or care about. Personal histories are a particular minefield. The lives of grandmothers are not as interesting as people tend to think, but of course it's the telling of the story that makes the difference, doesn't it? Anyway, many people seem to believe I could help them if I felt like it. Lord Bodwally was a prime example of someone whose hopes I'd probably have to dash. And . . .'

'And?'

'And I don't think he would've taken no for an answer, or with any grace. We parted on good terms, but I was sure I hadn't heard the last of it.' A pause, as what she had just said sunk in. 'I guess I had heard the last of it, even though I thought I'd have another chance to let him down gently. Oh, my. How perfectly awful.'

'Awkward,' St. Just agreed. 'Anything else?'

'Nothing that jumps out at me, but I'll think more on it. What he had basically was a bullet list of interesting things but tying it all together into a book would require more focus than he seemed to have.'

'Not to mention patience.'

'Yes. More important than talent in many ways.' She added slowly, 'He seemed quite nervy and scattered when we met – he did seem unwell, didn't he? I wonder if the book was just a pretext.'

'Why would he . . .?'

'Why would he waste my time? Do you know, I had the strangest feeling he just didn't want to be alone. I suppose even lords get lonely.'

'Did you get the sense he was *afraid* to be alone?'

'I've been asking myself that very thing,' she said. She ran a hand through her hair and said, 'What's really going on, Arthur? Should I be worried?'

Although policemen had to keep sensitive information about a case to themselves, it was a given they would talk in general terms to their wives or partners. St. Just often discussed cases with Portia, and as often was rewarded with new insights. He could always trust her discretion.

Briefly, he summarized the several areas of the lord's life where people might have taken against him, ending with 'women'.

'Uh-oh,' said Portia.

'My words exactly. I'm off to speak with one or two of them now.'

'That could get messy. Be careful.'

'I will. It's you I worry about.'

He drew Portia to him, enveloping her slight frame. Even knowing the world was too full of hazards to be able to save her from them all, he was determined to try. He didn't know what he would do without her, without knowing she was alive and safe, at large somewhere in the world. She had slipped into the heart of his life so easily that he feared she might just as easily vanish.

He stood back, holding her at arm's length, searching her face as light from the bedroom window caught its every beautiful plane and angle. His sense of alarm was suddenly overwhelming.

'You should take the car, right now, and just keep going,' he told her. She shook her head. '*Yes.* Have your day trip if you want it but after that drive on to Truro station, leave the car, and head back to Cambridge. Stay in a hotel if the last train's already left by then. It's too dangerous for you to be in this small place with a murderer on the loose. We have no clue where the case is headed.'

'It's too dangerous for you as well, then,' she said. 'It's not your case but they need you; that much is obvious. Of course I'll not just leave you in Maidsfell. I'd do nothing but worry, probably ring you every ten minutes.'

'I would answer if I could. I'd have to be trapped under a lorry not to answer.'

'Perhaps I'll ask Sepia to join me for a drink or a meal if she's free,' she added casually. Seeing his look of concern, she added, 'I'll make sure we meet in a public place. Perfectly safe.' Having just come up with this variation on her plan, she saw the wisdom in it. 'But I promise I'll be careful, every minute.'

'Oh, good,' he said. Sarcasm wasn't a tone he used often but fear drove him. 'That's all right, then. You'll be careful. Portia, listen: Sepia is a suspect. Everyone's a suspect – you know that as well as I.'

'But Sepia? No way. I just cannot—'

'Portia, we don't know what we're dealing with here. A random thrill killer, or a methodical murderer with a set agenda we can't fathom. In either case, if you get in their way . . .' It was too awful to countenance.

But there he faltered. This was the strong-minded, smart, and determined woman he'd fallen in love with. Changing her wasn't possible. Would he want to? 'If you *must* stay, then . . .'

'I must. Only a coward would scuttle off and leave you to this.'

'At least promise me you'll stay well away from the investigation. I know your tendency to want to get involved. But this is not like Lucy Ricardo wanting to dance in Ricky's show. There may be lives at stake.'

'I know,' she said sombrely. 'Believe me, I know.'

She turned to gather her things for the day.

'It's anyone's guess if I'll need sunglasses today. Anyway, I have to dedicate myself to—'

She snapped her fingers and spun round. 'That's it. I nearly forgot to tell you. Bodwally showed me some pages from his work in progress and, just flipping through them, I noticed he'd already written a dedication.'

'Oh?'

'Yes. He'd done what most writers do – what *I* do, at any rate. They dedicate a book to someone even before the book actually exists. It gives a psychological boost – it's a promise to oneself, a motivator. That there actually will *be* a book one day. Anyway, his said something like "For my bright boy" or "For the sunshine boy" – something like that. It was in French.'

'Did you ask him about it?'

'No. Dedications can be rather personal – a tiny peek into the writer's mind and history. I will tell you this – you don't dedicate a book to some random person who does your dry cleaning; you dedicate it to someone or some group with whom you have a meaningful relationship, or to whom you owe a debt of gratitude. It's far too important – to the writer, that is; the dedicatee may not care – but to the writer it is too important to leave to chance. The book I'm writing now, well . . . it may well be dedicated to you.'

'It may?'

'Well, yes. It is. It was supposed to be a surprise . . . but since this comes up now and it may be important, yes.'

He was inordinately pleased. 'That is such an honour,' he said quietly. 'Thank you.'

'You're welcome. Of course I'd dedicate it to you. You're the mainspring of my life. *Do* you think it's important?'

He shrugged. 'Could be. I'll make sure Mousse's people have a look for those pages. Typescript or handwritten?'

'A mish mash. Maybe he was a true writer, after all. We thrive on bringing order out of chaos.'

'Not unlike a detective,' said St. Just.

'You see? You need me here. I might remember something else.'

'I need you somewhere safe.' He thought a moment. 'You're sure it was something about a boy?'

'*Garçon* was the word he used. He may have been talking about a waiter. But that doesn't make sense, does it? That pretty much puts it in the category of dedicating your book to your dry cleaner, unless he was totally infatuated with some young man he'd met in France. And that doesn't really tally with my impression of him.'

'His sexual orientation seemed to be almost insistently directed towards women. Extravagantly so.'

'Yes, it did. But that can be camouflage. I suppose some people still would try to hide being gay or bisexual, even in this day and age. On the other hand, Bodwally did strike me as being rather secretive overall. Perhaps a man who was all about appearances . . .'

'Could it be he had a son? He was dedicating the book to his son?'

'That would be *fils*. Unless his French was even more rudimentary than mine. Well, you'll find out soon enough.'

FOURTEEN
To the Lighthouse

The two DCIs chose an outside table well away from other customers.

'Preliminary results only,' Mousse told St. Just. 'As you know, that's all the examiners will release this early, lest they be called out on a mistake later. Even without the tox results, we're left with the obvious cause of death: Bodwally died because he was stabbed in the neck in his right carotid artery, the wound to his throat probably the fatal one. It was what you'd call a clean kill, with death almost instantaneous. Whoever did it had a rudimentary knowledge of anatomy, at least. But for good measure, they added six more wounds to the chest area, presumably once he'd been incapacitated.'

'A rage killing. They had the element of surprise?'

'Almost certainly. He was probably grabbed from behind and stabbed before he knew where he was. Apart from unleashing a massive amount of blood, the attack involved very little muss and bother. The other wounds were post-mortem, or as near as makes no difference. And before you ask, a very determined female killer could have done it.'

St. Just wondered if there was any other kind. 'Ex-military, do you think?' he asked.

'Could be. Or to explain the targeted neck wound, maybe someone with medical training. Or a hunter. Or it may simply have been a stroke of luck for the killer, so to speak, with the carotid artery being severed. Nasty business, that.'

'The killer must have got some blood on him or her, even with an attack from behind.'

'Certainly, they'd have blood on the hands or sleeve, if they wore long sleeves,' said Mousse. 'They may have come prepared, wearing something to shield them from the blood.'

He looked round him to make sure no one was playing attention.

'If they wore gloves, as I would be willing to bet they did – we're not finding fingerprints – they may have thrown the gloves in the fireplace. We'll look into that, sift through the ashes. The nights are cool enough that a fire wouldn't arouse suspicion.'

'This can't have anything to do with the fishermen's causeway. Can it?'

'You know as well as I do, murders have been committed because someone crossed a property line or their cows broke through a fence. An eyesore of a jetty – that has been stirring the blood for some time round here.'

'We were at the village meeting where it was discussed,' said St. Just. 'Lord Bodwally was in the vicinity, but he may have been sitting right at the back during the meeting, perhaps hoping not to be noticed. Can't say I blame him; it was a village free-for-all, only lacking pitchforks and torches to complete the effect.' He rubbed his jaw, remembering. 'I believe he was there when the crowd left. But the next day when we spoke with him, he didn't seem to want to admit it.'

St. Just recounted the conversation – the argument – he and Portia had overheard.

'There would be no need for him to turn up to the meeting itself,' said Mousse. 'He's holding all the cards in that game and all he could achieve would be to rile sentiment further. I don't think the fishers stand much of a chance, myself.'

'Someone mentioned Smuggler's Beach. They said Lord Bodwally held the key to solving the dilemma and was too lazy or selfish to do anything about it. What did they mean?'

'I'd actually forgotten that rather heated discussion of a few months ago. Smuggler's Beach is a small strip of sand Bodwally owns at the foot of the mansion grounds. Technically, the fishermen could use that or he could sell or rent them access but – n-o-o-o. It would be the neighbourly thing to do, to help resolve the dispute about having the action nearer the village. Not perfect, but better than what they have now, which is nothing. But he wouldn't sell the land and he wouldn't give them access rights, and as to parking – never, not ever. He said they'd create noise in the mornings and disturb his sleep. Just imagine. Yes, I suppose there's another motive, and a good one for anyone fed up with the situation, which is everyone. He said it would spoil *his* view.'

'That's as good a motive as the brides-to-be had. Almost an identical motive, come to that, minus the bridesmaids and forfeited deposits.'

Mousse mused, 'I suppose if a fisherman – or fisherwoman – knows anything, it's how to wield a knife to good effect.'

'Are there any known hotheads among them?' St. Just asked.

'There's Will Ivey,' Mousse said immediately. 'The very definition of a curmudgeon, but I've never seen much harm in him. All talk and bluster – you know the type. But then, there are others might take him at his word. He was angry, no doubt about it.'

'Who else comes to mind?'

Mousse considered. 'One or two of the young fishers are given to brawling when the pubs close, but I would say cold-blooded murder – the planning, the lying in wait, the sheer rage propelling the deed – was not in their skillset.'

'Still, we can't discount Smuggler's Beach as a motive. When a man's livelihood is at stake and the one person who could help refuses . . .'

St. Just conjured a picture of Will Ivey, the weather-beaten man with an air of command about him and a low regard for tourists. He supposed Will could rally a group of hotheads to his cause, start another Cornish Rebellion.

'Oh, I don't disagree,' said Mousse. 'Was anything actually decided at the meeting, or did everyone just see it as another opportunity to vent their grievances about the village jetty and so on? I'm a bit out of touch on the topic, I'm afraid. And since I don't live in the village and am miles from the water, I don't have a dog in the race. I tune out most of it to keep my own sanity. Privately, I side with the villagers, of course, but I can't be *seen* to be taking sides.'

'Only odd thing was, Morwenna, who was adamantly opposed to interference with the fishers, seemed to dither about speaking up. I've no idea why.'

'Not surprising,' said Mousse. 'Best she keep her head down. So, what was the upshot?'

'The council voted to send the matter over to the district council – the local planning authority – but they recommended English Heritage and the conservation groups be consulted first. At this rate, the winter will come and go with no resolution.'

'Ah,' said Mousse. 'So they kicked it down the road and threw in some "whereases" and a bit of "more study is needed". Thought they would; they always do. What a spineless bunch. They'll be debating that topic until the end of time.'

'Or until the last of the "true" villagers have gone or moved away.'

'To be replaced with rock stars and Russian oligarchs. I'm afraid you're right.'

'I did gather the council was hoping something would change if they stalled long enough,' said St. Just. 'And something has.'

'Indeed it has. Revellick House will go on the auction block or, more likely, get scooped up by the National Trust or similar.'

'Who inherits from Bodwally?'

'We're looking into it, of course, but as far as we know, he had no heirs. We're even having trouble locating a next of kin to identify him. Anyway, if he did have a proper will leaving the place to someone, the taxes on the place will do their heads in.'

'Why did you say that just now, about Morwenna Wells's backing down not being surprising?'

Mousse began to play with his used sugar packets, arranging them just so on his saucer. 'For one thing, she may be trying to plant a flag on both sides of the issue, which can't be done. Also . . . Morwenna can be a bit tricky to deal with. It's no wonder, given what she's been put through. I'm not sure I'd be all right in the head myself after such a tragedy. She had a daughter who died, you know. Tombstoning. She was here on holiday with a school group, and . . .'

'My God,' St. Just breathed softly. Sybil Gosling had mentioned the dangerous 'sport' of jumping off cliffs and sea walls into the water below, with the Fourteen Maidens site being a draw for that sort of thing. It was a pastime that tended to attract the very young, who are, as everyone knows, invincible. But no tombstoner can know what is hidden beneath the sea's surface – rocks, building debris, anything at all fallen overboard or dumped from shore, as people treated the sea like their own personal rubbish tip.

St. Just thought back to the tattoo on Morwenna's wrist – the initials GM – and her sudden steering of the conversation away from the subject of her daughter. Asking him and Portia about their own plans for a family must have been a knife to the ribs, but apparently it was better than revisiting her own sorrow.

Mousse went on. 'It was believed at the time that Gwithian tried a tombstoning stunt and died, but no one dares mention that theory to Morwenna. Nor even suggest the girl may have fallen by accident. Let alone that she may have been a suicide.'

'If she won't countenance the possibility it was suicide – and who can blame the poor woman – that means she believes someone pushed her daughter?' asked St. Just. 'That it was murder?'

'Murder or horseplay that led her to fall, and that no one is willing to own to, even now, when kids' horseplay might almost be forgiven. Teenagers, you know the sort of thing they get up to. But Morwenna doesn't draw a line between accident and murder. To her it's *all* murder if the cowards who did it won't come forward.'

'Like a hit and run. We see it all the time, especially when drink-driving is involved. They speed away and how they live with themselves later, no one knows, but somehow they manage.'

'We see it too often out here, too,' said Mousse. 'Sometimes they just drink more to try to forget.'

'I suppose the memory fades. "The murder being once done, he is in less fear and more hope that the deed shall not be betrayed."'

'Shakespeare?'

'Thomas More. Always the national expert on guilt and the workings of conscience. So, who does Morwenna think did it?'

'Unclear. There were a lot of teens hanging round together in a mob, like they do, travelling in packs, so the field of suspects was wide. The girl had fought with her boyfriend, so Morwenna turned the heat up under him for a while, or tried to get us to.'

'Do you recall his name?'

'I'd have to look it up, but I'm quite sure he moved away. We're talking nearly twenty years ago.'

'So, the case is still open?

'Officially? I believe so, yes. In Morwenna's mind – no question it's as open as the can of proverbial worms.'

'What exactly do police know about her daughter's death?'

Mousse sighed, gazing upward in recollection. He took a sip of his coffee but quickly set it down in disgust. 'Cold,' he said. 'Well, alcohol and drugs were in her system. Kids partying that night, the usual. Sybil spends an awful lot of her time patrolling against that sort of thing, but they slip past her. I would have to go back and read the report for the full tox screen. I do remember there was initial conjecture whatever she had in her system had caused her to hallucinate – made her believe she could fly. You know.'

'LSD?'

'Something like that. Again, I'd have to pull the report – some drug with a Latin name. But I can give you the broad strokes. We know she didn't die immediately – that was the worst of it. By the time she was being airlifted to hospital, she was no longer conscious. But she was alive when she hit the base of the cliff.'

St. Just winced. 'Jesus Almighty. Poor girl.'

'Yes. The fall on the rocks shattered her spine. If she'd lived . . . ah, God. It doesn't bear thinking about. Thankfully, there were men working on the path to the lighthouse who saw what had happened. They rang nine-nine-nine and everyone who could respond, responded. Lifeboats, the ambulance service, rescue heli-copters – the lot, practically in each other's way. A lifeboat managed to drop two men on to the rocky beach below; a paramedic was winched in. As always with these rescues when the weather is rough, they were risking their own lives, but they got her airlifted out of there. It was too late. She died on the way.'

'And never regained consciousness to say what had happened.'

Mousse shook his head.

'Sudden death by accident is not an uncommon story round these parts – it's a dangerous place to live and work, no question. The Townies come here – no insult to you intended – for the sun and scenery yet somehow they miss what lies beneath, if you know what I mean. What is actually involved in putting food on the fancy restaurant table. But even when people just want to relax and enjoy themselves . . . well. People fall, people swim too far out, people get caught in the riptide.'

'Yes, we had a taste of that when we first got here.'

'Right, so I heard. But it's the idiots ignoring the warnings and going in for tombstoning who should get a stiff fine and a jail sentence, in my view. The rescue services have their hands full without risking their lives rescuing fools half the time. If a *dog* falls off those cliffs or down an old mineshaft – and they do routinely; they get away from their owners – the rescuers will absolutely risk themselves to save it.'

'So Gwithian's accident – or whatever it was. Did the workmen actually see what happened?'

'No, worse luck. They saw her sort of in mid-fall. No way to tell what she was up to, or if any foul play had been involved. Well, Mark thought he saw a figure left standing at the top of the cliff, then running away.'

'So Morwenna was right?'

Mousse shook his head. 'He wasn't sure. All eyes were on the girl, quite naturally.'

'Are the workmen still around?' said St. Just.

'Mark Halpern's been dead these two or three years past. The other man was Morgan Goldsworthy. You can generally find Morgan at the Parrot. Best get there early, if you catch my drift, before he's several pints in. His memory, never good, is shot to bits now.

'Now, are you ready to go empty a few heads of background information now?'

St. Just nodded. 'Let's see what Sepia Jones has to say, as planned. But I think someone should go and talk with Will Ivey before too much time passes. At the meeting he seemed to be the alpha fisherman, if you will, and he might have a sense of whether someone has gone from nursing a grievance to taking action to cure it.'

'Will Ivey is sure to be out on his boat; we'll have to wait on that interview. But sure, Will's worth talking to; he does tend to have his finger on the pulse.'

Mousse began flipping through pages of his notebook. Finding what he wanted, he read aloud: 'Sepia Jones, forty-four years old, divorced. For now let's get in touch with our artistic sides, shall we? Sepia should be open for business by now.'

FIFTEEN
Romancing the Lord

They found Sepia wrapping a large, flat parcel in her art gallery – no doubt a painting being shipped to a customer. St. Just thought her drapey dress with its muted pattern might be designer. He was willing to bet it cost a packet.

'You've heard what happened to Lord Bodwally?' DCI Mousse asked.

'Yes, of course I have. Mobiles are alight with the news. The wonder is it took more than five minutes for it to filter through the village. That's why I was late opening – every other person wanted to ring to chat about it. They've not had news like that since . . . I don't know. Since the last time a Viking warship was spotted along the coast.'

'Really? I'm a bit of a history buff but I didn't know Vikings were ever spotted round here.'

'I couldn't swear to it personally,' said Sepia, smiling. 'But they seem to have got everywhere. Their ships were the party yachts of the day, without swimming pools and helicopter pads.'

'I'm sure you're right,' said DCI Mousse, smoothing back his hair. 'I wonder if you've read Bronson's latest? He maintains the Vikings were—'

'I wonder if we could return to the topic?' said St. Just. It was awkward, this not being his case, but at the same time he couldn't see how the Vikings were involved, thugs though they may have been. And these two – unless he was very much mistaken – were flirting. And Mousse a married man with a grandchild. Interesting, that.

'Right,' said Mousse. 'We're here to ask some questions of you, Sepia. You knew Lord Bodwally well, did you?'

'I can't say I did. He bought a few paintings from the shop but mostly as gifts. Seascapes tended to clash with his décor.'

'So he was a customer,' said St. Just. 'Just a customer?' He let the question lie on the counter between them undisturbed, wondering if she would tell a bit more of the truth, unprompted. DCI Mousse looked decidedly uncomfortable.

'We went out to dinner a few times last year,' she said, her tone light. 'But as a date, especially as a prelude to "romance", it was a non-starter.' Little air quotes around the word 'romance'. Her bracelets clattered at the gesture.

'Oh? And why was that?' St. Just was relieved she wasn't going to waste their time in denials. Having to establish a relationship existed could be a tedious if necessary part of the investigation. Her preference for the straight answer put her in the plus column.

'Do you know,' she said, massaging the cleft in her chin. 'I could never quite put my finger on it, what was wrong.' She was speaking now more to DCI Mousse, whom she probably knew well. Shop owners could probably thank him for Maidsfell's low crime rate.

'I was supposed to be all excited, right? Like a character in one of Ramona Raven's rubbishy books. *Passion's Proud Promise* or whatever. I actually read one of her books; she had a signing when she first came to the village and I went along to support the bookshop. It was like bathing in candy floss, that book – it stuck to the skin somehow. You know: gorgeous woman in reduced circumstances rides out on to the moor to escape the attentions of some drooling halfwit from the village and falls off her horse and into the arms of a dark, brooding, very rude – but wealthy! – bloke. The wealth presumably making up for his rudeness.

'Anyway, here was this rich nobleman, not bad-looking, with his big house and his fancy cars, wanting to take me out. We went to Jake Trotter's restaurant – not a bad start, wine with each course. But somehow . . . well, his anger, simmering just below the surface, came through loud and clear. He was bitter about something; I've no idea what it was. But by the end of the evening he'd recovered his charm so I agreed to a second date. Same story – this sort of Jekyll and Hyde quality he had. I began to wonder if he was bipolar, you know? Finally, on the third date, I called him on it. What was wrong? I asked. Because he didn't seem to be with *me*, you know? He might have been sitting alone, tortured by his own thoughts.

'He hemmed and hawed, and finally told me I reminded him of a woman he once knew. By the bottom of the wine bottle, he'd admitted it was a woman he'd been engaged to, a woman who'd left him standing at the altar.'

'Literally?'

'Uh-huh. I didn't think things like that happened in real life. A bit *Jane Eyre*, when the wedding is interrupted because, wouldn't you just know it, there's a madwoman in the attic. Hate it when that happens, don't you? Only this, I gather, was different – the woman simply changed her mind and never turned up.'

That, thought St. Just, might explain why Lord Bodwally wasn't all that upset by people's losing their wedding deposits. He'd had a similar disaster befall him – actually, something far worse had happened. How mortifying to be left in the lurch like that. How easy for a man given to pettiness, his mind perhaps filled with images of revenge, to wish the same fate on others.

He stole a glance at DCI Mousse, who seemed to be having similar thoughts.

'Where did this happen?' St. Just asked.

'The non-wedding? I don't know. Somewhere in London, I suppose. I don't know when.' Leaning toward them across the counter, she said, 'Look. You'll get a lot more out of talking with Ramona Raven. They had a real thing. Quite real – at least in her mind.'

'I did not know that,' said DCI Mousse.

'Of course, it's only natural when you think about it. Ramona would never pass up a chance to snag a peer. Only she would call it "research".'

'I see. That makes sense.'

'Only to a romance writer does that make sense.'

'How did it go? Between her and Lord Bodwally?'

'You'll have to ask her that yourself.'

'Plan to. Thanks.'

'I only know it didn't last long. As I say, he was generous in his way but he was also a difficult man to like.'

The home of the romance writer was about what one would expect, thought St. Just. From what he knew of Ramona Raven from the fisher meeting, understated was not her style.

From what he knew of writers, for that matter. He'd been involved in a tricky case in Scotland where he'd been surrounded by writer types, and 'highly strung' didn't begin to describe them. The publishers, publicists, agents, and reviewers attached to the industry seemed to him as bad but in different ways. He wondered still what it was about publishing that sent people off the deep end like that. Portia, generally level-headed and calm, seemed to him the exception that proved the rule.

Ramona's cottage was perched along the coast not far from where he and Portia were staying, and it took twee to an entirely new level. Laura Ashley hadn't been active in decorating for some time, as St. Just recalled, but this was clearly a scheme inspired by Laura's daydreams of no rose left unturned, no wall left bare, no chair or sofa left uncushioned with a dozen patterned pillows. Everything that could be embroidered or branded in some way displayed a large initial *R* or two entwined *R*s.

Ramona had thrown open the door to Rose Cottage with – it must be said – passion, as if every visitor carried the promise of a glorious new adventure which must be – and again, it must be said – embraced. She smiled her glittery smile and waved the men inside to her padded living room, which overrode the twee-cottage default setting by featuring a large overhead crystal chandelier.

It was difficult to imagine this woman as someone newly returned from murdering an ex-lover, but St. Just had seen worse – men who'd carved up their wives and gone on to a meal and pint at the pub without a care in the world. That sociopaths walk among us was not, to him, news. What was frightening was how very good sociopaths were at wearing different disguises as a sort of outerwear – schoolteacher, dentist, farmer, barber, and, of course, romance writer.

Ramona dazzled the eye in daytime wear more suitable for a night out in Soho. An embroidered Moroccan caftan, beaded Indian slippers, and elaborate gold jewellery established her international traveller credentials, although with the advent of online shopping, he supposed she might just be a dab hand at the keyboard, in between pounding out scenes of raw abandon.

'You're in luck – I just woke up!' she cried, doing a passable imitation of Margaret Thatcher with her rounded vowels. 'Won't you join me for coffee? Tea?'

But she must have been up for hours, thought St. Just, unless she slept in full makeup. Her eyebrows and lips were painted with a precision requiring a steady hand and a determination to distract the viewer from the first signs of age. She had, however, missed a tiny spot of pink lipstick on her unnaturally white teeth.

'Thank you,' he said, with a glance at Mousse. 'I wouldn't mind a coffee. Breakfast was rather rushed this morning.'

'Black or white, DCI St. Just?'

'Black, please.'

'And you, DCI Mousse?'

'I'll have the same.'

'Have we met, Ms—'

'Call me Ramona,' she said, her eyes carefully taking the

measure of St. Just. 'No, it's just that the word is out. I had a phone call just now from . . . a friend . . . telling me the police were making the rounds. I recognize you from photos in the media, of course – oh, you needn't look so surprised, Inspector! Your fame precedes you. It's frightfully thrilling for us all that you should honour us with a visit to our little village.

'Besides, you're here with that *mar*vellous author, Portia De'Ath, and of course I know her well by reputation – even though we plough very different fields, in a manner of speaking – crime versus romance. So by process of elimination – I know you'll appreciate my methods, Inspector! Using ze leetle grey cells! – I knew it had to be you. And simply everyone round here knows DCI Mousse. Terrible thing, about Titus.' She held a hand to her heart. 'I'm absolutely gutted.'

But she didn't look absolutely gutted. She looked like a woman having the time of her life. She was probably among the many who had a rather morbid, even ghoulish, interest in crime. St. Just wondered how much more melodrama they'd have to endure before they got down to cold hard fact.

It was Mousse who asked, 'You were on first-name terms with the deceased, were you?'

'Oh, my, yes,' she said. 'But of course! I was his confidante, you could say. I had his *utter* and *complete* trust. Do we have to call him "the deceased"? Too awful to think of Titus that way. Garrotted, I was told. Now, please take a seat and I'll be right back with a tray.'

And she twirled off, all the little crystals and bells and beads of her clothing making a gentle music, the subtle *ching-ching* of a million tiny tambourines. At least, thought St. Just, the police could rule her out as a cat burglar.

'Garrotted?' whispered Mousse.

'The grapevine must have got it wrong,' St. Just whispered in turn. 'Not the first time.'

'Jammie Dodgers or Hobnobs?' This from the kitchen.

'Nothing, thanks,' said the men in unison.

She emerged with a plate of Jammie Dodgers, the biscuits with the little red hearts St. Just had loved as a child. He loved them still, probably, although he'd not had one in decades.

There was something a bit childlike about this woman, he

thought, watching her float about the uber-twee room, fussing with the tray and napkins and spoons and the pouring out of the coffee. Of course the Jammie Dodger brand, decorated with hearts, would be her first choice, the red jam nearly matching the colour of her hair.

As she moved, she dispersed her perfume about the room like a human atomizer – some kind of tropical scent which, in the small, overstuffed room, was overpowering. He'd read somewhere that people who overdid the perfume had a poor sense of smell so they kept reapplying it. He recognized the rosy scent from the village meeting, where it had permeated the atmosphere, circulating as she flapped about in her pink garments.

'Do you know,' he said, 'I've changed my mind. Do you have enough to spare if I take a Jammie Dodger?'

'Yes! Of course! Save me the inches round my waistline, anyway. I shouldn't be having them at all; my doctor would *not* approve! But I believe a full figure is a sign of health, don't you?' Standing tall, she ran her hands down her sides, smoothing her waistline.

She seemed to be fishing for compliments on her figure, which both men wisely chose to ignore. St. Just, selecting a biscuit from the plate and taking a bite of the shortbread, doubted not that her writing would be as sugary and, like her speech, littered with exclamation marks.

The biscuit wasn't as transporting as he'd hoped. He sank back onto his mound of cushions, balancing his coffee on one be-jeaned knee. It felt strange interviewing a witness in clothes he'd brought for a summer holiday. Could he carry any authority, he wondered, without the shield of a suit and tie? Probably gnawing on a biscuit designed with children in mind didn't enhance his image.

Ramona beamed at him in a rather disturbingly domestic way, as if sizing him up as a marital prospect. She crossed her legs, setting off a cacophony of sound. St. Just realized there were little bells on the toes of her slippers. How did she ever get any writing done, at the hub of all that racket?

Mousse perched on the edge of his seat, as if awaiting the moment he might be given a chance to speak.

Or more likely worried he'd never be able to dig himself out from behind his pile of cushions.

St. Just munched on his biscuit and sipped his coffee, observing Ramona over the lip of his rose-patterned cup.

'Your timing is perfect, gentlemen! My agent said he'd call in' – she paused to consult her little diamond-crusted wristwatch – 'in about one hour. He is hearing from film agents *around the world* about my Tessa Tobler series! But I have told him, it must be filmed in Switzerland. One producer wanted to change the setting to Leeds, which makes absolutely no sense. Does Leeds even have mountains, does anyone know?'

'A few hills,' Mousse told her.

'But Tessa is *Swiss*. What would she be doing in Leeds?'

'I'm sure I don't know. Now, to return to Lord Bodwally . . .'

'Oh, yes!' It was clear she'd forgotten all about him. 'Such a dear man. I tried to let him down gently, but of course, in matters of the heart, the male is so much fragiler – is that a word? – so much more *fragile* than the female. After all, the female of the species gives birth! If that doesn't make a man of you, nothing will.' She seemed to hear what she'd actually just said, and laughed. 'Of *course*, I mean, it toughens a woman up! Men, lacking that experience, well. They simply can't begin to—'

'Might we return to the topic?' asked St. Just, putting aside his biscuit. He was finding it was true: one can't go home again. What his eight-year-old taste buds craved, his adult palate found gluey and cloyingly sweet. A bit like Ms Raven. Which reminded him: 'Ramona Raven. Is that your given name?'

She flushed a bit at this. 'Clever you, Inspector. No, of course not. I knew from the time I was a girl I wanted to be a writer and I needed a proper writer's name, one people could remember when they ran in to demand my books from their local booksellers. A name they could spell, too! When I divorced Mr Moran, I legally took the name by which I knew my fortune would be made. I had already written twenty books as Ramona Raven, books which had been translated into twenty languages, so naturally I stayed with it. I knew it was going to be lucky.'

'And your given name? Your Christian name, if you like?'

She regarded him from across the antique white coffee table, as if weighing the pros and cons of lying to him. A group of teenagers could be heard walking by outside, shrieking and giggling. Her eyes, heavily weighted with mascara and false eyelashes, slowly closed. As St. Just was thinking they had glued themselves shut, the eyes opened.

She sighed and said, 'Medguistyl Buglehole, if you must know.' DCI Mousse had produced a notebook from somewhere, and she spelled out the name for him. His expression suggested this was not the worst he had ever heard.

St. Just's face must have shown a different reaction.

'I know,' she said to him. 'Can you credit it? My mother must have been barking mad – and my father mad in love to have indulged her. I was their seventh child, you know. My other sisters were Anne, Betsy, and Carol. Normal names. I asked my mother once when she was in a good mood why in the name of God and she said, "Because I knew you would be special and I wanted a good Cornish name for you." Well, that was nice, but I ask you. The teasing I took in school. Not to mention the mix-ups applying for a driving licence!'

'I can imagine. So tell me, how did Lord Bodwally enter your life?' St. Just shifted forward in his seat, all ears. She clearly was a prolific talker (as well as writer) so he wanted to set the stage for her to ramble on. He gave a slight nod to Mousse with his notebook and let her rip.

Mousse had also produced from somewhere a pair of eyeglasses with thick black frames. He settled them more firmly on the bridge of his nose to show he was getting down to business.

'Lord Bodwally rode in on the proverbial white steed, Inspector! I was out riding on Bodmin Moor and it was raining, raining, raining. Which is what it does in those parts, especially. Rain and rain and rain! I had just decided I'd had enough when through the mist appeared . . . a shadowy black figure. A man wearing a black cape and riding a white horse! *Ever* so romantic. As he approached – just then! Just then! – I fell off my horse. Fortunately, it was a short little horse. More a pony, actually. But I fell at the lord's feet, literally, and of course as a gentleman he had to stop and see if I had been hurt.'

'Um-hmm. And were you? Hurt?'

'I had a twisted ankle. I was in such agony, Inspector! The next thing I knew, he swooped me up in his arms and put me behind him on his saddle and the two of us – well, counting the horses, the four of us – returned to the stables. The rest is history.'

It seemed to St. Just there were a few blank pages in her history book. It was Mousse who asked, 'You didn't fall deliberately, did you? In order to meet Lord Bodwally?'

'Oh, Inspector, you are naughty! Of course not! Well, I'd heard he'd be out there that day but it was the most *amazing* coincidence I should happen to be there, too, and that I should fall quite literally at his feet. I'd never ridden a horse before – well, not since my school days. It truly was the purest accident! But know this: there are no accidents when it comes to affairs of the heart. It was *fate.*' She sat back in her chintz-covered chair, beaming at them in turn, lying through her phony eyelashes. St. Just didn't imagine it really mattered how she managed to arrange an introduction to the lord, and the setup she described was no doubt something ripped from the pages of one of her own books. But whether she realized it or not, her equine adventure on Bodmin Moor aimed a powerful lamplight into the workings of her mind. The sort of woman who might stop at nothing to get her way, a cunning sort at best . . .

'So,' he said. 'You two met and . . . what? Went out to dinner?'

'Oh, my, no. Nothing as pedestrian as that, Inspector.'

'Why not? I have found in my limited experience that ladies enjoy being taken out for a meal.'

'No, no. *Mais non, mon cher inspecteur!* We found we were so simpatico he ended up inviting me to his *manor house* for dinner. The world-famous Revellick House.' She paused to spell Revellick for DCI Mousse, who was well ahead of her. 'The place is of medieval origin with later Tudor additions, you know. How could I resist? Around these parts it's usually all boring white Georgian this and that. Bodwally's place is a real gem. Those are my specialties: the medieval period, the Tudor age. I wrote Regencies at one time but, my goodness, the research involved! I find when I conjure a medieval setting, no one can be bothered to check back that far. The university types are the only ones who might catch a mistake. Not that my books have mistakes.'

And not that university types would read them, thought St. Just.

'It really just doesn't matter to my readers when spectacles were invented and so on. It's all people riding horses and dancing and falling in love and dealing with jealous types who would *do one down* – the timeless, universal themes. Human nature does not change.'

'I see.'

'We had lobster thermidor and champagne.'

'Very nice. Now, I—'

'And later that night our souls melted into one indissoluble, er, hazy, um, *thing*. It was a rare, earthy communion, the likes of which neither of us had never experienced before.'

He didn't dare look at Mousse, who with a flourish turned to a fresh page in his notebook and looked expectantly up at her.

'And the rest is history,' she concluded demurely.

More history.

From her expression, she'd been transported back in time to what he was certain she would call that 'fateful night'.

'That fateful night,' she began . . .

Bingo.

'. . . my future was sealed. As was his.'

'Sealed in what way?'

'Why, when love strikes – yes, yes! It was *love*! – when true love strikes, one questions it at one's peril.'

'You questioned it?' St. Just asked. At her nod, 'What exactly did you question?'

'Hand me one of those serviettes, if you would. I rather fear I may weep . . . The memories . . . so traumatic.' She seized one of the napkins he offered and began dabbing tentatively at her eyes. It was important, it seemed, not to dislodge the eyelashes, but she aimed a token pat at their moorings. Her eyes were devoid of tears. 'My life might have been so different. And needless to say, the publicity opportunities afforded me by being Lady Bodwally, well . . .'

'You questioned him?' he prompted.

'Well, yes. I had told him over dinner I'd been married and afterwards – in bed, you know . . . after – I asked him if he had ever been married. Just pillow talk, you know.'

'Mm-hmm. And what was his answer?'

'He said he'd been married. And that in fact, as far as he knew, he was married still.'

SIXTEEN
Forbidden Love

'Oh,' said St. Just and Mousse in unison.

'Yes. It was a shock, I don't mind telling you. I rather wish he'd mentioned it *before* we . . . you know. But there you are. Men were cheaters ever.'

'Deceivers,' St. Just corrected automatically.

'What?'

'It's Shakespeare.'

'That, too,' she said. 'A deceptive cheater, that he was.'

'Did he happen to say anything more – the wife's name, where she lives now?' Mousse asked.

'I don't know, do I? And what's more, I don't care. I have bigger fish to fry. *Much* bigger.'

'Oh?' they said again.

'Callum Page. *The* Callum Page, one of the most desirable men in the *kingdom*. The heart-throb adventurer, as he's known. Those shoulders, those pecs, those abs! That manly bearing. Brought here to little Maidsfell. By chance? No, I assure you, not by chance. By *fate*. He was brought here by the very gods of love. Driven in the very *chariot* of a god of love.' St. Just hoped the sheep had stayed out of their way. She sighed. 'Never was a man more suited to my temperament. Gorgeous, and sensitive with it. *And* intelligent – you'd be surprised.'

'He's not just a pretty face, then.'

'No, indeed!'

Given the age difference – she probably had ten years on Callum – it would seem the gods of love were running behind schedule. But ten years wasn't that big a gap – St. Just reminded himself not to be so sexist. If the man was older by ten years, no one would blink.

They said their goodbyes not long after. Once the door to Rose Cottage was firmly closed behind them, DCI Mousse said, 'Jesus Christ.'

'I know. Unlike Sepia, who seemed to want to downplay her involvement with Lord Bodwally, Ramona painted a portrait of star-crossed lovers.'

'It only lacked a mad wife in the attic to complete the picture.'

'But not in the attic, like Rochester's wife. Living blamelessly, we hope, perhaps somewhere in a flat in Notting Hill, where she never, ever thinks of her ex. We'll need to get that looked into.'

'On it,' said Mousse, adding, 'That perfume. Does she bathe in it, do you think?'

'She probably bathes in milk, like Cleopatra. But why would she carry on like that?' Slowly they made their way down the lane from Ramona's cottage. 'Ramona, I mean, not Cleopatra. It puts her rather in the frame, does it not? The jilted lover, the romance gone wrong, the blameless victim deceived by a cad – all of that.'

'Right,' said Mousse. 'Why go on and on about her "romance" with Bodwally? I don't think she can help herself, if I'm honest. Her brain runs along in those little grooves and she probably can't claw her way out of the mindset. Someone told me she's written nearly a hundred books; she writes several a year, apparently. Publishes like clockwork. My wife's read a few of her books; she thinks I don't know – she hides them in the laundry basket. I reckon she doesn't want to hurt my feelings. What man could live up to the ideal of manhood presented in those stories?'

'I thought the cliché was of a rude and churlish berk who is brought to heel in the end,' said St. Just. 'You should have nothing to worry about.' Having said that, he thought of the mild flirtation with Sepia he'd witnessed that morning. He hoped Mrs Mousse had nothing to worry about.

They passed the fishmonger's, where that morning's catch was being laid out on ice in the window, dead eyes glaring balefully at the world.

'Ramona's handed us a ready-made motive, hasn't she?' mused St. Just.

'That Bodwally wasn't honest with her up front about the wife? Yes, that might anger even a more, shall we say, down-to-earth person than Ramona Raven. It might anger anyone, come to that. He seems to have been more of a cad than I realized.'

'She'd be much wiser to play it cool with us, as Sepia seems to be doing,' said St. Just.

Mousse clearly did not like this idea. 'Oh. You think that's an act? Sepia?'

St. Just decided it best to smooth his way past Mousse's too-obvious concern for Sepia's reputation. 'I'm not sure,' he said. 'Sepia seemed to be cooperating fully. I am just saying a smart woman would play down the whole thing. She wouldn't bare her soul as Ramona did just now.'

'I don't think of Ramona as being a particularly smart woman. Manipulative, perhaps. A bit sly – all that horse nonsense. But I also don't think she could get through breakfast and a trip to the shops without baring her soul at least twice to someone. It's how she's made.'

'She claims to be over her fling with Bodwally and to have bigger fish to fry. *Wink, wink.*'

'Question is, should we believe her?'

'I don't know. Let's go and see how Callum Page, star of stage and screen, feels about this, if he's not too busy heaving furniture about to keep fighting fit. It may come as news to him that he is the other half of a romance for the ages.'

'I didn't know Callum Page was a stage actor, too. Or was that just an expression?'

'Portia knows something of his . . . achievements,' St. Just muttered. 'You could ask her.'

'What did you say? I missed that.'

'Portia knows a bit about him,' St. Just repeated. 'She has to keep up with what her students are obsessing over this week.'

'I don't see why.'

'I don't, either. I guess she wants to establish rapport.'

'What subject does she lecture on? The Romantics?'

'No. She's attached to the Institute of Criminology at Cambridge.'

Mousse whistled. '*And* she writes crime novels? Perhaps we should hand over the keys right now and let her solve this.'

St. Just smiled. 'Probably she could. But her speciality happens to be recidivism. Why old lags remain old lags. Now, where is Callum staying, do we know?'

'Follow me,' said Mousse.

SEVENTEEN
Beach Baby

Much as Ramona Raven had done, Callum Page threw open the door to his cottage with a staged flourish, as if he had been expecting them. St. Just wondered how long it had taken Ramona to fill him in on their visit to Rose Cottage.

He was wrapped in a snowy white beach robe, his hair wet and his feet bare. The robe was monogrammed in a flowing script. St. Just speculated on what the 'O' in *C.O.P.* stood for. It would turn up in whatever background Mousse was having run on him, but he was betting on Oscar.

St. Just and everyone on the beach the other day had already been treated to the sight of Callum's toned body, the planes and ridges corded in his stomach like the proverbial washboard, the massive thighs and legs like those of a Roman legionnaire.

Now St. Just took a moment to study the face of Adventure Guy, as he had come to think of him, whose angular features would undoubtedly have captivated a Renaissance sculptor. Yes, the straight nose, the deep eyes – not too deep – set just the right distance apart, the curve of strong lips, the cleft in the chin. St. Just was looking for a flaw and unable to find one. Even Callum's feet had long Jesus toes. It was simply ridiculous.

But wasn't such perfection a bit boring? Surely Portia, for example, wise woman that she was, would appreciate the flawed human being as more interesting. More human. More of a challenge. Someone with more to talk about over dinner than death-defying treks through the Amazon and being outfitted with new equipment for his next scuba dive. Or his next solo sail across some ocean or other in a hurricane. His next potholing adventure down a forgotten mine full of treasure.

Well, perhaps, the man's conversation *would* be above normal chats about taking the car for a tune-up and weeding the back garden, so perhaps it was best simply to hope physical perfection in and of itself would prove boring over time. And, of course, handsomeness doesn't last, and the maintenance becomes non-stop. There were tons of film stars keeping facelift doctors in Mercedes and ski chalets to prove it.

The result was all too often a man or woman whose skin was pulled back so tautly they looked to be continually under the influence of G-force.

But was Callum a killer? A reality star seemed miles from anything happening in peaceful Maidsfell. St. Just supposed the only suspicious thing about him was that he was here alone. Shouldn't he be surrounded by bikini-clad women, like a man in one of those ghastly American detective shows from the sixties?

Callum offered them coffee and St. Just accepted, wanting the chance to take in Callum's surroundings and look for whatever personal touches he may have shed on the rental.

He could see Gull Cottage had not been spared the nautical holiday décor. But the furnishings were all of a higher quality than those at Seaside. Also, the cottage was minus the vibrant tartan element; Callum was surrounded by the oatmeal neutrals of a Danish hygge setting.

St. Just wondered what had brought the man here – apart from the chariot of Ramona Raven's imagination. He began to ask Mousse when he noticed Callum had returned. Would they like anything to go with their coffee? A biscuit, perhaps? St. Just (still coming down off his Jammie Dodger sugar high) and Mousse declined.

He must use a tanning bed, thought St. Just, taking a seat in the insistently neutral, spacious sitting room, which in addition to being expensively furnished for a rental was larger and better sited than Seaside Cottage's. The obsession with having a tan was rather vain, thought St. Just, even though Callum blended in nicely with the hygge colours.

Struggling to be fair-minded, St. Just allowed that since the man was an actor, his looks were his stock-in-trade. The way a carpenter would own a hammer, Callum Page would own self-tanning cream and a gym membership and would pay to have his teeth whitened. Surely smiles left to their own devices were never so blindingly white?

Callum returned with a tray bearing two cups and all the

accessories needed for drinking coffee. The tray also held a single large glass of water.

'Let's have this on the patio,' he said, leading them out to a small round table with four chairs set round it. The view was stunning, clear to the horizon, where a passenger ship made its stately progress to the next port. St. Just realized he was unused to seeing such ships afloat. The cruise lines had been among the last industries to recover from the Plague Time.

'Only two cups?' Mousse asked. 'I wouldn't have put you to the bother, sir, if I'd realized you weren't having any.'

'I don't drink coffee or tea,' said Callum. 'Never have – it stains the teeth. Also red wine.' He smiled to show the happy outcome of this abstinence. St. Just was reminded it was time for his next dental checkup. 'Also I find stimulants hard on the system and I need to keep a steady hand.'

'Steady hand for what, sir?'

'Oh, you know. Sports. Training. Running.'

Single-handedly lifting vehicles off the near-lifeless forms of old-age pensioners, thought St. Just. Rescuing cats and toddlers.

'But I have no problem with others drinking coffee or tea, of course. It's become such a part of our culture, hasn't it? Which is why I keep all the necessary on hand.'

He smiled at them again and it was as if the sun, already bright and warm on their faces, had been dialled up on a dimmer switch.

To St. Just he said, 'I will say again, that was some fast thinking you did on the beach.'

'Well, thank you, but I had a lot of help. By no means can I take all the credit.'

'That girl caught in the riptide?' asked Mousse, reaching for the sugar bowl.

'Yes, St. Just here figured out how to get a flotation device out to her. In this case, a beach ball. Quite good thinking.'

'Thank you, Mr Page.' A pause and he added, 'It's certainly high praise coming from you.'

'No one understands the force of the tides, do they?' Callum launched into a story that ended with his own near-death adventure the year before off the coast of Molokai.

St. Just decided the word to describe Callum's personality was 'affable', even though a man so supremely good-looking might be expected to have a large ego. He was simply likeable, in the way of people who want very much to be liked, who want to please others. But he managed it without seeming needy or nerdy, and that was the real gift. People would probably fall over themselves to help out such a nice bloke. Women, it went without saying. But men, too. Men wanting some of that glow to reflect on them, even if it meant being relegated to a wingman's role.

Although St. Just supposed he had that wrong. Callum would be the wingman, drawing in females for his friends.

To all appearances, he was what he was – a nice fellow. Maybe not the brightest, but then he didn't have to be. He could pay other people to do his thinking for him.

It's all too much, thought St. Just. *He's a reality telly star, for heaven's sake. He should be unable to carry on an intelligent conversation with anyone over the age of seven. He should be a vain egomaniac, besides – an unfeeling rat no woman in her right mind would admire.*

Instead, here he was. Being nice, like some bloody Canadian. Complimenting St. Just on his role in the rescue like a true gentleman, not trying to seize the credit.

He probably donates generously to all the animal causes and rings his mother weekly and spends his free time serving dinner at a homeless shelter, fumed St. Just. Pointless to wonder what woman would be interested in him. They would all be interested and yet somehow, miraculously, Adventure Guy – Callum – didn't seem to have a big head about it.

It was all so maddening. Why didn't Callum go back to London? Why was he even here? Didn't he have movie commitments and contracts to sign and meetings with his agent? With his business manager? With Trixie the publicist?

St. Just reminded himself he was forming these opinions based on very short acquaintance. There was still hope Callum would turn out to be something other than he seemed. St. Just's instincts were good; it was what made him a good policeman. But he wasn't infallible and he knew it.

'The worst is the people on holiday who simply ignore the warnings,' Mousse was saying.

St. Just became aware of Mousse's eyes on him – he was a trained observer, after all, and St. Just hoped he could not read any of his inner turmoil. He relaxed his shoulders and neck and reminded himself he had a job to do.

'They either don't understand or they pretend not to,' Mousse went on, returning his attention to Callum. 'More likely, they underestimate the danger. There will be a red, no-swimming flag displayed on the beach when it's foggy. "If we can't see you, we can't save you," as they say. But some pay no attention.'

'Fog!' said Callum. 'That would've been all we needed.'

Setting aside the coffee he didn't want, St. Just asked, 'What brings you to Maidsfell, Mr Page?'

'Why, the surfing, of course.'

Mousse, with a lift of his shaggy eyebrows, said, 'Not here in Maidsfell. The conditions are wrong for surfing this time of year. At most times, in fact. Were you thinking of trying Porthleven?'

'No,' said Callum. 'It's too flat there in summer.'

Mousse nodded sagely, as if Callum had passed a test, thought St. Just.

'I thought I might try Gwithian Beach, near Hayle.'

'Ah,' said Mousse. 'You can get in a good run there. Mind, much of the coastline is for the professionals. It can be quite tricky.'

'Oh, don't I know it,' Callum replied easily. 'But it's the challenge I'm after.'

'And you probably are a professional. I was forgetting.'

'Anyway, I don't suppose you're here to talk about surfing. You're here to talk about Lord Bodwally.'

'Quite. How did you come to hear of it, sir?' Mousse asked. 'The murder?'

'It was murder, then?'

'No question it was, sir.' St. Just noticed the slight emphasis on the 'sir'. This was Mousse getting down to business at last. Indeed, out came the notebook and the glasses from his pocket. He unfolded the frames and put the glasses on his nose. 'How did you hear?'

'There's a woman comes to make up the cottage every morning,' Callum replied. 'She was agog with it. I wasn't sure how much of it was her imagination, to be honest.'

'That would be Nora.' Mousse addressed St. Just with this information. 'She cleans for most of the rental-cottage owners round here.'

'Straight yellow hair like uncooked spaghetti?' asked St. Just.

'The very one,' said Mousse. Turning again to Callum, he asked, 'What did she tell you? It is sometimes interesting to hear the "whisper down the lane" versions of a story that pass for the truth here.'

'She said he had been found with his head "done in" with a tyre iron. Had he?'

'No, sir, not at all. He'd been stabbed. The villagers can be gifted storytellers. Anyway, it was quite a brutal death, no matter the details.'

'Yes. How horrible. Those final moments . . . it doesn't bear thinking about. It's not a normal happening for these parts, is it?'

'It is not,' answered Mousse, 'and I'd like to see there are no repeats.'

'Of course.'

'It was an attack requiring considerable strength.'

'I see. And I'm strong, therefore . . .'

'Not really, sir. We have considered that under considerable duress, the human body is capable of incredible feats. The mother lifting a car off her child – that sort of thing.'

'Or the scorned woman stabbing her cheating lover with ferocity. Of course.'

'Interesting you should use that as an example,' said St. Just. 'The lover taking her revenge.'

'Was it a lucky guess?' Callum asked. 'Actually, from what little I know of Bodwally, that sort of end would not be unexpected.'

'Felled by the woman scorned?'

'Something like that. Perhaps the only way to stop him gadding about would be to stab him to death.'

'Really,' said St. Just.

'I'm sorry. That sounded rather harsh, didn't it? I try not to judge; I'm not entirely blameless myself.'

I'll bet.

'But the man was beyond saving in that department, or so I've heard.'

'I'm surprised you know as much as you do, sir. You haven't been here that long in Maidsfell.'

'Well, I got my information from a local writer. Lovely woman. That's not to say she didn't embellish things a bit. In fact, I gather embellishment is in her job description. It's her stock-in-trade.'

'You are speaking of Ramona Raven.'

'Yes.'

'And how do you know her?'

'I threw a party when I first got here – a way of saying hello, letting the villagers get to know me. I do find my celebrity can be rather off-putting to people and I wanted them to have a chance to get to know the real me – or at least as much of the real me as I wanted to show. "Callum Page at home, friendly guy, nothing to see here" – you know the sort of thing. That way I could get to meet people and at the same time avoid the stares in the street.'

'It must be hard having to live like that,' said St. Just.

That earned him a quick, hard gaze.

'Celebrity has its pluses and minuses, Inspector. The pluses are that I never have to make a dinner reservation; I can just turn up at the door. But so what, really? The minuses are you are always on display, always expected to perform somehow, and you know that every encounter will be reported, sometimes – most times – inaccurately. The day I found myself in total sympathy with Meghan Markle was the day I knew my fame had gone viral.'

'On social media, you mean.'

'That and the mainstream press, what's left of it. But social media can be a real nightmare, the photographers – amateurs and pros – in particular. Just waiting for you to put a foot wrong so they can document it. They don't want the shot of you looking your best. They want the shot of you spilling your drink, the shot of you with spinach in your teeth. It must be a bit the same for policemen. You don't dare get caught not being a credit to your profession.'

'Quite so,' said Mousse.

'You threw a party,' St. Just prompted. 'Who was there?'

'Bodwally, as it happens. Ramona. Morwenna barely popped in – it's hard for her to find time away from the restaurant. Sepia, the woman who owns the gallery – a few others. I don't recall all the names right now but I can try to come up with a list for you.'

'We heard from Ramona that you two are now an item.'

He laughed. 'Oh, God. Is that what she told you?' He seemed to pause to consider this. 'She's an attractive lady. But Bodwally spent the entire evening trying to avoid her. It was rather hard to watch – it was so obvious what was going on. I guess I took pity on her; I was the host, after all. I fetched her a drink and a plate of something to eat. We talked. We flirted a bit. OK, a lot. She made sure – I helped her make sure – Bodwally noticed. Not that he cared. She could have done the dance of the seven veils – she practically did, in fact. He wasn't having any.'

'He had other fish to fry?' St. Just realized he'd just borrowed Ramona's own cliché. The woman was contagious.

'I'll say.'

'For example?'

'I'd rather *not* say.'

'It's a murder inquiry,' Mousse reminded him. 'We're not after gossip.'

Actually, that's precisely what we're after, thought St. Just.

Callum shrugged. 'It's not that important. First he went after Sepia, who was clearly not interested, which of course drove him wild – her indifference. If there was ever anything there – which, according to Ramona, there had been – those flames had long been extinguished on her side.'

'Anyone else?' Mousse gently tapped his notebook with his biro. St. Just stole a look at what he'd written: pure chicken scratch. He hoped the man transcribed it all into a computer. St. Just was reminded of his faithful sidekick back in Cambridge, Sergeant Fear; the ranking system he used while taking notes included stars by certain comments. Fear's system was: 'One star = may be true; five stars = lying.'

It wasn't infallible but ever since Fear had attended a course on how to tell if a suspect was lying, his bullseye rate, already good, had improved dramatically.

'Morwenna,' Callum said slowly, reluctantly.

St. Just perked up at that. 'What about Morwenna?'

'Do you know, I couldn't really say. She didn't seem to care for him any more than Sepia did. The estate agent, on the other hand . . .'

'Cynthia Beck, yes,' said Mousse.

'There was some tension there. Sexual or otherwise. You know how it is with some couples. They look like they want to kill each other but it's just foreplay.'

'You don't say,' said St. Just. 'Interesting, that. Also interesting that you call them a couple.'

'It was just an impression I got. I'm telling you, this is the worst form of gossip. Actually, if there's a good form, I'd like to hear of it.'

'It's a murder in—' began Mousse.

'I know, I know. A murder investigation. And believe me, I want to help you catch whoever did this. We can't have people running about knifing other people in one of the most peaceful villages in the UK, if not the world. I want to base a show near here, you see. Holywell Cave near Newquay is said to be amazing, and if they'll allow me to film at low tide, I shall. Even better, an escape at high tide might make for some fantastic footage.'

Clearly Callum saw life as a series of filmable opportunities, the more dangerous the better. 'You think they may have been quarrelling?' St. Just asked. 'Bodwally and Cynthia?'

Callum seemed to be making a greater effort to recall the night of the party. 'I don't know. There was a tension you could cut with a knife. She just kept staring at him. He kept staring at Sepia. After a while, Ramona kept staring at me. It was, on the whole, rather an awful party. Once Bodwally left, it got better.'

Interesting. 'So it eased some of the tension when he left.'

He shrugged, a gesture which seemed to engage every muscle in his broad shoulders, and settled himself more firmly in his chair. 'It redistributed the tension, more like. Ramona transferred her affections to me. Sepia looked relieved he'd gone. Cynthia – I'm just not sure what that was about. It was more like he'd run over her dog or something than a lover's quarrel.'

'I'm not sure I'd know the difference, myself,' said Mousse.

'You had to be there. Let's see, the only other woman of suitable age and inclination was the padre, and she didn't appear to be in this race. If she even noticed Bodwally, I didn't notice her noticing.'

'Padre?' asked Mousse.

'I mean to say, the Anglican priest. We used to call them padres in school but I guess she's a madre. Anyway, Judith is her name. Judith Abernathy. I saw her in the village shop one day and invited her to the party. She seemed rather fun with the Hawaiian shirts and all. Priests in my school days were more into black and white and didn't worry one jot about being relatable. Anyway, she hasn't lived in the village long and she seemed really happy to have a chance to meet more villagers. I rather feared she might see it as a chance to convert people – drag them along to her services; baptize them forcibly, if necessary. But she just had a drink, chatted a bit, and left early. It was on a Saturday night and, of course, Sunday was her "big day", as she put it, so she had to work on her sermon. For the same reason, she only had one drink. Although I think most sermons I've heard could have been improved with a bit of drink all round, don't you?'

'It could often help, yes,' said Mousse.

'It's an interesting story, how she came to be here,' Callum continued.

'Her husband's death,' said St. Just, nodding.

'That is sad, of course, but what I meant was she was being stalked by an unwanted suitor and had to flee London for her life. I think it just creeped her out more than that she was in real danger – that sort of thing is a mind game for the most part, but I suppose you police would know more about that than I do. Anyway, the vicar gave her a place of safety here – to hide out until it blew over.'

Mousse made a note of all this. 'Did anything else at the party strike you as unusual?'

'Not really. If my guests weren't staring daggers at Bodwally, all they wanted to talk about was parking and the sea wall and tourists and second-home owners. I probably put a damper on much of that discussion by being a tourist myself. They also wanted to ask about my show and I'm always happy to oblige. Oh, my.'

'What's that?'

'Nothing, really. I just remembered: I seem to have promised Ramona access to one of the live tapings. She said it would help her research. I've no idea how I'm going to wriggle out of it.' He hesitated, adding, 'I don't think she's a woman to take "no" for an answer.'

'No, sir,' said Mousse. 'I'd be surprised.'

The two detectives left not long after.

'Why did you ask him where he was planning to surf?' St. Just asked.

'I was just making sure that was what brought him here. It was a bit of a test.'

'I thought so. But I wasn't sure *why* you wanted to test him. You think he has another motive for being here, do you?'

'I find it a bit odd that he's here, yes. An attractive man in the prime of life normally seeks the bright lights of a city – especially this man, who seems to spend half his time in hard-to-reach places.'

'I would say Cornwall qualified as that.'

'What? Oh, I see, yes. We're a bit off the beaten path. Still, Callum doesn't come across as some loner looking for revenge. He seems to have established himself quite quickly in the village with parties and whatnot.'

'And romance writers.'

'That, too. I wonder if he even realizes Ramona's got him in her sights.'

'I can see no way to warn him.'

'Of course,' Mousse added slowly, 'just because he knows a bit about the best places to surf in summer doesn't mean much. He would have that sort of sporty knowledge at his fingertips, wouldn't he? But I'd bet anything he's a superb surfer.'

'I'd bet it, too,' said St. Just ruefully. 'Probably surfs standing on his head.'

'You don't seem to like him much,' Mousse observed.

'Actually, I like him fine. It's not often you get to meet a perfect specimen of humanity. He's cordial, polite, bright – or bright-ish – and, of course, blindingly handsome. Nothing to say against him.'

'I understand,' said Mousse. 'It's irritating, isn't it? Perfection.'

'Quite. But you're saying his reasons for being here are a bit glib. You think he has another purpose? A darker purpose, perhaps?'

'I don't know. It's just this feeling you get, when a suspect isn't telling you *all* the truth or giving you the entire story.'

'Ah. What my sergeant back home would call a three-star statement.'

'Hmm?'

'Sergeant Fear has his own rating system. He tends to pre-judge suspects. The problem is he's so often right.'

'Must come in handy,' said Mousse. 'Well, it's all very interesting and Lord Bodwally clearly was not loved but where is this getting us?'

'We'll get there in the end,' said St. Just. He always did, although each new case haunted him with a fear he might fail. After a pause, he added, 'I'm afraid my judgement of Callum may be clouded, to be honest. So I'm going to go slowly where he's concerned.'

'Clouded?' asked Mousse, his expression an attempt at childlike innocence that would not have fooled a child.

'Clouded,' St. Just repeated. 'So, who's next?'

'I think we should have a talk with some of the other people who were at the party. The Reverend Judith for one. Morwenna for another. Which lady do you fancy speaking with first?'

St. Just looked at his watch. 'This time of day we might find Morwenna taking a break between lunch and dinner services. I don't know what the curate's schedule might be.'

'The curate will be out making pastoral calls,' said Mousse. 'Morwenna lives in rooms behind the restaurant – if she's around, we'll likely find her there.'

EIGHTEEN
De Rien

S ybil Gosling did not know what to do.

She had just returned to her cottage from attending the wedding of a former pupil. The reception had been held in the home of the bride's parents, a large cottage halfway up the cliffs of Maidsfell, overlooking the sea. Food, wine, a perfect setting. A perfect start to a new life for the happy couple.

Half the village had been there, because half the village knew the bride, Lynda. It was not as if life could not go on 'just' because there had been a murder. Life went on, regardless.

But Sybil's mind was disturbed.

More than the usual, Sybil's mind was disturbed.

That big policeman from Cambridge was much in her thoughts. She supposed she should talk to him. Or to the other one. But the big policeman had an air about him that said she might be listened

to. Mousse was a local man and had absorbed the locals' preju-
dices. He might send her away: just another silly old woman with
ideas.

But it was nothing, really. It was nothing.

It was such a small thing. Surely she was imagining it, her mind
paying tricks. Who would disturb the hallowed site of the Maidens?
Who would even know it was there? She had left the flowers
centred before the fourteenth maiden but when she went to do her
final inspection for the day, after the wedding celebration, they'd
been moved to the left. *Someone* had moved them.

Nonsense. Besides, the big policeman wouldn't care about this
as long as nothing had been damaged or stolen.

She made a cup of tea and carried it out to her little patio. The
sea and the sky above it stretched tall and wide, bursting every
boundary, wrapping the world in a mysterious circle.

Light and dark.

Of course, everything that went on in 'regular church' was a
mystery to her, too, today's ceremony being a prime example, but
she hoped she could remain ecumenical in outlook. She had
been raised in the Anglican tradition and still remembered
holding her parents' hands as they walked together to St. Cuthbert's,
her brother bringing up the rear. Every Sunday, barring illness,
they would sit midway up the aisle in a left-hand pew. She did
wonder from a young age how the stained-glass artists had got it
so wrong. Mary had never looked like a blonde Italian, the baby
Jesus had never looked like a shrunken old man.

Later, of course, her faith had been shattered. Irretrievably,
irredeemably. Her belief in the stories she'd been taught during
sermons and Bible study – gone. She would wake up every morning
from a dreamless sleep and realize the horror of her living nightmare was still with her, that it would colour her existence
throughout the day. Pulling herself from her bed she would sigh,
wishing that one day her first waking thought would not be of
Ruthie. Praying for the memories of her to go away, even though
that prayer was quickly chased with guilt. For if she forgot Ruthie,
who would remember her once she herself was gone? Who would
tend her grave? Her daughter, that gift so rudely taken back, like
an invitation to happiness withdrawn – 'Sorry, Sybil, we miscounted;
there won't be enough room for you after all.'

One moment of carelessness by a driver pulling away from a pub after one pint too many. One split second. And Ruthie was gone.

Sometimes she would try to picture life with Ruthie still there, still with her. Imagining a future for her, what Ruthie would do out in the world – how clever she would be, how many men would fall hopelessly in love with her, how she would come home on visits to tell her mother of her latest triumph. It was like those drawings they showed on the telly of a person who'd gone missing – age progression, they called it.

Ruthie at thirty-five. Ruthie at forty. Ruthie with children of her own.

Sometimes this parallel life seemed almost real, and Sybil would set out two cups of tea and a plate of scones in the afternoon, hoping the scent of the Earl Grey, Ruthie's favourite, would draw her only child back to her, make her come and sit across from her mother as she'd always done after school. Sybil could almost imagine it; it was real.

So nearly real.

Sybil would see other mothers with their daughters and try to see what made them so special. She would stare, trying to puzzle it out. That was when her reputation for being a bit odd got started, but she didn't care; *she* knew she wasn't being rude. She wanted to see what these perfect mothers had done that allowed them to keep their children.

Did they chastise them to keep them in line? Did they ignore their misbehaviour? Did they bribe them with sweets to get them to behave?

What was it?

All Sybil had done was adore her child from its first breath, and it wasn't enough.

What sin had she ever committed? She'd been a good girl, a good wife, a blameless widow – and a fat lot of good any of it had done her.

What sin had *Ruthie* ever committed?

So Sybil chose her own path, going her own way in religion as in so many other things. Today's wedding was the first time she'd been to church since the funeral of another pupil. Once the Plague Time came to an end, Sybil felt as if she'd gone to a funeral every week – everyone catching up with services that could not be held when people passed.

It had been strange, being at St. Cuthbert's again, like witnessing a ceremony from another culture, the words foreign to her, the priest in a costume chosen for the festive occasion, looking as if she had on a medieval white nightgown, its ruffled sleeves tied at the wrists. The bells and smells of a High Church service were gone, however. They'd changed things to be 'relevant', trying to attract the young ones.

At least this Judith person didn't drink, not like Peder Wolfe, who was always half sozzled, spilling the communion wine and scattering the wafers and losing his place in the service. Fortunately, he had the sense never to drive. If she'd ever caught him at that, Sybil would have made a formal complaint to his bishop.

After the service, on her way to the reception, she had seen Morwenna in the Maidsfell allotment garden near the church-yard, spraying insecticide on the cabbage. *That* she felt she should report. It was supposed to be an organic garden and it was forbidden to use pesticides. Didn't Morwenna realize poison salted the ground for who knew how many years – even centuries? But there she was, serving her produce to tourists and the villagers, claiming everything from her kitchen was organic.

But that didn't really explain why she was spraying poison in *someone else's* allotment space. Sybil wasn't sure whose it was; she just knew Morwenna's space was in the northern segment. Sybil puzzled over that for a moment, but decided it didn't matter. Using chemical insecticides anywhere in the allotment was *forbidden*. And everyone knew it.

Would that policeman, St. Just, realize this was a crime and act accordingly? Sybil supposed he was busy with other things such as Bodwally, but what could be more important than deliberately poisoning the planet?

What if someone had pulled up the cabbages – 'borrowed' them from someone else, as so often happened in those allotments? And then had not had the sense to rinse them thoroughly? It was a risky thing for Morwenna to do, however you looked at it.

And wouldn't it be murder? Maybe St. Just would be interested then, if someone fell sick and died. If she could just frame things the right way, he would see the danger. He would understand that

Morwenna was being reckless, so keen to keep her restaurant in business, even though – oddly – Morwenna was always backing the fishermen and that ruddy car park they were always on about.

Always until recently, that is. She'd done that abrupt stand-down at the council meeting. Morwenna must suddenly have realized she needed the big spenders to keep coming to Maidsfell so she could sock money away in case hard times returned.

Of course, she'd take shortcuts like spraying pesticide. It was the sort of woman Morwenna was. Sybil had always known that. All pub owners were alike. All people who traded in alcohol were alike.

In the garden allotment, Morwenna hadn't noticed Sybil and some instinct – no doubt a warning sent from the Goddess – had told Sybil it would be best to slip quietly away.

NINETEEN
Toxic

On the way to Morwenna's, Mousse began slapping at his pockets, like a man fighting a sudden attack by bees. St. Just correctly guessed Mousse's mobile had started vibrating.

Just then a giggling crowd of tourists surged past. They were headed for the beach, to judge by the array of coloured plastics tucked under their arms. To get away from their noise, Mousse stepped off the high street into an alleyway, followed by St. Just.

'Say again?' Mousse said. Then, 'You're certain?' He listened a moment. 'What do you mean, unknown?' Another pause, a streak of swear words, then, 'Well, call me when you do know something.'

Mousse had switched to Cornish at the end of the conversation. St. Just knew enough of it to guess much of what had just been said was unprintable.

Mousse rang off and said, 'For the love of God. That's just what we needed.'

'Yes?'

'That was the pathologist.' He paused, clearly digesting what he'd just been told, struggling to make sense of it himself. 'He says – wait for it – he says . . .'

'I am waiting.'

'It's just that – Bodwally's tox scan is back. Routine, even in cases where the cause of death is as apparent as in this case. As you know.'

'Yes?'

'Yes, and the pathologist says there was some foreign element in his system that had just about worked its way through to – you know. The end of the line in his plumbing. It's an unknown substance but they know it's weird and no doubt shouldn't be there.'

'What, drugs? I'd be surprised. He struck me overall as a man too in love with himself to risk his health with drug abuse.'

'No. None of that. It's a poison – well, as the pathologist always points out, everything taken in too large a dose is poison. But this is not the usual street drug, and you're right in thinking it's unlikely he would have been experimenting with it. It was a fish, you see. A poison fish.'

'A poisoned fish?'

'No, no, it seems to be that the fish in and of itself was poison.'

'O-kaaay. So we've got a fisherman angry with Bodwally and a poisoned fish – sorry, a poison fish. I'm going to guess the two things may be connected.'

'Not just Will Ivey was angry, mind, even though he's by way of being the Godfather of the fishers round here. They all were angry. That makes, just scratching the surface, fifteen to twenty-five new suspects. More if we extend to nearby villages, family members affected, and so on.'

'You think Will Ivey – or someone – might have found it in his catch?'

'It's possible. No idea, really.'

'What sort of fish are we talking about?'

'They can't say yet. It's not a type of fish normally found in these waters. They're going to have to run DNA on it, especially since it's – well, I suppose since it's not in its original state after it travelled through the ins and outs of Bodwally's digestion.'

'If it's not native to these waters, maybe it was flown in from somewhere else. Frozen, perhaps? Do you think they can tell that?'

Mousse shook his head. 'They simply don't know much. The subject doesn't come up in their experience. If there's money in the budget for that sort of high-level testing, we're still not going to have specific answers like that for months, given the backlog.'

'I know. The magic of DNA testing does seem to take forever.'

'They run tests for things like alcohol levels, arsenic, metals – as well you know. There are standard runs. But no one searches for poison fish unless they're told to, and even then, not knowing the species . . . Well, you see the difficulty. They'll figure it out, but not soon. Does it matter, really?'

'Oh, certainly it does. But the real question is, did he consume the fish by accident or was someone trying to poison him? And the poisoning having failed, did they go for the more direct method?'

'I'm with you,' said Mousse. 'Almost certainly a poisoning and a stabbing of the same individual in such a short span of time defies the odds.'

'Could they say when the poisoning occurred?'

'The day before he died. Died for real, that is, by the more direct and guaranteed method.'

'So that would be some time on Monday. Dinnertime, perhaps?'

'They can't narrow it down to the minute.'

'Of course not. It's always up to us plods, isn't it?'

'Always. So, what next? Do we start sorting the fishers?'

'I wish I had a better sense of which direction we should go,' said St. Just, leaning against the stone wall of the narrow alleyway. 'We've only just scratched the surface of the interviews. Let's go have our talk with Morwenna. See what she knows about poison fish.'

'Of course, it spreads out beyond the fishers, doesn't it? The pool of suspects, if you'll pardon the pun. Jake Trotter would know a lot about fish, too. It's his business, after all. He serves nothing but fish and seafood in that restaurant of his.'

'All right. Let's have a word with him, too.'

Mousse consulted his too-large watch. St. Just imagined he could use it to track the planets and order grocery delivery. 'I need to check in with the office,' he said. 'See how they're doing on background, and make sure they include restaurateurs while they're about it. Why don't you go ahead, maybe grab a pasty somewhere, and we'll meet at Morwenna's in, say, half an hour.'

TWENTY
Bake Off

St. Just first tried the main door of the Maiden's Arms and, finding it locked, followed DCI Mousse round the side. There they found a cottage attached like a carbuncle to the back of the restaurant. Its small green door had a video doorbell at one side, with a nameplate labelling the occupant as Wells. Mousse rang and identified himself; a crackling disembodied voice answered: 'It's open.'

St. Just looked quizzically at Mousse. Surely all the village was behind locked doors by now? Morwenna was either very brave or . . .

Mousse pushed on the green door and together the men made their way to a room illuminated by lamplight.

Morwenna Wells sat in a swivel chair at her desk, apparently going over the accounts for the restaurant, a stack of receipts to one side of a green desk blotter, a ledger to the other. The detectives sat in in two spindly chairs across from her.

'You've not heard, then?' said Mousse.

'About Bodwally? Yes, of course I've heard.'

Of course. 'And you're not worried?' St. Just asked. 'The door to your place here was off the latch.'

'He's dead, isn't he? Why would I be worried?'

The men exchanged glances.

'Oh, come on,' she said. Putting down a gnawed pencil, she resettled a pair of reading glasses on her nose, pushing the bridge up with her index finger. 'Of course I'm not daft. I don't think he walks the night or anything – or walks the broad daylight, in this case. For that nonsense you should consult Sybil.'

'Our concern is more . . . earthly,' Mousse told her.

She scoffed, her face creased in a look of contempt. 'You don't think there's a serial killer on the loose, do you? Surely this was a one-off.'

'You think the killing was targeted, Morwenna?' St. Just asked.

'I do.' Her chair creaked as she leaned forward. 'I'd be hard pressed to think of anyone in the village who got people's backs up the way Bodwally did.' She licked one finger to sort through a pile of pages covered in figures, pulling out the sheet she wanted. 'Good riddance, if you ask me. But don't read anything into that. Of course I had nothing to do with this.'

Interesting, thought St. Just. Usually, people involved even peripherally in murder will take a second to mourn a man's passing before breezing on to the next spreadsheet. Or at least display the common curiosity attendant on a sudden, mysterious, and horrific death.

She caught his eye just then, peering over her spectacles; his expression must have shown a trace of his dismay.

'Oh, *do* come on,' she said. 'If you don't know how unpopular he was, you should get Tomas here to fill you in. I don't have an hour to spare or I'd do it.'

'She's right,' said Mousse. St. Just gave him a *Whose side are you on?* look, then realized Mousse was simply playing out his line.

'The fishers all hated him,' she said, 'and there are dozens of those. They were given planning permission for improvements and now they've had them snatched away, or as good as, by the do-nothing village council – all with Bodwally's connivance. Delay after delay, send it here for review and there for review – it amounts to the same thing, doesn't it? For the fishers, those improvements are essential to their livelihoods and safety, and what's essential to them is essential to me, to my business. We've not forgotten the Plague Time, and we've none of us recovered yet. I did everything in the world to keep this place going, and to get it started again once we got the go-ahead. The government's "Eat Out To Help Out" discount scheme was a well-intended disaster but a disaster nonetheless. We had to turn people away for safety and legal reasons, they weren't happy – *and* they went straight online to say so. As if it was somehow *my* fault!'

'How does it affect their safety, the fishermen?' St. Just asked.

He decided now might not be the moment to call her out on her about-face at the very village meeting she was deriding. At her glare, he added, 'Sorry, I'm not trying to be clever. I don't understand the business of fishing.' He shrugged. 'I'm a city bloke. I've never even fished in the Cam.'

Morwenna relented. 'As things are now, they have to haul their catch across the beach in punts. It's dangerous. The rocks are strewn with seaweed – it's slippery, hazardous. A jetty and a slipway would make their lives so much easier.'

'Do you have any grudge against Bodwally yourself?' he asked.

'Don't be silly,' she said. Again the glasses slid down her nose and again she pushed them in place with one finger.

St. Just didn't feel he was being silly in the least but let it go. Looking round the office, he noticed there was one vital accessory missing. 'You don't use a computer?' he asked.

'I have a girl from the next village comes to "key in the data", as she puts it. Personally, I like to see numbers on paper. That way I know without scrolling about where we stand.'

'And how do you stand?'

She shrugged. 'We're making it. It was a long climb out from the Plague Time but we're on the mend.' She stared at another printout and repeated, 'On the mend. Last weekend was stellar.'

'That's good,' he said. 'A friend of mine's place in Cambridge very nearly had to close its doors permanently, which would have been a pity. St. Germaine is my favourite.'

'St. Germaine? Garoute's place? I'm so glad to hear he made it.'

'You know him?' asked St. Just.

'It's a very small world of upmarket restaurants in the UK. His is one of the best.'

Mousse looked like he wanted to interrupt but St. Just carried on. He had found a topic Morwenna could relax into.

'Constable Porter, a member of the special constabulary in Cambridge, works part-time there as a pastry chef. Has done for years.' It was also where St. Just had first set eyes on Portia, but he didn't feel like sharing that memory, even for the greater good of softening up a suspect. St. Germaine was where he planned to celebrate many of their birthdays and anniversaries in future.

'I must ring him one day,' Morwenna said. 'Find out how he got through it all.'

'How did you?'

'How did I what?'

They had wandered far from the topic of the murder, but now she was using the stalling technique of answering a question with a question. St. Just wondered if something had gone on during the Plague Time that she didn't want to talk about with the authorities. A bit of cost-cutting, perhaps. A bit of off-the-books negotiation. It wouldn't surprise him. People did what they had to do to save their businesses in those days. It made him wonder if she was in some way beholden to a fisher or two who had looked the other way as she ignored some regulation or other.

From the direction of the restaurant kitchen, seeping through even the thick stone walls of the old structure, came the intoxicating odour of onions being sautéed in butter. St. Just hoped they might stop for a bite once they'd concluded the interview. He'd spent his 'pasty break' sitting on a pensioners' bench, thinking.

'How did you get through the Plague Time?' he clarified. 'So many restaurants and pubs closed, and many could never find traction enough to reopen once they'd announced the all-clear.'

'Well, I got through it, that's all,' she said. 'But it wasn't easy. One customer tested positive and we had to close for a deep clean. One lousy customer, one probably faulty test, and the entire staff had to isolate for fourteen days and be tested before they could return to work. We had to throw out tons of food that would have gone to rot in the meantime. I thought we were out of the woods but next thing you know one of the waiters came down with it – nearly died, he did; young bloke, too – and we had to close, go through it all again, contacting customers to let them know they might have been exposed. That time we hired some outfit to do deep cleaning including fogging. Guess how much that cost? I came to be on intimate terms with the people at the test-and-trace system. Total nightmare.'

'I can imagine,' said St. Just.

'Can you really? The worst part was, of course, we lost the public's trust for a long while, and through no fault of our own. I tell you, I've always run a clean kitchen, since well before all the trouble started. There was nothing to "catch" at the Maiden's Arms. But that virus was so tricky.'

'I remember,' said St. Just. 'I kept wishing the enemy droplets glowed in the dark like phosphorus so I could see where the stuff was and avoid it.' He noticed Mousse had stopped taking notes and was studying the framed foodie awards hanging on the walls of Morwenna's office.

'Nightmare,' she said again, shaking her head. 'And then came the order: all restaurants had to close. And off we went, downhill all the way. If we weren't closed entirely, we had a curfew. Or we could only serve drinks, not food. No one knew which end was up. It's small wonder customers chose to stay home.'

'How did you get by? I know there was some help from the government.'

A snort at that. 'Don't get me started.'

'It could never be enough, could it?' he asked mildly.

'Could've been if they'd tried harder. But still, I'm not one to just sit about wringing my hands and hoping money will magically appear in the till. I set to it, seeing what I could do for myself. I began teaching classes online – I saw other chefs were doing it and I thought, why not? The marketing was the important thing – no use putting on a show and no one knowing about it – but I had experience getting the word out about restaurants, so I just reprogrammed the wheels, as it were.'

'My wife saw the show you did about how to fillet fish,' said Mousse, his attention returning. 'I am personally grateful to you. We wasted a lot of fish in my household before she figured out what she'd been doing wrong for twenty years.'

Morwenna smiled and sat back in her chair.

'Thank you,' she said, softening a bit. 'That's gratifying to hear. I found I quite enjoyed the process. Got a lot of good feedback, as the kids say. The lobster show had over one hundred thousand views. Now I wish I'd charged more – who knew it would catch on like it did? – but it was good advertising for when the End-of-Times times actually ended. I didn't do too badly if I do say so. People stuck at home were bored and they were especially bored with their old recipes, so I taught classes in making curries, breads, pasta dishes – whatever I thought the market would bear. I got a village lad who'd done a course in cinematography at Truro to run the video machine thingy for me.'

St. Just noticed how voluble she was when it came to her cooking and good business sense, silently applauding the good

play by Mousse. St. Just, winding up for his next pitch, didn't
want to stop the flow just yet.

'I also set up a meal-delivery service of my own – the local
options were unreliable, half their blokes always the worse for
drink,' she continued. 'More often than not it meant delivering the
food myself but you do what you have to. I was never just running
the local boozer, with a load of regulars, so I had to get creative.
Not that anyone had regulars anymore; it was a desert for the
restaurant scene.'

St. Just saw his opening as she paused to draw breath.

'And the wedding scene, too, I'd imagine. Big impact there.'

'Oh, of course! When they limited the number of guests, the
cancellations for receptions poured in. I—' She stopped, suddenly
having made the connection. 'Has anyone told you about what
Bodwally did to those couples? If you're looking for a motive,
you won't have to look far.'

Far and wide, perhaps. 'Is that why you quarrelled with him
at Callum's party?' St. Just put in smoothly. 'His treatment of the
wedding couples who wanted to use his property?'

'Who says we quarrelled?' Instantly, she'd gone from expansive
to truculent. St. Just didn't know her well enough to tell if these
swings were routine. He did know master chefs had a reputation
for diva behaviour.

Or Bodwally's death may simply have thrown her for a loop.
The sudden demise of a man in one's known circle is disturbing,
even when there was no love lost.

Her expression, lips taut and brow knitted, betrayed a nice
mixture of wrath and worry.

'We have lots of witnesses who overheard you,' Mousse put in.
'You may as well tell us, Morwenna.'

In fact, no one had told them they'd overheard much of anything,
but it was a lucky strike, saving them countless hours of her denials.
That the police were allowed to lie during a murder investigation
always came as a shock to the great British public. St. Just always
reconciled his conscience by remembering how many murderers
the technique had put behind bars. How many innocent lives had
been saved by small deceptions.

He noticed there was a cobweb in the corner behind Morwenna;
its creator, small and shiny black, was working from home. St.

Just watched the tiny creature for a count of ten slow beats. *Busy busy busy.*

Meanwhile, Morwenna deflated like, well, like a soufflé, thought St. Just. She reached for her mobile phone, seemingly out of habit: the security blanket of the twenty-first century. She stared at the blank screen, turned the instrument this way and that.

And then, 'Morwenna.' Not threatening. Cajoling. He waited. 'Were you thinking of phoning a friend? It's not that difficult a question, is it?'

'He was a dreadful man,' she said at last, in a voice even huskier than normal. St. Just realized she'd been afraid all along they'd arrive at this moment. Finally, she said, 'We had an affair once. Are you satisfied now? Enough dirt there for you to paw through?'

Well, this was a nice bonus. St. Just and Mousse exchanged glances as Mousse jotted briefly in his notebook.

In a way, it came as little surprise, thought St. Just. He'd sensed she'd been withholding something, wrapping her testimony in dark reminiscence of the Plague Time.

'It was a long time ago, in London. I was naïve, not much more than a girl. He took advantage, that's all. Nothing new, right?'

St. Just prompted. 'All?'

'I wasn't his type, he said. That was the only explanation I got.' She sat back, again making the chair creak. 'It's probably just as well. Some people aren't cut out for double harness. Certainly not Bodwally.'

Very philosophical of you, thought St. Just. Was anyone ever that accepting of rejection?

'Did he come here because of you? Perhaps wanting to rekindle the romance?'

She paused to consider, as if this was a novel idea. She swung her head upward, gazing at the beamed ceiling for a long moment. Finally, she returned her eyes to them and said, her tone brittle, 'He did mention he'd seen my cookery shows online, on YouTube. It didn't take a mental giant to figure out where I was, since I mentioned the restaurant before, during, and after each show.'

'Was he hoping to renew the acquaintance?' St. Just persisted. 'Maybe he thought being a life peer increased his chances of winning you back.'

'Oh, come on. If so, he was out of luck. I like people who work for a living, not people who sit back waiting for things to be handed to them on a plate.'

'Actually,' said Mousse, 'we gather he earned his peerage.'

As surely she knew, if she and Bodwally went that far back, thought St. Just. She had lied about that, hadn't she? Perhaps tried to win him and Portia to her side using the whole fisher dispute, making it a case of the never-hads versus the born-to-riches types.

'You can be sure it wasn't a case of winning me back,' she said. 'I knew his reputation by then and I thought he was a creep, peerage or no.'

'"No man ever steps in the same river twice, for it's not the same river and he's not the same man,"' St. Just quoted. 'Actually, I've never quite believed that.'

She looked at him. 'What are you saying? You think he'd changed? You'd be wrong. But whatever. I wasn't having any.'

'So what was the fight about?'

'I just told you, it wasn't a fight. He just needed to be set straight on a few things.'

Mousse underlined something in his notebook. 'So, Morwenna, you're saying he wanted to pick up where you'd left off. And you weren't having it.'

'Now you're *entirely* putting words in my mouth.' She sounded bitter – and more than a little angry. St. Just thought he wouldn't have used such an incendiary tactic. Morwenna seemed much more amenable to flattery.

'Actually, you just said you weren't having any,' Mousse persisted, glancing at his notes. 'Your exact words. "I wasn't having any."'

'Do I need a solicitor?'

'That won't be necessary,' said St. Just, standing. Mousse reluctantly followed suit, peeling himself from this chair. 'Thank you for your time, Ms Wells.'

As the two policemen walked away, Mousse asked, 'What do you make of it?'

'On the face of it, she's being honest.'

'Really? I think she's holding something back. He just turns up in the village where she's opened a restaurant, buys a big house to impress, and so on?'

'It's not outside the realm of possibility. It's an attractive place to live. People can be drawn to the same place for different reasons.'

'Maidsfell is too obscure for the likes of him,' insisted Mousse. 'But whatever they talked about – and I nearly forgot, we don't actually know, do we? – I suppose she might have come home still angry, thought it over a while, dug around in her own mind through all that old history, and snapped. Here he was, being served up to her on a platter, so to speak. It could have happened like that. We do need to know more about the man, apart from what's in the media archives.'

'She's a fighter,' mused St. Just. 'As she said, she didn't just sit about wringing her hands during the Plague Time. She set to and tried to fix it. All hands on deck. It makes you wonder, doesn't it?'

'Wonder about what?'

'If Lord Bodwally needed "fixing", just how far would she go?'

TWENTY-ONE
Like a Prayer

The two policemen again decided to split up: Mousse to update his team, and St. Just to see if he could find the Reverend Judith Abernathy.

St. Cuthbert's was a small perpendicular building typical of its time and place, not as resplendent as some, carved rather unimaginatively out of solid wood and stone, which at least meant there were fewer bits of it to break off. The door was unlocked, and St. Just entered a gloom little dispelled by the light sifting through stained-glass windows. Sealed into the walls were the smells of centuries of candles and flowers and wood polish and communion wine.

A small pamphlet, *A Brief History of St. Cuthbert's Church, Maidsfell*, was offered for sale at twenty pence on a table at the foot of the nave. St. Just slipped a one-pound coin into the payment box.

Flipping through the pages, he saw the church claimed foundation in the fifteenth century. He thought he detected the fine hand

of Horace Bude, author of the Maidsfell village guide, in some of
the grander rhetorical flourishes:

> Standing firm against the winsome tides of mankind's foibles
> and follies, St. Cuthbert's has endured as a beacon of hope
> for centuries, guiding its fishermen home, and finally, at day's
> end, casting them off to meet their Maker.

The church wore its age well after six centuries and, despite its
plainness, seemed as much a part of the life of the village as the
cliffs and rocks surrounding it – the sort of place where generations
of fishermen and miners and their families had prayed for a good
catch, for the safe delivery of a child, for the soul of a beloved
parent.

They would have prayed for all the same things as the generations before, and probably, like them, had wondered why some of
the most earnest prayers from the most deserving had gone
unanswered.

Judith Abernathy, the woman charged with answering the unanswer-
able 'whys' of her congregation, was in the process of cleaning
the area round the altar. A vacuum cleaner stood at the ready in
the nave, but for the moment she was polishing the altar's wood
railings. At her feet was a bucket of soapy water and a mop.

St. Just wondered that the curate had taken on these domestic
chores, that the church didn't hire a cleaning service or a solitary
charwoman. But he thought he knew – like all churches, St.
Cuthbert's ran on fewer and fewer resources as the faithful died
or otherwise fell away. Churches in the UK could often only be
saved by the generous benefactor who wanted, in return, his or
her name painted on to the stained glass. But St. Just imagined
there were few of those sorts in a village this size – or had the
influx of people owning second homes meant more pledges and
more loose coin in the collection plates?

What were the odds Bodwally had been a benefactor? For so,
according to a call received by Mousse just as he and St. Just
parted, he had proven to be. He had left thirty thousand pounds
in his will to the church. Not a huge sum, nothing near what he
could have afforded, but large enough to be most welcome.

Surprisingly, the bequest had been made with no demand for

his name on a stained-glass window or at the head of a pew. Instead, Bodwally had specified the money go to repairs to the bell tower, 'in honour of my friend and confidant, the Reverend Peder Wolfe'.

It was odd, thought St. Just, and out of character for a man so lacking in humility – let alone piety.

Out of character for what he knew of the man's character, he corrected himself. Perhaps he'd found in the Reverend Wolfe one man in the village who could tolerate him.

Judith looked up from her polishing with a welcoming smile. Her reading glasses glittered in the filtered blue and purple light from a stained-glass depiction of the Madonna holding the Christ child. It wasn't possible that window had survived the attentions of Cromwell's men, thought St. Just; it had to be a later addition. Here and there, coloured windows had been repaired with clear glass, making him wonder if the village had been damaged in the war; he knew thousands of bombs had fallen on Cornwall, its harbours being particular targets. Perhaps Horace Bude's colourful little pamphlet could tell him.

'You came for the cook's tour, did you?' she asked.

'Not exactly,' said St. Just. 'I'm sorry to interrupt your work, but I have a few questions I'd like to ask. About Lord Bodwally.'

'Of course, of course. I just now learned from the woman who runs the Post Office in the village. She couldn't seem to take it in. Nor could I. It's . . . it's madness, is what it is. Plain madness – and wickedness. Who would want to kill him?'

'Lots of people, apparently.'

'Well, yes, let me rephrase that. He was not what you'd call a Christian man. But he was one of God's children. It's hard to remember that sometimes, even for me, when dealing with difficult people. We all came innocent and pure into the world.'

St. Just, wondering what would qualify a person as Christian if thirty thousand pounds did not, asked, 'What makes you say that – not a Christian man?'

'Well, he was never to be seen at services – so I heard from the vicar. The occasional wedding or funeral, you know. But that was all.'

'Not a regular churchgoer.'

'No. *Nooooo.* We had hopes he might turn to us – most people do in time of need, you know – but now . . . it's too late.'

Apparently, she hadn't heard about the bequest to the church, and he didn't think it was his place to tell her. 'The vicar – will he be returning soon? I'd really like to speak with him about Lord Bodwally.'

'Funny you should mention it. I got a text just this morning. Peder will be back next week.' She turned to look at the altar. 'And my job here will be done.'

Her words made St. Just think of the film *Poltergeist* and the medium's famous line, 'This house is clean.' But the medium had been wrong about that.

'Do you know, I am going to be sorry to leave,' Judith was saying. 'My husband and I visited Maidsfell years ago on our honeymoon and, like so many, we fell in love with the village. When I came across St. Cuthbert's Facebook page, it felt like a sign, you know? Some would say it was pure chance – I was simply flitting randomly about Facebook – but of course it was not. It was my *destiny*. That was how it felt.'

Just like Ramona Raven, thought St. Just. Another hostage to fortune.

'I rang the vicar, hoping he could find a spot for me even if temporarily. I explained about losing my husband and that I was looking for a peaceful spot in which to recover. Peder jumped at the offer – as I think I mentioned, he wanted – rather, needed – to go on retreat. Alcohol addiction is such a curse, is it not? Anyway, I spoke with my vicar at St. Mary's and asked permission to take up Peder's offer. They couldn't allow a temporary and indefinite departure, they said; I should have known it was too much to ask. But God was calling me. So I decided I must make the leap or stay forever sunk in mourning.'

'Where will you go now?' he asked.

'Oh, you know. Wherever they send me. Wherever *God* sends me, I mean. "Whither thou goest", etcetera.'

St. Just doubted it was as random as all that. The Church of England didn't just fling its clerics about hither and yon. Although prayer was undoubtedly involved, there would be some sort of process. Not that he knew a lot about that.

'Isn't there some sort of process?' he asked, voicing the thought. 'For finding you your next parish?'

'Of course. But I shall wait to be guided, as I was guided here. You see, I was on something of a sabbatical myself when I was called to St. Cuthbert's, dealing with . . . you know, all that must be dealt with when someone dies.'

St. Just, who did know, nodded.

'Anyway, St. Mary's was merging with another church, so I was given some time to think about my future. To pray over it. Go or stay. That's happening all over, churches closing, mergers. It's simply tragic.' She aimed her polishing cloth at an imaginary mite of dust. He noticed she hadn't really answered the question about the process and wondered if she'd left her London church entirely under her own steam. He made a mental note to have Mousse look into it.

'It's a not uncommon story,' said St. Just. 'The struggle to fill pews.'

'In hindsight, I could have worked a bit harder,' she added. She had a way of driving her own train of thought, as if he hadn't spoken. The last person he'd interviewed with that habit of mind had been a drug user. Surely that was not the case here? Her outward physical signs were normal; her eyes had rather an intense focus but the pupils were not dilated; her skin was clear with a high colour at the cheekbones. Mousse had told him she would soon be fifty.

Judith's was in fact a look he associated less with drug users and more with a sort of bloody-minded determination to dominate the conversation. It couldn't be a trait that went down well with parishioners.

'We could all say the same,' he said mildly. 'There's never a case I don't feel I'm missing something.'

'There just aren't enough believers these days to keep the show going, so to speak,' she said. 'And not enough hours in the day. But – sorry to go on about my own worries. You wanted to talk about something in particular, did you? I will have to tend to some of my shut-in parishioners soon.' She glanced behind her at the waiting mop, clearly an invitation for him either to help or get out of the way.

'I don't suppose you've been here long enough to have formed

firm opinions about people,' he said. 'But when you heard of Lord
Bodwally's death, what was your first thought?'

It was a useful interviewing technique, he'd found, to get people
to talk about their initial reactions. It was often enlightening.
Always, of course, assuming they were telling the truth.

'Well, I've told you my views on Bodwally,' she said. 'But it's
other people's relationships with him you'll be wanting to hear
about, am I right? The difficulty is, I can't say I've met anyone
in the village I think capable of murder, so I can't help you there.
I only know a lot of people were changed by the Plague Time.
They simply came undone; there's no question about it.'

'And never recovered?'

An eloquent shrug. 'They did all these surveys, the social
services types, and I remember reading that adults with no previous
experience of poor mental health were showing symptoms – something like a quarter of that population.' She shook her head. 'They
felt God had deserted them.'

'There's a predictable logic to that,' said St. Just.

'But that is when the devil works his way in,' she said, eyes
shining. They were unusual eyes, nearly the dark blue of Portia's.
'It's how the evil gets in – *not* the light. The devil. When people
despair and feel God has abandoned them.'

There was something unyielding in her posture that gave him
pause. St. Just felt a slight quiver of unease. Altogether, she had
the look of the fanatic about her.

The Church tended to weed out the worst of that sort but a few
inevitably slipped through. And perhaps they thought in such a
tiny parish as Maidsfell, she could do little harm. The occasional
dispute over the literal meaning of Mark, Chapter Five, with the
Bible study group – that sort of thing.

'True,' he said mildly. 'But I did see people at their best, too.
There were some real heroes in the National Health Service, for
a start.'

As usual, she wasn't quite finished. It was almost as if, while
she might wait politely for a person to finish speaking, it was a
mere formality. She was waiting for their 'noise' to stop.

It was possible she was hard of hearing, he thought. People in
that condition often chose their own topics and ran with them
rather than admit they couldn't hear the conversation.

'The vast majority just got on with it,' she concluded. 'That's what you have to do.'

He could see he wasn't going to get much further here. He needed someone who'd been in the village longer and, more importantly, someone not given to speaking in generalities about people in the congregation, all tinted with a rosy Christian wash. Someone more willing to spread the dirt would be helpful.

His mind turned immediately to Morwenna.

He fished a card from his wallet. 'If you think of anything that might be useful, here's my mobile number.'

'I thought I *was* being useful.'

'I meant to say, anything more useful. You've been very helpful indeed.'

He took his leave of her, keenly aware of those dark-blue eyes on his back. At the notice board just outside the entrance, he stopped to read the call for donations to the Harvest Fayre to be held in autumn on the church grounds. There would be games and a gymkhana and face painting and demonstrations and all manner of food for sale. Pasties, no doubt.

The local bobby, trapped in the stocks, might be the good-humoured target of the wet sponge throw.

He was sad to think he and Portia would not be in Maidsfell to enjoy it.

TWENTY-TWO

Fire

That night St. Just was wakened from a deep sleep by the sound of fireworks. The phosphorescent glow of the hands of the bedside clock told him it was three a.m.

He and Portia had rendezvoused over dinner at the little Greek restaurant, its location outside the village affording some degree of privacy. She filled him in on her visit to Bodmin; he told her what he could in good conscience reveal about the investigation. They shared a bottle of red wine and twice the food they would have eaten at home, mussels saganaki with ouzo and feta and Greek yogurt cake infused with cognac.

Later they had fallen into deep slumber, lulled by the rumble of distant thunder.

But that, he quickly realized on waking, was not thunder.

What sort of fool . . . this time of night?

Sirens carolled stridently in the distance. They sounded as if they were headed into the village from the main road.

He shot from sleep as if he'd been drowning and was suddenly pulled by unseen hands through the ocean's surface to safety. He had in fact been dreaming of trying to swim through black waves, the shore maddeningly out of reach. He'd grabbed a beach ball as it floated by and it exploded in his hands.

The cacophony of high-low wails tore through the still night – there had to be at least two, perhaps three appliances responding. Every dog in the village was barking its head off.

Jumping from bed, he ran through the cottage to the dining-room window.

Tugging open the door to the patio, he saw flames shooting into the night sky.

The sirens bleated, more and more frantically, like lambs who had lost their mothers.

Not fireworks, then, but an explosion. More than one explosion.

Wearing only a dressing gown over his pyjama bottoms, he ran in bedroom slippers down the lane towards the harbour. He didn't need a lantern or torch – a skyful of flames illuminated his steps. This was a good thing, he decided; it had been a mistake not to stop to put on his trainers. The cobblestones bit through the soft leather into his feet.

Reaching the bottom of the lane as fast as the slippers would allow, he could see why the night was floodlit, and the reason for it was terrible. A fishing boat in the harbour, close to the shore, was engulfed in flames, with plumes of smoke from a major conflagration shooting up into the sky. The wheelhouse was well alight, fuelled by everything within reach, devouring anything it touched like matchsticks thrown on to a hearth.

It was like the scene from Van Gogh's *Starry Night* – a swirling blend of grey smoke and blue flame and yellow bursts of light. Surely no boat could survive this, not even a modern one built to

withstand more than the old wooden ones could bear. Those picturesque old boats could be death traps, and St. Just feared that was
what he was seeing now.

He couldn't be sure, but he had a terrible suspicion the boat
he was looking at – now merely a collapsing outline, the suggestion of what had once been a sailing vessel – had belonged to
Will Ivey. *Please*, he thought. *Surely*, he thought. *Certainly*
anyone on board would have wakened in time and jumped overboard. The explosion would rouse him. He could easily have
swum for shore.

He had a sudden, sharp recall of Will Ivey telling everyone in
the meeting he was sleeping on his boat most nights to protect it
from 'pirates'. St. Just had thought he meant tourists, which actually made little sense. Or pranksters defacing the village with
their spray paints. But had Ivey felt he was in danger – this sort
of danger?

As St. Just was wondering where in hell the fire crews had got
to, he saw an appliance inching its way down the narrow street
into the village from the main road. On its heels was another
appliance. And then another. They were letting out the intermittent
bleeps they used to warn anyone passing by. The fire engines were
trailed by a vehicle branded with the signage of the Coastguard
Rescue Team, and by two police cars. The swirling lights of all
the rescue vehicles joined the radiant coils of Van Gogh lights
against the dark-blue sky.

The firemen, sheltered in breathing apparatus, commandeered
the spot nearest the harbour and began unfurling hoses. They
aimed the spray at the blaze, two main jets, seemingly to no effect.
The fire looked likely to burn itself out before they could quench
the flames.

St. Just could hear over the discord (the village dogs having
entirely lost their minds by this point) a Coastguard man shouting,
'Do we know what happened?'

A long answer, cut off by the noise: '. . . wait for daylight.'

'The one time we need bloody rain, we don't get any.'

St. Just glanced at the sky, where, high above, dark clouds huddled
uselessly, conferring, blocking the stars. The lightning and thunder
display of the night before had apparently decided to move on.

Another voice, a woman's. She was in full fire gear, displaying

so many stripes and stars she had to be in charge. St. Just, straining
to hear, caught the last of her words.

'. . . calling this already. It's arson, has to be.'

A babble of voices, shouting: '. . . not Ivey. Was he here? He can't—'

'Eccentric. Quite mad, of course. But we all knew—'

The smell of petrol permeated the air, even though the boat's
engine didn't appear to have exploded. Black smoke as from a
fire fuelled by accelerant curled up to meet the sky.

Somewhere a woman sobbed. A wife or family member? Perhaps
someone reminded of previous disasters.

From round the cove came a fireboat, just as the firemen appeared
to be making headway from the shore and the flames were nearly
extinguished. But in an *As long as we're here, might as well*
gesture, the little boat began squirting water at the stricken
vessel. The crew on shore started hosing down the nearby vessels,
in case the fire jumped. They still dared not get too close to the
inferno; the reddened faces of the two men on the fireboat
were lit from below as if by a bonfire.

St. Just felt someone touch his right elbow. He turned to see
Portia beside him.

'That was Will Ivey's boat, wasn't it?' Her face shone a blood-
less white as moonlight broke briefly through the clouds; her skin
shimmered with light from the flames. She placed her hand more
firmly on his arm. 'We saw him docked there on our way to the
beach yesterday. Please tell me he wasn't on board. No one was
on board, right?'

St. Just shook his head. 'We won't know for a while. But at
this time of night, I doubt he'd be on his boat.' He didn't want to
remind her of what Ivey had said at the meeting.

'Hadn't he taken to sleeping on his boat? For safety?'

Of course, she'd got there already.

'I think so. Yes.'

'This is awful. *Awful*,' she said, pressing her other hand to her
lips, eyes wide.

He watched as the firemen kept dousing the flames, making
sure there were no flare-ups. Even surrounded by water, St. Just
knew, a boat fire could be tricky.

This was exactly what it looked like, he thought: an utter
disaster that could not end well. The best to be hoped for was

that Will Ivey was not on the boat. But the boat, his livelihood, was gone.

The crowd watched, waiting, helpless. It seemed as if the fire crews could never get enough water into the hoses to douse the flames without emptying the sea. St. Just and Portia stepped back under the eaves of a gift shop away from the chaotic noises of the firefight.

'Is it arson?' she asked, turning to him. 'It *can't* be arson. If it's arson, it's murder.' The word caught in her throat. She wanted this to be anything else, an accident. For Portia, crime needed to be confined neatly to the pages of whatever she was writing. And murder, especially, couldn't touch a man she'd seen hale and hearty and blustering – what, not two days before?

'It's manslaughter if he was on board,' she continued. 'Whether intentional or not.'

'I am hoping not,' said St. Just. 'He has a flat or cottage some-where, I gathered; he made it sound as if sleeping on board was not a normal thing . . . He could be at his place now, sound asleep. He could be oblivious to this. Someone has to go and see—'

'But why? If this is deliberate – sabotage or whatever we might call it. Why? Over fish, for God's sake?'

'I don't know but we can't avoid thinking it's related to Lord Bodwally's death. The chances against the two things not being connected are astronomic. In a village this small? Astronomic,' he repeated. 'But I can't *see* a connection. There never were two men more different, at opposite ends of the social scale, different in temperament and values. Unless . . .'

'Unless?' Portia was shivering from the cold – they both were. She'd at least had the presence of mind to throw on a jumper over her nightclothes. He held her more tightly and she wrapped her arms around his waist, taking warmth from his solid frame.

'Unless the two were somehow in business together. Something shady, from the look of this.' St. Just flung an arm in the direc-tion of the now diminishing flames. But it didn't make sense. Will Ivey would never do business with the likes of a toff like Bodwally.

Would he? Could there be some form of blackmail involved? Extortion?

'How were they connected?' he said aloud. 'Bodwally and Ivey. I'm quite certain nothing—'

A memory of something to do with fishing was slowly emerging in his mind. What was it?

Portia waited, not taking her eyes from the scene of controlled mayhem before her, but listening intently as the gears ground on, as it were, inside the head of her beloved. He'd figure it out; he always did. He'd catch whoever did this.

'There is one other possibility,' he said. 'They weren't in business, but Will knew something he shouldn't have known.'

'Right,' she murmured. 'But personally, *I* can see them in some business. Fishy or otherwise. Will Ivey was in a risky job with a narrow margin of return even in a good year. He would know better than most what it was to live on the edge. Maybe Bodwally was paying him for something. And the money would be welcome. Until . . .'

He hadn't really heard her, so intent was he in following the train of his own thoughts. 'This is either an attempt to warn him off, or—'

'Good Christ.' DCI Mousse came upon them, at a run. 'Were there . . . was he . . . Will?'

St. Just shook his head. 'We don't know.'

'I just came from his cottage in the village. He's not there.'

There was shocked silence, as their minds cycled round the implications. St. Just could give no reply but a tense nod.

They watched as the fireboat continued dowsing the little boat with chemicals, extinguishing any chance of a hidden flame sparking up. But they also heard the creaking sounds of wood giving way. It wouldn't take much now for it to sink.

'Will told a roomful of people he was sleeping on his boat,' St. Just told Mousse.

There was a loud retort, a sharp release like a rifle shot, as the small vessel began to list at its moorings.

As with one voice, they said, 'Oh my God.'

TWENTY-THREE
Chickens Come Home

Friday

Early in the morning – no one had slept, no one felt they ever would again – St. Just slipped out of the cottage to fetch coffee and pastries to bring back to Portia. Dawn light was just creeping in from the east, a pearlescent promise outlining the clifftop church.

He and Mousse had capped off a dreadful night with a visit to Will Ivey's cottage, seeking clues to help them unravel what had happened. The eighteenth-century cottage was unlocked, in keeping with the village tradition of scoffing at big-city burglary concerns, and was remarkable only for its spotless orderliness. No stereo-typical bachelor, Will, with beer bottles strewn everywhere and unwashed dishes in the sink or stacked, barely rinsed, helter-skelter into the cabinets. Everything in the compact space was shipshape, as most certainly had been the case on his trawler.

Many books lined the built-in shelves – all adventure stories, men-at-sea tales – and a Bible lay open at his bedside. St. Just noted the passage, which had to do with lost sinners, which seemed to offer no clue to the conflagration that had probably taken Ivey's life.

Turning the place over took little time. They found nothing to suggest the man had been manhandled or threatened in any way. A shopping list tacked to the fridge with a sailboat magnet listed only tea and milk. He had evidently planned to return to his little home and had foreseen nothing to hinder that return.

After about an hour, St. Just returned to Portia at Seaside Cottage. They rehashed what had happened into the early dawn hours and while they may briefly have dozed in each other's arms, both stayed on high alert. For what, they weren't sure. Surely no one would set fire to their little haven? Just in case, St. Just's nervous system wanted him conscious for whatever might happen next.

In dire need of strong coffee, he walked to the Lighthouse Café the minute it opened.

Along the high street he ran into Sybil Gosling, a covered shopping basket slung over one arm. She had to be headed to the Fourteen Maidens, either for some light gardening or – more likely, thought St. Just – some vaguely neo-Druidic ceremony to greet the new day. Apart from the Lighthouse, no shops would be open so early.

'Awful news,' she said in greeting. 'About Will. *Such* a nice man – in his way.' She'd wound her hair in a topknot stuck through with what appeared to be chopsticks; strands pulled loose by a mild wind off the sea flew about her face.

She looked thin – too thin – and weary. She looked like the ageing woman she was, her shoulders hunched, her shawl held against her chest by wrinkled, veined hands.

'I live outside the village, you know. I'm just now hearing what happened. I'd have slept through the commotion, being so far away.'

He hadn't asked where she'd been, but high emotion could make the most innocent person garrulous. He said, 'People seem to have liked him.'

'I'll say a prayer the Goddess receives him.'

St. Just recalled the music he'd heard coming from the top of the cliff the other night. The flute, the drums.

'I thought I heard music coming from the Fourteen Maidens,' he told her. 'Quite late it was.'

'Music? I'm not sure . . .'

A guilty look shifted the lines of Sybil's face. There was no way she couldn't have known what he meant and no reason he could imagine for not owning up to it. Assuming, as he did, she was the High Priestess round these parts, she would have been a key participant in whatever rituals were held up there. And he had no doubt what he had heard.

'Music,' he repeated gently. 'People chanting. Musical instruments. All coming from the direction of the Fourteen Maidens. That narrow path going past our cottage funnels the sound clearly.'

'Ah!' Her worried expression was transformed by a look of awe, a new-age Moses receiving the tablets. She said cryptically, 'Not everyone has ears to hear nor eyes to see.'

St. Just gathered from this that he was among the chosen. The whole neopagan business was so cobwebbed with nonsense, but he could see how people were drawn in. Everyone wants to feel special; everyone wants to have access to ancient, secret knowledge.

She seemed to him a harmless enough woman. Everyone was a suspect, yes, but unless Sybil was more unhinged than her mild nonsense would suggest, he'd have said the necessary venom required for murder wasn't part of her makeup.

He needed to ask about her whereabouts during the supposed time of Bodwally's murder and was thinking how best to frame the question. Although a motive could only be guessed at, it was as well to cast a wide net.

Meanwhile, she was trying to tell him something. He tuned back in at the end of what may have been a lengthy speech. Investigating on mere minutes of sleep, he realized, was going to be a challenge.

'I've been wondering whether to speak with you about it,' she said. 'I don't like spreading gossip. Only it's not gossip – it's fact. I went to this wedding service for an old pupil, you see, or I wouldn't have been in the village that day at all.'

She was continuing to over-explain all her whereabouts, he noted.

'It was a beautiful ceremony, blue and gold for the flowers and bridesmaids' dresses. Judith left out the bits in the service about procreation and avoiding fornication but I suppose that's not a popular notion these days. That's not what I wanted to tell you, though. I—'

'I suppose you're right,' said St. Just, again barely listening. He was supposed to meet up with Mousse for an update on the crime – now crimes, plural – and he didn't want to be late.

'I wanted to tell you about the poison. It's most concerning.'

'Yes, I'm sure it is but I really must— Poison, did you say?'

Her radiant smile engaged every wrinkle round her eyes. It was all she could have asked for by way of a reaction.

She told him of the 'skulduggery' she'd witnessed in the allotment garden, concluding, 'I do not imagine it. Morwenna was up to no good.'

'Well,' St. Just said. 'Yes. Surely that's unethical at best, tinkering about with the allotment garden. But really, if you'll pardon the expression, I have bigger fish to fry today.' Again, as Ramona Raven would say.

'There will be no more fish in the sea to fry if we carry on spoiling the planet like we do. She had *no* business. It's not just a small crime, as some may think. It's a crime against humanity as well as nature.'

'Thank you, Sybil,' he said, anxious to be gone. 'I'll see what can be done.'

'Promise? You'll talk with Morwenna?'

That hadn't been his intention, but he found himself saying, his innate politeness winning out – that and his desire in any investigation to dot all the i's and cross the t's – 'Promise.'

'It's important,' she insisted.

'Yes, I'm certain this could be valuable information. Thank you for telling me. We police rely on citizens being our eyes, as it were.'

He realized he'd not asked her a crucial question, a question he might be asking many people before the day was out.

'What exactly was your relationship with Lord Bodwally? Were you friends?'

'Friends? I should say not.' Her voice turned sharp in an instant. 'Most *certainly* not.'

'I mean to say, since you're such a part of the preservation efforts for the village, it would be natural that a man of Bodwally's stature would have crossed your path.'

'Stature, is it?' she said, folding her arms, suddenly avoiding his eyes. *Interesting.* 'That's a nice word for a man pretending to be a gentleman. Pretending, and fooling no one.' She tucked in a stray lock of hair and said, 'Of course he crossed my path.'

He waited for her to go on. The longer her silence stretched, the more curious he became. He copied her movements, folding his own arms across his chest. His jumper suddenly seemed insufficient to meet the morning chill.

She was hiding something, ready to lie about something. Tempting as it was to slot every woman in the village into some role as Bodwally's paramour, regardless of age difference, there were other relationships where Bodwally might have run afoul of people. There were the brides and grooms Bodwally had let down through his selfishness, and the fishermen who had similarly been let down by his refusal to offer them a place on his property to land their boats. And what of his business relationships? Surely a wealthy man had made enemies along the way?

How *had* plain old Titus Bodwally become Lord Bodwally?

'So,' he said gently, sensing she would not yield to any heavy-handed *Come, come, now, I'm conducting a murder enquiry* approach. 'In what way did you have anything to do with Lord Bodwally? If it helps, I have come to understand he was a bit of a, shall we say, scam artist.'

'Scam artist? That's rich. I wouldn't say he was an artist, no. A true artist gets away with things undetected. It would seem his misdeeds finally caught up with him.'

This sounded promising.

'He was . . .' she began. 'I know him well because . . .'

'Yes?'

'I suppose I must tell you he was engaged to my daughter. Once upon a time.'

St. Just remembered that Bodwally had been left at the altar.

She stared defiantly up at him from dark, clouded eyes. In the morning light he could detect the certain signs of cataracts beginning to dull the lenses.

Evidently, it was not a topic she relished discussing, and he reached for something to say that wouldn't distress her further. Someone with knowledge of Bodwally's past could be a crucial witness and he didn't want her shutting down on him.

'It didn't go well, the engagement?' he hazarded.

'Of course it didn't go well,' she said. 'There was no way it could ever go well, no matter what my daughter tried. And she did try. But he was a horrible man, his aura dark, his chakras all out of alignment.'

'I see.'

Since he clearly did not, she explained. 'A chakra is a main energy centre of the body.' Her tone was pretty much what a person might adopt in explaining nuclear physics for the hundredth time to a roomful of bored sixth formers. 'It's a concept that dates from the early days of Hinduism.'

'I see,' he repeated. 'Thank you.' She certainly was wide-ranging in her beliefs. It could be the sign of either a broad mind or a disturbed one. Perhaps a needy one, vulnerable to exploitation. 'I didn't know you had a daughter.'

'We didn't see each other as much as I'd have liked. She lived in London.'

'Where she met Lord Bodwally.'

'Yes. Some party or other. She worked in public relations.' More than a touch of pride, here. 'Even though she was just getting started, she was very much respected in her field. She was honest in a profession full of charlatans, you know.'

St. Just noticed the 'lived' and 'was' – the past tense.

'You fell out of touch with her?' Clearly, from the flush flooding her face, this was her least favourite topic. But he had to press on.

'A bit.'

He hazarded a guess.

'You tried to warn her off Lord Bodwally.'

'I did.'

'And how did she take that?'

'Not well. We never quarrelled but then . . . we quarrelled.'

'Please help me out a bit more here. A man's been murdered. He doesn't seem to have been universally liked or loved, but it was a horrible death, and no one deserves that.'

She seemed to struggle with that concept, possibly thinking Lord Bodwally was the exception to undeserved deaths that proved the rule. Her expression contorted briefly with anger.

Finally, she said, 'I tried to warn Ruthie, as I say, and at first she wouldn't hear a word against him. He was going places, all the places she wanted to go. I don't, if I'm honest, know how I raised a child to think only of the superficial and never about why we're put on this earth. And I told her so. It was a mistake.'

'But she seems to have listened to you.'

'In the end, I suppose she did. Yes. I heard about that in a roundabout way. I wasn't invited to the wedding – by that point we weren't speaking at all. It was a friend told me how he stood at the altar as if he was waiting for a bus, repeatedly looking at his big fancy watch. She never showed. So she figured it out for herself, right enough. But by then . . .'

'The damage was done in your relationship.'

'That's it. Exactly – that's it.' She shook her head in confusion, seemingly not knowing how to begin to explain. St. Just, not yet having children of his own, could only guess at the pain. 'There seemed to be no going back. It's not like on the telly when families all get together at Christmas and have a good cry and say they're sorry. Send a text saying, "If you'd like to talk, I'm here," and everything's grand again. I daresay she felt foolish for having got involved with him. Ashamed. Embarrassed. As if she'd let me down.

She was still in many ways a child, barely out of childhood. Didn't she know I would never hold that against her? *Didn't* she?'

St. Just felt there was more to the story.

'Where is your daughter now?'

She stared at the ground, as if a neutral surface could absorb the memory. Tears began to gather at the corners of her eyes; roughly, she wiped them away.

'I begged her to come home, you see. And she did.'

'So you reconciled. That's won—'

'Hit and run,' was all she said.

No. He had not expected this. 'Drink?'

'What? No, she didn't drink. She was a beautiful girl, careful of her looks, her figure. She didn't drink.'

'She was the victim of a drink-driver?'

'I don't know, do I? They never caught who did it, never charged anyone.' In case he couldn't grasp this concept either, in case he might share some of the blame for blind justice, she restated it. 'The police never charged anyone.'

St. Just had a sinking feeling, remembering Morwenna's daughter. Gwithian Wells, her young body soaring off a cliff, through the air. By her own disturbed will, or at the will of another? His mind wouldn't allow him to complete the arc of this moving, flailing image to her lifeless body crumpled on the shore. An accident?

Now Ruthie, the victim of a car accident.

Two young women who had met with untimely deaths. Two grieving mothers – Morwenna and Sybil. It was as if something was going on beneath the surface of Maidsfell, something eerie . . .

He hesitated, considering how to phrase the question, but finally the best he could do was: 'How long was this after the wedding? The wedding that never happened, I mean?'

Finally, she seemed to say. She looked straight at him, acknowledging he was approaching the same conclusion she had reached.

'One month,' she said. 'One month to the day it was.'

'And you told this to the police?'

'Yes, of course I told it to the ruddy police!' She paused, her colour again hectic, as if she was reliving the still-simmering outrage. A hard look came into her eyes and again it aged her. All the mantras in the world were not enough to kill this kind of pain.

'Of course I did. Some young calf of a sergeant not yet dry

behind the ears, only good for running the copy machine and making coffee. I told him. Do you know, I'm not even sure he wrote down all I said – he stopped taking notes midway through. I can still see him, his pencil hovering over his tablet, trying to decide whether to call someone for help. Mind, I wasn't in my right state of mind. No, I was not in my right state of mind. And talking to him, like talking to a wall, only made matters worse.'

She shook her head, clearly drowning in the memory.

'I'd just lost my child and when I mentioned Titus Bodwally's name – no lord then, just plain old Mr Bodwally – the sergeant had brains enough to recognize the name of one of the richest men in the realm. I knew from that moment, that very *second*, the police weren't going to touch it. They'd arrest the Queen's corgis before they'd trouble a rich man. I tried to kick it upstairs to someone with rank. I wrote to my MP – now, there was a joke. The case was closed. Well, officially it was unsolved.'

'How long ago did this happen?'

'Going on twenty years. One anniversary, if that's what you'd call it, he had the nerve to have a big dinner party in London. I saw it in that magazine for posh people. *Tatler*. Just as if nothing had ever happened. It was like a stab through the heart, I can tell you.'

'Surely not . . . not a deliberate provocation.'

'Oh, you credit him with having finer sensibilities than that, do you? But I daresay he just forgot.'

'I'm so sorry,' he said, meaning it. 'I'm so terribly sorry.'

'Are you? Well, thank you for that. But if you're wondering if I'm sorry he's dead, I'll have to get back to you on that. My religious beliefs encourage forgiveness and leaving the past and harming none but do you know how hard that is to do? So, yes, I'll get back to you on that.'

Tears once again had filled her eyes to the brim and her breathing was ragged, uneven.

He put out a hand to touch her arm, a gesture that, since the pandemic, still felt unnatural and awkward with anyone but Portia. Sybil Gosling tolerated his touch for only a moment before quietly shifting her arm away.

'I suppose your next question is whether I killed him. But really, don't you think your question should be, who wouldn't? In my shoes, who wouldn't?'

He looked straight at her, willing her to meet his eyes.

'You're not confessing?'

'Don't be daft. Of course I'm not confessing. I don't know when he died and I may not have an alibi. I was probably either with the Fourteen Maidens or at home.' She paused, added, 'I didn't kill him but I'll help the person who did, if it's in my power. I wish I'd had the courage to kill him myself.'

'You really mustn't go around saying things like that.'

'Too late. I'm sure the entire village knows what I think by now.'

Making her the perfect person to set up for the killing of Bodwally. And Will Ivey? He covered his mouth in frustration, scratching against the stubble he hadn't had time to shave. He could picture her stabbing Bodwally, knew she was capable of it in some sort of frenzied, adrenaline-fuelled attack.

It didn't explain Will Ivey's death, though. Not at all. That additional murder called for a special kind of psychopathy, especially if the point of his death was to aim the finger of suspicion elsewhere, or simply to muddy the investigation.

Was Will's death a revenge killing, in retaliation for Bodwally's? Was that even a good working theory? It seemed improbable, given Bodwally's unpopularity, that anyone would go to the trouble to avenge his death. His connection to Will Ivey seemed tenuous – from what they knew so far. St. Just thought there might be something more than the disputed fishers' plan behind the killings. Still, the only way Ivey had drawn any negative attention to himself was over those plans.

'Last night when Will Ivey's boat went up in flames. Where exactly where you?'

'I already said. I was alone in my cottage. Where else would I be?'

He wondered again if she'd offered that information preemptively. Now she was saying firmly she'd been at home. A slight change of emphasis, a shade of a distinction. Did it matter? Most suspects, guilty or innocent, improvised a bit in retelling their stories, simply out of boredom from repeating exactly the same thing.

Answering another question he hadn't asked – *How did you know Will was dead?* – she said, 'I saw the mess by the harbour. They told me what had happened. The people . . . the people cleaning up told me. I knew it was Will Ivey's boat and they told me the poor man had been on it.'

Even though undoubtedly true, it was more than he himself knew for certain. Ivey could for whatever reason have spent the night outside the village. But Sybil was a known figure in the village; no secrets would be kept from her.

She almost didn't seem to understand why there would be questions as to her whereabouts: She was in her cottage because that's where she always was that time of night.

'I'm so sorry about what happened to your daughter,' St. Just said again. 'Let me know if—'

'You can't know what it's like,' she said. 'How would you know? Being a policeman, you see terrible things, all right. Sometimes you *cause* terrible things to happen.'

He bridled at that truth, but he let her run on.

'If you don't have a child, how would you know?'

His mind was crowded with a dozen answers to that. He could tell her how often he'd sat with parents who'd lost a child, and how that sort of pain was infectious. No one built up an immunity, no matter how often exposed. And it ripped the heart open anew, every time. The car wrecks, the overdoses, the suicides – the endless grief of those left behind.

He could tell her above all about losing his wife, and the empty days and nights when he could not see anything ahead of him but his own long, slow slide to an unmourned and lonely death. The nights when ending his own life seemed like a rational solution, something that might be best for all, a plan whispered in his ear by a voice of cool reason. It sounded so logical that he almost . . . almost wanted to buy into it.

But he knew it was pointless to tell her any of this, because each person's grief was tailor-made for the owner, stitched together with memories no one could share.

He said nothing. He thought of her cloutie tree at the Fourteen Maidens, and of all the hope and love and despair it represented. She had turned aside from him – why bother with the likes of him? – and stood looking across the high street, down the lane to the sea. The wind switched up a notch; it would soon be shaking the cloutie tree with its worthless, priceless treasures.

She turned back to face him and said, 'Just you find whoever killed the bastard. I'll pin a medal on him myself.'

TWENTY-FOUR
All That Glitters

Gossip in the village in the hours following the boat fire was rife with fanciful theories, particularly once they were able to confirm (someone had a cousin who knew the son of the pathologist's housekeeper's uncle) that a body had been found among the ruins. People barricaded themselves behind doors, refusing entry to anyone not a family member. As in the Plague Time, an invisible danger could be anywhere, unseen and ready to strike.

Mousse came to find St. Just at Seaside Cottage and motioned him outside for a talk.

'If anything, the fire upsets people even more than the murder of Bodwally, and – much like the police – they're stretching to see the connection between the two men. Meanwhile, panic has taken hold.'

'It's not surprising, is it?' St. Just asked, leaning with arms crossed against the cottage door. 'What happened to Bodwally they probably saw as a one-off event. Maybe we'd catch the culprit, or we wouldn't. Some vagrant would be arrested, or some bloke he'd cheated in some way, and that would be the end of it. And since no one really mourned Bodwally . . .'

'Yes,' Mousse agreed. 'Easy come, easy go. Sad to say about anyone, but that's the general tone. Will Ivey – now, that's a different case. He was eccentric, the original curmudgeon who called BS when he heard it, but there was no menace to him.'

'When will we know for sure the body was Ivey's?' asked St. Just.

'Sometime this afternoon.' Mousse checked his massive watch. 'It's just gone eight now. But the pathologist knew Will personally, and as the body was not burned beyond recognition . . . By the way, he was stabbed, possibly in his sleep. If so, he wouldn't have felt a thing from the fire. He may not even have died from smoke inhalation. Either way, if the killer had any skill with the knife, it would have been a relatively painless death, thank God.'

'That suggests to me someone who cared for the man. Who didn't want him to suffer, but for whatever reason needed him silenced. On the other hand . . .'

'Yes?'

'On the other hand, it may have been someone who wanted to make sure he didn't escape the fire.'

'With the rest of the carry-on meant to destroy whatever evidence there was. Yes.'

'The fire raises things to a whole new level for the villagers. And for us. Now anyone could be a target. If the villagers are paranoid now, it's justified.' He thought of Portia, tucked safely inside the cottage behind him, her thoughts hopefully deep inside the book she was working on. Her writing was her escape, she'd often told him.

'They'll be locked and loaded, that's certain. Literally – in the country, having access to a firearm isn't unusual. We do have something that may prove the fire was deliberately set. CCTV footage. Would you care to see it?'

'Yes, of course.'

Mousse went down the lane to where he'd parked his car and came back carrying a black backpack. St. Just held open the door to Seaside Cottage.

Portia greeted Mousse briefly and returned to the bedroom where she'd been trying all morning, unsuccessfully, to get some writing done. She'd resigned herself to attempting to answer some of the emails that were pouring in. Maidsfell was suddenly in the news and her friends knew she was there.

Softly, firmly, she shut the door behind her.

The men settled themselves at the cottage's dining-room table, St. Just clearing the space by moving a centrepiece of artificial flowers over to the kitchen counter.

'The citizen dashcams for which we put out a call when Bodwally was killed have so far turned up nothing. Now we've put out a similar call for dashcam footage from last night. It all, as you know, takes time. This video I'm about to show you was taken not from a car but by the bank's cashpoint surveillance cameras across from the harbour. Constable Whitelaw, zipping through the footage, managed to find a segment for the time when Will Ivey was killed. Or at least for the time the boat burst into flames – not the same thing, but near enough.'

'It's on tape?' St. Just asked. 'What a stroke of luck.'

'Yes, but don't get excited. It's virtually useless in terms of identifying a suspect.'

Mousse cursored the video to a spot at about the halfway mark.

'At least we know the timeframe now,' said Mousse. 'To the minute. God bless CCTV and DNA, law enforcement's new best friends.' He pushed the play arrow and they both leaned in for a closer view.

Video footage was often grainy and dark, like viewing fish through an aquarium filled with used dishwater; even so, St. Just was amazed at the poor quality of the thing. Digital technology had improved matters vastly from the days when a proprietor would reuse a tape until it was in shreds, but the quality of the camera lens itself mattered, and he could see at a glance that this had been done using antiquated equipment that hadn't been very good to start with. For a bank it was shockingly lax but he supposed Maidsfell was remote enough not to qualify for the sort of flashy surveillance equipment Exeter, for example, would have splashed out on. Maidsfell just didn't have the criminal traffic of the larger towns and cities.

The recording did show enough of what happened and, as Mousse had said, the timing of it, for them to be able to say definitely someone – some two-legged, two-armed creature – had boarded Will Ivey's boat as it rested at harbour, and less than ten minutes later that someone had disembarked, considerably faster than he'd boarded, unencumbered by the satchel with which he'd arrived. A satchel presumably containing the tools needed for arson.

And murder – unless the knife he used had belonged to Ivey.

He or she used, of course – the pronoun 'he' being a placeholder for the figure prowling about in the dark. If Ivey had been taken by surprise, put at ease by the sight of a friendly face, it opened wide the possibilities of their investigation. The person in the black-and-white video wore a hooded garment like a yellow fisherman's raincoat – the fabric stood out stiffly from the wearer's body, suggesting an oilskin-type fabric. On the feet were what looked like a pair of black wellies. The lower part of the face was covered by a dark face mask. And who didn't have a spare one of those sitting around since the Plague Time? Just in case? Even with all the mask-burning parties that had swept the globe when vaccines had helped eradicate the virus.

The two men watched as the figure came aboard, slowly, stealthily, literally trying not to rock the boat. The figure went inside the cabin and disappeared. The vessel was about thirty feet LOA – length overall. There was no way, St. Just surmised, the skipper didn't know his ship had been boarded unless he was passed out cold asleep – always a possibility. More than sufficient time elapsed for him to have been murdered or the fire to be set, or both. Which raised a question in St. Just's mind: had the vessel been searched for some reason? Or had the killer just taken his sweet time for reasons of his own?

'Did Ivey drink?' St. Just asked.

'Did the sun come up this morning? He drank far too much – famous for it. He went to AA but he was an off again/on again case. As soon as he docked his boat of an afternoon, offloaded his catch, and squared things away for the next day – he was meticulous about that boat – he'd be holding up the bar down the pub. It's a habit that would have carried him away one day with cirrhosis or the like. As it was . . . well. You can never say going one way is worse or better, can you? It's the going that's sad. I'll say this for him: he never quit trying to quit.'

'Did he ever do time? Drink-driving?'

'Once or twice, yeah. Third time he'd probably have had to hang it up for good. So he quit driving. Problem solved.'

'Let's watch it again,' said St. Just.

He scooted his chair closer to the table, leaning in as Mousse moved the cursor to the start of the relevant part of the video: masked figure creeping about, boarding the ship, leaving the ship, more creeping about. Impossible to say where the figure had gone next. The only thing St. Just could spot as a potential clue was that it was a person whose movements were reasonably fluid. Could have been a young person. Could have been a middle-aged person used to clambering around boats. Could have been a fit elderly person, used to hiking or using his or her body in manual labour. That was nothing rare for this part of the world.

Whoever it was would also have to have the eyesight of a cat: at the time of the video there was no glint of moonlight or light from any other source. The recording was so opaque, the face so hidden, there was no way to guess at eye or skin colour, dark or light. And, of course, any hair or baldness was concealed by the hood.

'The bank only has one camera?' St. Just asked, eyes still on the screen, when Mousse hit the stop button a second time.

'There are three. One aimed at the cashpoint, this one pointed at the harbour, and one covering the car park at the back.'

'Can we have a look at the footage of the car park?'

'Well, certainly, it's here somewhere, but it . . . oh. Of course. Will's cottage was across the road from that car park.'

'It's worth a look if for no other reason than to establish a timeline for his movements. Can the constable be trusted with this?'

'Whitelaw? Certainly – it's more his line than mine. He loves video games. A colossal waste of time if you ask me. But his eyes are keener and his bones more able to sit for hours.'

'All right. Let's get him on it. I don't suppose we'll ever know if Will was specially summoned to the trawler or was there already, but in case a meeting with someone was pre-arranged, a look at his phone records might be in order, too.'

'Already on it, for his mobile records,' Mousse told him. 'He had no landline.'

'So, where are we, theory-wise?'

'All over the place, if you're asking me, personally. We had a million suspects when it was just Lord Bodwally murdered. Now . . . in a way, Will's death narrows things down. Put that in the plus column.'

'Does it really, though, narrow things down? All right: let's assume all this has to do with Bodwally's stance with regard to the fishermen's cause. And since Will was a fisherman and thus in favour of the cause . . . well, that would make sense as a theory if he'd killed Bodwally and in remorse killed himself.'

'The pathologist says not. And besides, the video pretty much proves not. We saw him being murdered, as good as. It wouldn't hold up in court but whoever that was, if they were innocent, should already have come forward.'

'Right. But now we have to tie two disparate murders together.

The men were basically sworn enemies. So what if this had nothing to do with the fisherman's cause? We're back where we started with the million suspects. Although how the frustrated wedding couples figure into this – into killing Will Ivey – I cannot begin to guess.'

'Nor Bodwally's angry ex-lovers.' A thoughtful look had come over St. Just's face. Mousse had noticed whenever St. Just was concerned or worried, as no doubt he was now, the hawk-like profile and high cheekbones became more pronounced.

'It seems most likely the visitor was unexpected, uninvited,' St. Just said after a moment. 'The poor man had announced to a roomful of people where he could be found, especially late at night. Not at his cottage, where normally they'd look, but on his boat. In a harbour which is essentially deserted after midnight.'

'Yes, I agree he—' His mobile, which he'd placed on the table, buzzed loudly in the quiet room. Seeing the caller's number, he said, 'It's the pathologist again.'

He listened intently to the voice on the other end.

'He what?' A few moments later: 'And what's that when it's at home?' A pause, eyes widening. 'But it didn't kill him. Right. No, it doesn't help, but thanks anyway.'

He rang off and looked at St. Just.

'Thanks a bunch,' he murmured. 'Curiouser and curiouser.'

'What is?'

'Fish,' he said. 'He's got a name for the fish.'

'Not Moby Dick?'

'Ha. Some Latin name. He's emailing me details now. It's Salsa something. I quote: "Poisonous as the apple the Evil Queen gave Snow White" – the pathologist is the proud father of a five-year-old. Anyway, he said we need to talk with an expert on fish in these waters.'

'Great. That would have been Will Ivey.'

'Good God,' said Mousse. 'You don't think the murder really was done over some sea wall?'

'I don't know what to think, if I'm honest. Who else can we ask? Any fisherman worth his salt is out fishing right now. But someone who prepares fish all the time might know something.'

'Time for another talk with Morwenna Wells?'

'I did promise Sybil I'd speak with Morwenna, anyway.' St.

Just summarized for Mousse the highlights of the 'poison' conversation.

'Typical,' was Mousse's comment. 'Village politics at their finest. Nothing is too petty for sides to be taken. Those allotment gardens have been the scene of more than one skirmish. I can't tell you how many nine-nine-nine calls have been made over stolen carrots and watering cans and whatnot. Sybil will work herself into a froth over it but I wouldn't pay much mind. Next week it will be something else.'

'People don't tend to take the word of women like Sybil seriously, and that's really all they want,' said St. Just. 'All any of us wants, yes?'

Mousse sighed. 'Where we're supposed to find time for ruddy community relations, I—'

'We were going to Morwenna's, anyway. I'll tell Portia where I'm headed. Meet you out front in a minute.'

On the way to the Maiden's Arms, Mousse summarized the message he'd received from the pathologist, quickly scrolling through the text in his smartphone's email app. 'It's a fish out of water in these parts, in a manner of speaking. It shouldn't be found anywhere near England. But with global warming, all manner of fish are turning up where they're rarely found, if at all.'

'Do you have a photo?'

'Yes, sorry, of course you'll want to see. The pathologist provided a link to Wikipedia.'

Mousse punched at the mobile a few times, then held up the screen to St. Just.

'It's actually quite a beautiful thing. *Sarpa salpa*, it's called. Known more commonly as the dreamfish. A flat, oval body, as you can see – about twelve inches long on average, depending on male or female. Did you ever?'

The fish was bluish-silver but with brilliant gold stripes running in an evenly spaced design along its body. Its eyes were gold, as well. It looked like something out of a fairy tale, a creature of immeasurable worth, fit only for a queen.

'My goodness,' said St. Just, suitably impressed. He handed back the mobile. 'But at the end of the day, it's still a fish. What's so special about it?'

'Well, as we now know, it's actually quite dangerous to eat.'

'So it's not something a restaurant would offer.'

'Not unless they wanted their customers to hallucinate. Or die.'

'You're not serious.'

'Serious.'

St. Just shook his head. 'Go on, then.'

'It tastes all right, apparently, if not wonderful. The pathologist says Bodwally didn't consume a great deal of it, so perhaps he didn't care for the taste or texture. But the trick to avoid total disaster is in the preparation – it must be quickly gutted, because it's a herbivore and lives off a toxic seaweed. That's where the danger in eating it lies, and whoever prepares it for cooking must know this. Also, the head must be removed – the toxins collect there especially.' Scrolling some more, he said, 'But it's commonly found and served in the Mediterranean and on the Eastern Atlantic coast. The ancient Romans used it for "recreational purposes".'

'I'll just bet they did. It sounds like something the Romans would do. Too much time on their hands, the upper-class ones, anyway. But I don't understand. If it was in Bodwally's system . . .'

'I don't understand what's going on, either. It's definitely time to talk to an expert.'

TWENTY-FIVE
Something Fishy

Morwenna was in her restaurant's spotless kitchen, all shiny metals and stainless steel. As it happened, she was setting a large fish on ice in a tray when they arrived.

'What sort of fish is that?' asked St. Just conversationally. He supposed it was too much to hope he'd caught her red-handed preparing a dangerous fish.

'It's just bream.' Using her wrist, she pushed a shiny lock of dyed dark hair back from her forehead. She didn't look pleased by the interruption. 'Nothing too special on the menu today.'

She turned away to wash her hands in the kitchen's double sink.

By the time she came back to the prep table, she had pasted a neutral expression on her face. Drying her hands on a white tea towel, she waited to see what they wanted this time.

Her expression suggested it was one time too many.

'Bream,' said St. Just, as if hearing the word for the first time. 'How interesting. Have you ever come across bream with a sort of gold stripe pattern?'

'Come across? In what way come across?'

'Oh, you know. Stepped on one as you were walking down the high street. Come on, Morwenna.' This was Mousse, recognizing the stalling tactics.

'It's an odd question to ask,' she said defensively. She crossed her arms across her chest. 'Very odd.'

'It could be important,' said St. Just. 'We're dealing with murder, and we've little time to waste.' He debated adding, 'In case there's a third,' but discarded the warning as too baldly dramatic. 'Would you mind just answering the question?'

'It's quite a delicacy, if it's what I think you mean. *Sarpa salpa.*'

'Delicacy?' Mousse looked at St. Just. 'Would *you* classify it as a delicacy?'

'Not from what I've heard,' St. Just answered.

They both looked at her expectantly.

'Yes,' insisted Morwenna, 'it is. But a chef has to know what she's doing – it has to be prepared just so: a bit like pufferfish. Now, what else can I do for you?'

'I've already said. You can help us solve a murder.'

'I don't see how—'

'Or two.'

This brought her up short. Was it possible she hadn't realized the extent of the situation until St. Just put it like that? She pulled back in confusion, tilting her head to one side as she settled her gaze on him.

'Will Ivey, d'you mean? You're sure?'

'I am. And Bodwally, of course.'

'That's two, if you've lost count,' said Mousse. 'If you know anything about this, Morwenna, you need to tell us now.'

'Murder? Of course I don't know anything. Don't be—'

'*Anything* you know. About anything. Let's have it.'

She tried on a mulish silence, resting a hip against the table where she'd been working. St. Just became aware of the sharp fillet knife just inches from her right hand. The pathologist thought a kitchen knife – probably a utility or paring knife – had been used to kill Bodwally.

'Would Jake Trotter know anything about it?' he asked, guilelessly casting on the water the name of her business rival.

She took the bait, just like a *Sarpa salpa*. 'Jake? Don't bother asking him. He knows half what I know about fish. The prep *or* the cooking.'

'Is that so?'

'We're in Maidsfell, for God's sake, not Paris, but Jake wears a *toque* – how pretentious can you be? Wearing a toque doesn't mean you know *anything* . . .'

'If you do, tell us now,' said Mousse.

Not quite through with Jake Trotter's choice of headgear, she sighed. 'All right. If it helps you find who killed Will Ivey. What I know is it's rare for these waters but it's been turning up here and there. More and more.'

'Where is it normally found?'

'The Mediterranean. Africa.'

'It is very far from home, then.'

'Yes, indeed. Christopher Carew got hold of it somehow – do you remember, Tom?'

Mousse shook his head.

'Sometime last year it was. His dementia has well and truly settled in now and he'll need to go into care soon. The village has looked after him for years but anyone can see he's getting worse. Last year he had an episode, and as it turned out, it wasn't just the dementia; he'd got hold of the dreamfish.'

'From Will Ivey?'

'Who knows? Chris was on the St. Cuthbert's Delivers roster for food delivery but since he was the only one took ill, he must have got the fish from elsewhere. My restaurant participates by donating meals but he certainly didn't get it from here. I'd know it if I saw it and I'd certainly remember. I'd say go and ask Chris but he's as mad as a goose these days.'

A signal passed between the two men. Mousse nodded, giving St. Just his lead.

'An autopsy shows Lord Bodwally was poisoned by eating this

rare fish, known for causing delusions, which fact seems to point to a fisher. To Will Ivey in particular, perhaps?'

She hesitated before answering. 'Will Ivey hated the man, yes,' she said. 'With good reason. All of us had reason.'

He clocked the 'us' but let it pass. 'So you can see Will poisoning the lord, and when that didn't work, stabbing him to death?'

'No.' She shrugged. 'Oh, I guess. Maybe. Will drank a lot. No telling what a man might do when he's drunk.'

'What sort of delusions?'

'What?'

'What sort of delusions would the fish cause? Enough to lead to someone's death?'

'I wouldn't know about that,' she said sharply. 'Plenty of people have eaten dreamfish by mistake and survived.'

This was true in Bodwally's case, thought St. Just. He survived long enough to be stabbed to death.

'What exactly happens when you consume dreamfish?'

She tried for a nonchalant shrug, but St. Just could tell she wasn't enjoying this line of questioning. 'Pretty much what the name says. You dream. You hallucinate.'

'It's a sort of LSD of the sea?' asked St. Just.

'Clever,' she said. 'But I wouldn't know. I'm not a clubber; I'm too busy working.'

'Does something happen immediately – do the hallucinations start right away?'

'Two hours after.' Her fingers inched toward the knife.

'You do seem to know a good deal about it,' Mousse observed.

Her annoyance again rose at that. Now she clasped both hands tightly at her waist, as if to keep ahold of herself. 'I've been to the Mediterranean lots of times. I enjoy the cuisine; I study the preparation. It's not a crime to know things. It's my business to know these things.'

She was becoming agitated and St. Just recalled how her daughter Gwithian had died, perhaps under the spell of some chemically induced delusion she could fly.

'We don't care about any of that,' said St. Just in his most soothing voice. 'Can you think why it would have been in Bodwally's system? And can you tell us what the effects on him might have been?'

'It was in his system because he consumed it, obviously. Maybe he was experimenting – people do,' she added, crossing her arms. 'Foolish people. Young people. Rich people with too much time on their hands.'

'I see. How long would the effects last?'

'How long the effects last, and their power, depends on how much he ate.' There was a slight catch now in her melodious voice. She obviously found the topic distasteful. She also clearly wanted them to leave. She began fussing about with a bunch of herbs that had been soaking on her worktable in ice water, plucking away the unsightly bits. Her profession called for a streak of perfectionism, St. Just knew. In his experience, perfectionism carried to extremes could lead to all manner of mental illness.

'What would happen, exactly?' he asked gently. 'Would he see pink elephants, or what?'

'That depends on the individual. There are auditory and visual effects – people hear and see things that aren't there. It can last a few hours or up to a day and a half. But again, it depends—'

'On how much is consumed. Right.'

'Yes. And on the person's age and health.'

St. Just was trying to puzzle this out to the end, to see the possibilities in the tangled, murderous skein. Was it possible she and Will Ivey had been in cahoots? Had Will caught the fish and brought it to her to prepare? Did Jake Trotter come into this somehow – had *he* connived with Will Ivey to bring down Bodwally? Had some business deal between Trotter and Bodwally gone sour?

Maybe the intent by the poisoner hadn't been to kill, but to give Bodwally a few anxious hours. To teach him a lesson. Prepared carefully, by an expert poisoner, the fish might disable rather than kill the victim.

It may all have been a prank. A prank having nothing to do with Bodwally's later death.

Meaning, they might be looking for two different suspects. One mischief-maker, one killer.

Again, St. Just eyed the knife on the table.

'Oh, and by the way,' he said. 'Speaking of poisons . . .'

'Yes?'

'The allotment.'

'The allotment,' she repeated numbly. 'What?'

'I thought the village garden allotments weren't meant to be used commercially. They're to be used by families to feed families.'

Her shoulders sagged with relief. They had reached clear water. 'I'd say it was a fine line. No one is going to complain as long as there is adequate space for anyone who wants a plot.'

'I'm not worried about the little land grab you've got going on, Morwenna. Nor your turf war with Jake Trotter. I'm worried about the poison. Before you say anything, Sybil Gosling, for all her star-gazey ways, misses nothing.'

'Poison! But it's not—' St. Just watched closely as Morwenna's face flooded with a hectic colour. A pot that had been simmering behind her threatened to overflow. Mousse stepped over and turned down the dial.

She threw down the towel she'd been using to wipe her hands. 'That interfering old bat. I don't care what she says she saw. She's always been a bit floaty, they say – comes with the territory, teaching toddlers all day probably does your head in – but her daughter's death made her much worse. Not that I can't sympathize . . .'

'I can only imagine.'

'No, you can't. It guts you to lose a child. And I don't think Sybil was ever quite . . .' She tapped an index finger against her temple. 'She became unhinged when Ruthie died. She *is* unhinged, I tell you. Maybe she needs an exorcist.'

'What exactly happened to her daughter?'

She lifted her shoulders, gaze downward. *Who can say?* Finally, she looked at them both and said, 'Ruthie was an only child, extraordinarily beautiful. A natural beauty, so photogenic. I've been in pageants, you know, and I never saw a girl to match her. She was probably killed by a drink-driver. How you could ever be going fast enough on these lanes – pulling out of a car park from a standstill, mind – to actually kill someone, I'll never understand. But he or she managed it. Because the lanes are so narrow. She . . . she couldn't get out of the way in time, she tried to scramble over the low stone wall, but there was no escape.'

'This happened here? At the Maiden's Arms? The driver had been drinking here?'

Mousse was nodding, his gaze captivated also by the fillet knife; he knew the answer already.

It was clear Morwenna had very much wanted to avoid the direct question.

Finally: 'Yes, just outside. But it was well before I even thought of buying the Maiden's Arms. I wasn't even living here, I was in London and it was nothing whatsoever to do with me. But since I now own the place . . . I don't know. I think just seeing the building sets Sybil off. She certainly never comes in. I think she's sworn off pubs altogether.'

'They never caught who did it,' St. Just said flatly. He knew what Sybil had told him, but he wanted to hear it from Morwenna as well.

'No. Again, before my time, but I don't think so, no. DCI Mousse here would know.' But Mousse ignored her, in favour of studying a knife rack on the wall behind her. It was a magnetic holder without assigned slots, making it difficult to say if a knife had gone missing.

'If it was before your time, why are you so reluctant to discuss it?' St. Just asked.

'Jesus!' she said. 'Isn't it obvious? Who needs that sort of publicity?' She planted both hands on the counter, leaning towards him again. 'It was an old scandal, nothing to do with me, and to tarnish this place' – she swept one arm about her – 'this place with its starred reputation that I've killed – sorry – that I've worn myself to a shadow to build – well. It would be madness to dredge up the old sad history. I'm barely back on my feet again and Sybil . . . Oh, never mind. I suppose I shouldn't blame her; I should feel sorry for her, and I do, but . . . it's just that . . . Some of us move on. Sybil chooses to dwell in sorrow.'

TWENTY-SIX
Picture This

St. Just returned to Seaside Cottage, hoping to find Portia. She wasn't around, but she had said earlier she might have a late lunch with Sepia. He was glad she had found a new friend – Portia made friends easily – but in the middle of two murder cases he also was glad she was keeping to public places.

Mousse was checking in with the station but said he'd drop by within the hour.

The air in the cottage held a brackish scent, somewhat filtered by the constant sea breezes. Overnight, however, it seemed to have seeped into the little rooms and settled itself in corners. St. Just opened the French windows to the patio, taking a deep breath of the salt air beyond. The scene before him was like a tinted postcard from the thirties, except the blue skies for which Cornwall was famous in summer were overpainted with a slate-grey wash which portended more rain on the way.

He could hear the constant whoosh of the waves against the shore, normally a comforting sound. Sometimes – and this was his modern-day conditioning, he knew – sometimes he wanted to reach for the off switch or the volume knob. It was frustrating to realize how little control he had over that relentless churning.

How he had no control at all, in fact. The powerful pull and swell and release of the waves was the village's eternal soundtrack.

The dawn stain on the horizon had long since been transfigured by daylight's magic, perhaps seeping into some underground cavern alive with sea creatures never seen by man. The water was silvered with pale sunlight, a shining, undulating stripe.

He watched as a band of thunderstorms formed in the distance; the occasional flicker of lightning was reassuringly out of harm's way for now. As a child, he'd never feared the rain and thunder, however wild and unexpected, but it had sent his otherwise valiant little dog scurrying under the bed.

The wonder of that crackling sky opening to reveal the universe always stopped St. Just in his tracks. His hands itched to hold a brush or pencil, to try to capture that shifting scene. Portia had asked him once why he didn't take up photography. He didn't know why; for him, though, capturing something in the instant was a different creative impulse entirely.

He began to prowl about the cottage as he waited for Mousse, eventually stopping to study the contents of the bookshelf next to the fireplace. He found a copy of Shakespeare's *Romeo and Juliet* among half a dozen Rosamunde Pilchers and two copies each of Daphne du Maurier's *Rebecca* and *Frenchman's Creek*.

Daphne, who had written of the 'dark, diabolical beauty' of
Bodmin Moor.

He began leafing through the Shakespeare, and the pages fell
open to the scene between Romeo and the apothecary.

> Need and oppression starveth in thy eyes,
> Contempt and beggary hang upon thy back;
> The world is not thy friend, nor the world's law;
> The world affords no law to make thee rich;
> Then be not poor, but break it and take this.

Romeo was bribing the apothecary to give him poison, urging him
to break the law by accepting the bribe to become rich – dubious
advice, in any century. St. Just wondered if Landlady Penelope
had been taken with that scene, if that was why the spine had
broken open at that page from overuse. Or was it simply a book
left behind by a visitor, perhaps a book bought used at a village
fair or jumble sale?

It was Sybil who had turned his mind to poison and poisoners.
Morwenna who had been annoyed – angered? – at being caught
out.

Poison was a woman's weapon, it was said, but for Romeo it
was an equal opportunity weapon.

St. Just set the book aside.

What were they dealing with here? Blackmail? Revenge? Love
gone wrong?

Were there two people in cahoots, given the different methods
of killing? Stabbing and poisonous fish and arson – what were the
connections?

Male or female?

Was someone being paid or coerced – blackmailed – into murder?

He was mulling all this when he heard the expected knock at
the door.

'Got something,' Mousse said, popping open his laptop as he
headed for the dining table. 'At last, we've found a job Whitelaw
can do well. He was playing about with the video and took a
closer look at Will's cottage in the days leading up to the fire.
Scrolling through, patient as a hunter with a deer in his sights.
And bingo! Look at this.'

The two men closely watched the eight-minute segment. At the end they looked at each other, eyebrows raised, as if to confirm they'd each seen the same thing: A figure wearing a hooded fisherman's raincoat and carrying a woven shopping basket walking to the door of the cottage. Will Ivey opening the door to admit his visitor. Then an extended shot of the closed front door – nothing to see here, folks. But about eight minutes later, the same hooded figure departing – with that same basket hanging from one arm. Quickly, the figure moved offscreen, its face hidden by the hood. The camera offered a clear view of the basket, which was made of interwoven strands of fabric or plastic which appeared to be multicoloured. The design was distinctive, possibly unique, thought St. Just. In which case, they were in business with a clue.

'And then there's this, from a different angle.' Mousse opened a new video, paused at the door to Will's cottage. 'It was submitted via Operation Snap by a driver who caught it on the dashcam of his four-by-four and sent it along to us, thinking – quite rightly – we'd want to know all we could learn of Will's movements in the time leading up to his death.'

It was the same scene only from a different angle, the figure exiting Will's cottage.

'Again, no view of the face,' St. Just observed. 'Whoever it was may have realized that camera was on them. But it shouldn't be hard to find the basket. Or find someone who recognizes it.'

'Well, I'll give that a maybe. If you saw market day around these parts, you'd think differently. Everyone has a basket slung over one arm. That said, this may stand out as more colourful and different from the usual brown wicker or seagrass.'

'Would a woman be more likely to carry a basket like that?'

'I'm sure it's sexist to think so,' Mousse replied. His brown eyes in their wrinkled sockets held a look St. Just hadn't seen before. It was anger. 'That poor old man,' he said, catching St. Just's eyes on him. 'I think Will was in way over his head and never knew it. The bastards. But why would he get involved at all?'

'For money? You're looking into his finances, right? Or maybe he *didn't* know he was involved in anything serious. Maybe he thought it was a lark, a prank. Maybe he wanted to get even with Bodwally, teach him a lesson, send him a warning. A sort of horse's head, if you like. Only in this case . . .'

'In this case, a fish's head.'

'He may have wanted Bodwally to see those pink elephants, nothing more,' said St. Just. 'That basket, though – we're only assuming a fish was in it, and what's pointing to that idea is that it's clearly the same raincoat as in the boat video. As for the fish itself, it may have been coming or going. Being dropped off or picked up from his cottage, I mean.'

'Right,' said Mousse. His lips emitted a soft *pfft* of exasperation. 'Someone brought him the fish, or he was passing it along to someone else.'

'But when Bodwally was killed, Will realized he might have been dragged into something bad. Now it was no innocent prank.'

'And he was himself killed. Murdered on his own boat.'

'And for the usual reason, I expect,' said St. Just. 'He knew too much.'

TWENTY-SEVEN
Sweet Charity

She wasn't in the church and he realized how much he'd come to think of her as living there, like some colourful Hawaiian church mouse. All she'd need would be a ukulele for the children's Sunday singalong.

Mousse had gone to have another look at Will's cottage, particularly his kitchen, taking a member of the forensics team with him. St. Just, his mind on how the church dispensed food to people like Will Ivey, hoped a word with the Reverend Judith Abernathy might fill in some blanks.

He thought she might be in the vestry, counting communion wafers or whatever priests did in their downtime. The door into the sacristy gave a satisfying tales-from-the-crypt creak as he muscled it open.

Once inside, his eye was immediately drawn to a classic fisherman's oilskin coat hanging on a peg. It was damp and a small puddle of water had formed beneath it on the floor.

What would Judith be doing with a fisherman's coat? Then again, why shouldn't she have one? It was certainly a practical garment to have on hand given Cornwall's unpredictable weather. Perhaps it belonged to the vicar or had simply been left behind in a pew by a parishioner.

He had realized some time ago that Judith was from Cornwall – perhaps she'd gone to school here – for while the accent had worn away, certain acquired phrases had remained. What she'd said about her husband having died 'right in the Christmas'. Only a Cornishwoman would phrase it just that way.

What she'd told him about coming to Maidsfell on her honeymoon with her husband didn't mean she wasn't from somewhere else in Cornwall. He'd ask when he found her.

He stood back from the yellow garment, not wanting to touch it. It was the perfect surface to retain fingerprints or other evidence. He was just turning to leave the room when another colourful object caught his eye.

Of course, a splash of colour was not unusual in a room devoted to all the vestments and robes and accoutrements necessary to celebrate the seasons of the Church. Purples, reds, blues, whites, and yellows. This item was small, tucked into a corner under some overhanging robes, and multicoloured – woven using differently dyed strands of reed and fabric.

Like the basket in the video, of course.

What was Judith doing with it in the vestry? Along with that coat – perhaps the coat worn by the killer?

It was almost too much, too easy. He wondered if someone was setting her up. Or if someone had found an unlocked church a handy dumping place for incriminating items.

He recalled Mousse saying baskets were common in these parts, used in shopping to replace the ubiquitous, planet-destroying plastic bags which had now been largely outlawed. Trying to trace this particular basket might be challenging – thousands like it may have been made.

He'd start by asking Judith where she'd got this particular one.

This basket on which he detected the faint scent of a fish.

He gave Mousse a ring from outside the church, telling him to send someone to bag the coat and the basket and send them for testing. It was a case of acting first and asking permission

later – he didn't want to risk someone returning to collect what
they'd left.

'That rainbow basket? It's Morwenna's. I keep forgetting to
return it.'

He'd found Judith in the vicarage next to the church, a big
rambling cottage left over from a bygone day when the vicar was
a highly important personage. Most of the cottage probably
was closed off now to save on fuel. She let him into a little book-
lined study full of her predecessor's dusty old books.

'It's Morwenna's? She gave it to you. You're sure?'

'Of course I'm sure. Morwenna gave it to me, packed with
donated food for the poor of the village. Leftover food from
her restaurant.'

'I see,' he said.

'I'll return it to her right away.'

As if that was the point. 'It's not the basket we care about. Am
I to gather this basket is one that often gets handed back and
forth between the two of you?'

'Yes. The church runs a local charity, you see. A sort of meals-
on-wheels operation. We call it "St. Cuthbert's Delivers". People
like Agnes Ramsey and Christopher Carew benefit – Agnes's
arthritis put her in a wheelchair and Chris has dementia, but his
doctors have said he can live at home, with a bit of help. That's
where the church fills the gap left by social services. "Not enough
funding," they cry. It's shameful, you know. It's just shameful
how we treat our poor and our elderly. And even picturesque
Maidsfell has an unemployment problem. It's just we keep it well
hidden from tourists.'

'I see. Did she often do this?'

'Morwenna? Most weeks, yes. All the restaurants do.'

'Jake Trotter's restaurant included?'

'Yes, Jake's also. And the Athena. Why do you ask?'

'No reason. Just curious.'

But she wasn't put off that easily.

'Is there something wrong with the basket? Is it connected to
the crime you're investigating? Please don't tell me it's connected.'

He started to correct her – he was, in fact, investigating 'crimes'
plural – but decided if there was ambiguity about Will Ivey's death,

it would be better for now to keep quiet about it. If anything, she seemed to be the only person in the village who hadn't jumped to the conclusion that Ivey was a victim as well as Bodwally.

Perhaps it was an occupational hazard: as a priest, her mind just didn't run to serial killers.

Sometimes he wished his own mind didn't automatically trend that way.

He didn't answer her. Instead, he asked, 'When and how do you usually acquire the food? I mean, do Morwenna and Jake and the other restaurant owners always bring their contributions here, or do you go to the restaurants to pick up the donated food?'

'There's no set rule. If it happens to be convenient for me, I stop by the restaurant in question and pick up. Maybe share a cuppa with Morwenna. Sometimes they send one of the waiters or another member of staff to bring the donation to the church.'

'And is there a set day of the week all this happens?'

'Yes and no. Depending on what it is, the food might spoil, so the latest we accept certain items is Tuesday mornings. I'm talking about food that the restaurants would prepare on Sunday. Most often the food needs to be here for sorting on Monday – the day restaurants tend to be closed – for delivery that night or the next day. As I said, Tuesday morning would be stretching it but sometimes that has to happen.' She shrugged, palms up. 'It depends.'

'Did you collect the food from Morwenna this week – or was it brought here?'

A still look came into her eyes. Suspects preparing a lie sometimes got that look. 'Do you know, I really can't remember. One week for that sort of thing is much like the last.'

Except this week happened to contain murder, thought St. Just. While murder might make routine things fly out of a person's head, he thought she was being deliberately vague.

'That fisherman's coat hanging in the vestry. Where did it come from?'

'That big yellow coat? It was Will Ivey's. I should return it, I suppose, but . . . to whom?'

Again, not the point. 'Why do you have it?'

She might have rehearsed the answer, so swiftly did it come.

'He loaned it to me the night of the fisher meeting, when it was pouring down. I'd left my coat at home. He was a kind man. A bit of a heller, but a lovely, kind man.'

It was perhaps the mention of the shared cuppa made him ask, 'You're a particular friend of Morwenna's, aren't you?'

'I like her a great deal. Of course, I like all the people of the village.'

She loved all God's children. Of course she did. It was her job.

'She's not in any trouble,' he said, 'but it really won't help anyone if you try to cover for her. We have to get to the bottom of this. Because what it means right now is someone in this village is getting away with murder. And as we all know, "Thou shalt not kill."'

'Yes,' she nodded soberly. 'Honestly, I can't think of anything that might help you. Well, there's gossip and speculation, but I'm sure it's not relevant. Gossips are so often wrong, aren't they? As well as cruel.'

St. Just perked up at this. 'Go on,' he said.

Instantly setting aside all reservations, she said, 'Well, I guess it's not gossip if I heard it first-hand.'

'Oh, yes?'

'Morwenna told me someone was "putting the screws" on her – her phrase: she reads a lot of detective stories – because they'd learned she'd cheated on the government's subsidy scheme during the Plague Time. She spoke of "getting even", "teaching them a lesson", "warning them off". I talked her out of it, of course. No good could come of it.'

'What did she have in mind?'

'What *exactly* did she have in mind to do? I'm not sure. A bit of food poisoning, perhaps, at Jake's restaurant? Easy as pie to pull off, you know. And ruinous to his reputation as a fine chef. Again, I talked her out of it. As a friend, not just as a priest. I had to do right by her.'

'So Jake was blackmailing Morwenna?'

'Not Jake.'

It was too much to ask, he knew, but he asked anyway. 'I don't suppose she mentioned who it was?'

'Why, Bodwally, of course. It was his restaurant – well, he was Jake's backer. Everyone knows that.'

Bodwally a blackmailer?

It meant yet another visit to Morwenna's. Perhaps Mousse was with her even now, if he'd found anything at Will's cottage implicating her.

He needed to pass along what Judith had said.

'Have you told anyone else about this?'

'Of course not. I'm no gossip. Look, if I think of anything more, I'll give you a ring.' The finality of her tone made it clear she had said more than she'd meant to and was through with this subject.

Trying to drag it out of her might do more harm than good, so he had to be satisfied for the moment with what she'd told him.

Besides, she'd told him a good deal.

TWENTY-EIGHT
The Anchor

It was time for a visit to Jake Trotter, thought St. Just, the man he'd heard so much about but had never met. Fate – in the form of weariness from travel – had led him and Portia to favour Morwenna's place over Jake's on their arrival in the village. That had been Sunday evening; it was now Friday. How was it possible so much had happened? Even COVID time, that elasticity which had persisted even after the pandemic, could not account for it. An investigation always seemed to skew his sense of time passing.

Standing outside St. Cuthbert's, he again rang DCI Mousse, leaving a message for him to call immediately to discuss what Judith had said.

Next he tried Portia's number. They were not the sort of couple always in constant contact, but she'd been gone for much of the day now and he was starting to wonder. He got her voicemail, too, and left a message for her to call.

He checked the vestry and saw the basket and coat were still there. He decided to wait to make sure they'd been collected, filling the time with a stroll round the headstones in the cemetery. He was always surprised by how many wives men had had in the eighteenth and nineteenth centuries, when childbirth had carried off so many women – and their children.

Whitelaw turned up about fifteen minutes later, winded from his walk up the steep cliff path.

Too many hours at video games, thought St. Just. Still, he'd been able to put them on the right path with the security videos.

St. Just explained what was needed, then set off down the path in search of Jake Trotter, the famous proprietor of the Anchor.

It was just gone four and dark clouds had begun to spool by the time St. Just tried the door of Jake's restaurant. It was locked, in a departure from village custom, but St. Just supposed cash businesses like restaurants were the exception that proved the rule.

Quite sensible, thought St. Just, if not helpful now. He walked to the side of the building, rather hoping to find Trotter had attached living quarters, like Morwenna. No luck there, but he did find the back door to the kitchen standing open. A draft of warm, aromatic air assailed his nostrils, carrying the smell of meat and herbs and onions. His stomach reminded him his mealtimes were completely out of sync. Much in the way he'd sleep when he was dead, as the saying went, he'd eat an enormous meal when this investigation ended.

The man before him in the kitchen, rapidly dicing an onion, was recognizable to St. Just from many a photo spread in lifestyle magazines and online celebrity news sites. Trotter was the sort of superstar chef whose name and appearance had come to matter as much as the quality of the meals he prepared, although those were said to be very good indeed.

Trotter didn't look up as St. Just hovered by the door. To do so might have cost him a finger.

'You'd be that detective from away I've been hearing so much about, then.'

It was not said in a particularly belligerent way but everything about the man suggested he was always running at full tilt, expecting challenges and ready to meet them when they came. He had a plethora of tattoos on his bare arms, running up from his hands and into his black T-shirt. A dragon disappeared into his left sleeve; a Celtic cross dominated the right arm, a rosebud wrapping its thorns round his wrist. St. Just winced slightly – he had had to endure injections into his arms and hands following an attack by a suspect, and he knew exactly how painful that was. Submitting to it willingly seemed to him an act of madness but nowadays it was difficult to find anyone of a certain age who didn't have at least one or two tattoos. Many of those he'd seen round Maidsfell appeared to be Celtic in design. St. Just had not actually seen a tattoo parlour in the village but someone somewhere was doing a roaring trade helping people establish their Celtic credentials.

'I am DCI St. Just of the Cambridgeshire Constabulary,' he formally introduced himself. 'I'm assisting the local police in a matter I'm sure you're familiar with by now.'

'Right.' He pulled another onion towards him and starting chopping.

'And you would be Jake Trotter. Of course, I've heard of you. I can't imagine any food lover who hasn't.'

'Naturally.'

St. Just had never known an occasion when a bit of flattery had failed to soften up an interviewee, and despite that off-putting response Jake looked to be no exception. The man's already large, muscular chest expanded visibly as he sucked in his already flat stomach. He and Callum Page could hold a body-building competition, just the two of them.

'You are a foodie, then?' asked Jake.

'In my modest way and on my modest policeman's salary, yes.'

'You and your wife must come and dine with us. I'll make sure you get a discount.'

He didn't bother to explain Portia wasn't his wife – how had Jake known about her, anyway? The grapevine, no doubt – and he didn't stop to explain he didn't take bribes, if that was what this was. He merely said, 'Thank you, sir. I don't mind telling you, your way with Brussels sprouts has become legendary.'

Apparently, with Jake there was no such thing as pouring it on too thick. He beamed, grabbing another onion, dispatching it as quickly as the others. '"Trotter Sprouts", they call them. The secret is olive oil and muscovado sugar, but I trust you to share that tip with no one.'

'Your secret is safe with me, sir. Now, if you wouldn't mind answering a few questions.'

'About Titus Bodwally. Of course.'

St. Just noted the informality of the 'Titus'. 'You and he were business partners.'

'That's correct. Not exactly a full partnership but Bodwally fronted a lot of the money for this restaurant. And I was paying him back.'

'I expect you have records that will establish that,' said St. Just. 'But it won't be necessary right now for me to ask to see them.'

'That's good, because you'll need a warrant.' This was said evenly, if unequivocally.

St. Just thought he might have to tell the world about that secret recipe for Trotter Sprouts, after all.

'What I'd most like to talk to you about is the apparent competition between you and Morwenna Wells of the Maiden's Arms.'

Jake Trotter folded his massive arms beneath his massive pectorals, looked St. Just in the eye, and – clearly surprised – said, 'Whatever for? There is no competition. My restaurant is so vastly superior to her pokey little pub, the question doesn't arise. Any feeling of competition is strictly on Morwenna's side, I assure you. Served with a side dish of poison, to boot.'

'*What* an interesting choice of words,' said St. Just. 'That's precisely what I'm here to talk about, among other things. I have heard there's been some messing about with the garden allotments, for a start.'

'You must be joking,' said Trotter. 'The allotments are for personal use only, for one thing, and if you're accusing me of poisoning anything, we'll have to take a little break while I ring my solicitor.'

'Nothing of the sort,' said St. Just smoothly and – as it happened – truthfully. 'No accusation intended. But what I'd really like to discuss with you is a fish that happens to be poisonous.'

'The dreamfish, you mean,' Jake said immediately. 'They've been turning up here and there. Global warming, combined with mucking about with the waters British fishers and seamen are allowed in since Brexit.'

'What an interesting theory,' said St. Just, his voice ringing with admiration at Jake's astuteness. 'No one has actually mentioned Brexit as a culprit here.'

'So. Are you going to talk politics, Inspector? Because I've got work to do.' He scraped the chopped onions into a bowl and set it aside.

'You haven't by any chance seen a *Sarpa salpa* land in your kitchen lately?'

'If you're here about that daft old man, that wasn't my fault. Chris Carew tried to say he got the fish from my restaurant, but he was already barmy.'

Curiouser and curiouser. It was proving to be an informative interview. 'Morwenna Wells wasn't accused?'

'You'll have to ask her.'

'I'm sure I shall. But I thought you might like to cooperate, as she has.'

Jake set down the knife and, as Morwenna had done earlier, leaned forward against his wooden worktable – muscles rippling, elaborate sleeve tattoos on full display.

'It's like this,' he said. 'Carew probably got hold of it through the food charity. The distribution for that is handled at the back end of my kitchen; I don't get involved. My employees simply scoop up whatever is left over at the end of the day, portion it into paper bowls or whatever, and see it gets to the church on time. Now, where that particular fish came from, who knows? Morwenna's place or – if I'm honest – it could have been mine. Someone working for me may have made a mistake. What does it matter now? It certainly wasn't intentional, whoever did it. Old Man Carew was a danger only to himself.'

'It matters because Lord Bodwally got hold of some poison fish, too. And he's certainly not on the list for anyone's charitable handouts.'

This seemed to come as news to Trotter.

'Well, that *is* odd. The *Sarpa salpa* – it's not the sort of thing that could actually kill you, unless you were very old and decrepit or you ate a lot of it. Of course, it would have to be properly prepared . . .' His voice trailed off.

'Yes?' prompted St. Just. 'Properly prepared by an expert?'

'Well, sure. An expert chef. Or—'

St. Just could see the thought landing and finished the sentence for him. 'Or an expert seaman. Or seawoman.'

'Sure. Yes. It's the head you have to be careful of. The toxins collect there.'

'So I've been told.'

The conversation seemed to be making Jake unbend, just a bit. It had everything he could want, after all. A chance to share his expertise. And a chance to show the authorities how cooperative and above board he could be – just as long, presumably, as they didn't ask to see his records. When St. Just felt Trotter's ego had reached the appropriate heights, he tossed his next bit of bait into the water.

'Morwenna,' he said.

'Yes? As I've explained, whatever is going on is inside her own mind. You'd best go talk with her.'

'She seems quite hostile to you.'

He shrugged. 'Morwenna is a sore loser. She's just about got what it takes to run a pasty shop. OK, a bit more than that. But the Maiden's Arms will never hold a candle to the Anchor.'

'Star or no star? Sir?'

That seemed to hit the target.

'That Michelin star is so coveted, isn't it? Do you know, she suggested there might be a more . . . personal . . . reason for the animosity.' Morwenna had suggested no such thing, but St. Just was certain there was more to this High Noon showdown than met the eye.

'Oh, for God's sake,' said Jake Trotter. '*Women.*'

'"Can't live with 'em, can't live without 'em,"' quoted St. Just amiably. He pasted on the most man-to-man expression in his arsenal and waited.

'I was actually trying to be chivalrous, you know,' said Jake. 'But as long as she told you herself, well – yes, she and I had a thing. It was years ago, and it amounted to nothing, from my perspective.'

'And from hers?'

'I don't know. I guess she thought it was a "grow old together" thing. Where she got that idea . . . Wenna was a beauty queen in her day, you know. Men dropping at her feet. Me, I realized quickly she wasn't my type. End of.'

'I see.' Depressingly, he thought he did. No room would be large enough to contain two such egos.

Jake said, 'I have a wife and children now. Gretchen is half my age, which *really* gets up Morwenna's nose. I can't help any of that. But if she's worried I'll turn her in, she doesn't know the kind of bloke I am. She never did know.'

'I'm sorry,' said St. Just. 'I don't follow. "Turn her in"? Surely you're not saying . . .'

'Saying she's a poisoner? No. Nothing that dramatic. I was referring to her little trouble with the government. I mean her potential trouble with the government. I doubt they'd do anything at this point. Too hard to prove, and after all this time, the truth is, everyone just wants to seal the boxes and move on.'

'Could you be more specific, sir?'

He sighed. 'Wenna took advantage of the government eat-out subsidy during the Plague Time. She pretended people came to the restaurant who didn't, forging all the necessary documents, fiddling about with the orders. She seemed to think everyone was doing the same thing, which is how I came to hear of it – the restaurant business runs on gossip, and some bloke she'd fired came straight over here to see if I was hiring. He told me all about it. Any attempts she made at covering up what she was doing were completely lame, apparently.

'But I wouldn't turn her in. Gretchen is into karma and meditation and things. She talked me out of it. I mean, at the time it could have been quite serious.'

'She'd have been fined, certainly,' St. Just agreed, noting that Jake had at least toyed with the idea of turning Morwenna in until the idea had been meditated out of his chakras. 'She might even have done time for it.'

At the least, thought St. Just, it would hobble her restaurant career, and that seemed to be all she lived for. Her next meal might be in a prison kitchen. Was it enough to kill for – someone threatening to spill her secret after all this time?'

St. Just wasn't inclined to think it was. But the topic of blackmail kept rearing its head. Perhaps, combined with some other leverage, some old wound being reopened . . .

Perhaps then.

TWENTY-NINE
Dark and Stormy

Outside the Anchor the streets were dark and empty, the promised storm having driven everyone indoors. He thought of that yellow coat, wishing he had one. He made a mad dash to stand under a shop awning, where he pulled his mobile from his pocket to ring Portia.

Who didn't pick up. He called the landline at the cottage. No luck there, either. He decided to ring Sepia's gallery. He thought he might stop in there, on the off chance, as the gallery was on his way back to the cottage.

First he tried Mousse again, with no luck. This time he left a message relaying what Judith had told him, ending with, 'For what it's worth.'

He pulled up a browser on his phone and tapped the number on the gallery website. His call went to the shop's voicemail: 'Hello, you have reached Sepia's gallery. I'm unable to answer your call at the moment. Please note the shop is closed on Thursdays between four and six p.m. but reopens at six for late shopping.'

Great. She and Portia were probably at dinner somewhere. But did it really make sense they'd have lunch and dinner together in one day?

It was a long sprint through the rain. At first St. Just popped in and out of shops along the way, but in the end, soaked through already, he decided a little more rain wouldn't matter.

He found it strange to remember he was on holiday, and this wasn't his job anyway. But now he had the bit well and truly between his teeth and would see it through to the end. He had an inkling about the culprit, nothing more. Nothing to go on, but . . .

Where was Portia?

He could hear the ocean giving a good drubbing to the shore but the rain formed a curtain, veiling his view. Carefully, he made his way down the high street as rivulets of water threatened to overflow the pavements.

At Sepia's, a sign on the door confirmed she was closed, its adjustable red clock hands indicating she'd return at six.

Nonetheless, he peered into the shop through the front window past rows of canvases depicting boats at rest on sunny days in idyllic villages. It was nearly dark inside, a few nightlights on for security.

Recalling that Sepia lived over the shop, he stood back in the street, gazing at the upper windows through rain-washed eyes. It was dark up there, too. Not a light showing.

Damn.

Portia had to be at the cottage. Probably she'd turned her phone off for some peace and quiet while she worked. She wasn't checking her messages. It had to be something like that. Maybe she'd unplugged the landline from the wall.

He ran up the street to Seaside Cottage.

Wind sheeted rain against the windowpanes, scrubbing them clean, water pouring in an endless heavenly supply. Raindrops pounded against the roof and dinged the patio furniture, lifting and turning the lighter pieces for good measure. In the distance he saw lightning streak jaggedly against the sky, throwing the harbour out of darkness and into sharp relief like a photo flash.

The wind attacked the cottage in waves, as if a giant were giving it a series of mighty shoves, trying to topple the little structure, rattling its doors and windows. A sudden gust would make the door clatter on its hinges. St. Just began to wonder if it would hold.

He could hear tiles coming loose from the roof and sailing out to sea, like a deck of cards caught on the wind. The waves seemed to give out a keening complaint.

Not a soul was out there, of course.

No one would dare be out in this. So where was Portia? Safe indoors, please God – but where?

If not here, where?

Where?

Swirling his raincoat over his shoulders, he dived out into the rain, which began to gather more strength from the wind and hurl itself in a sideways attack, pushing and pulling him about at will. As large as he was, he struggled to stay upright against the onslaught.

He wasn't sure where to start; she could be in any of a dozen little restaurants or bistros. He'd got it into his head she'd be wanting a meal right about now. Why would she go out without him, though, and without a word?

He headed down to the harbour where the lights might have attracted her. Perhaps she'd stopped in a café or bar for a drink by herself, and although that seemed unlikely, it was the answer he wanted – to find her in a public place, fireside, perhaps with an open book in her hand, sipping a pre-dinner cordial in perfect comfort.

He ran splashing down the lane before turning left off the high street. Boats in the harbour tilted this way and that in the wind, bobbing maniacally. Where Will Ivey's boat should have been was a dark oily gap.

He'd find her and order a drink himself and perhaps she'd regale him with stories about Sepia – about her arrival in the village, her life before, why she'd wanted to open a gallery.

'I gather her husband was a bit of a rotter,' she might say. Or, 'She never married. No one could quite live up to expectations.'

But that wasn't right. Mousse had told him Sepia was divorced.

They would talk against the pop and crackle of the fireplace, her voice melodic, her eyes shimmering in the firelight. A *whoosh!* from the chimney might convince the owner it was time to put a damper on the fire before it could throw sparks on to the carpet. The flickering light of guttering candles would give the scene a Hitchcockian air. It would be a night for storytelling.

'And I thought we got storms in Cambridge,' Portia would say. 'That wind that blows straight from the north in winter into the bones. At least we're warmer here. But have you ever seen it bucket down like this?'

He stood under another awning, wondering whom to call. His mind running to places of sanctuary, he rang the number from the St. Cuthbert's website, which would likely ring through to the vicarage. It felt like the last place to try, the last place Portia might be.

No answer.

He tried Mousse again and at last was rewarded with the sound of a live human voice.

'I haven't been able to reach Portia,' he told him. 'She's not at the cottage and she didn't leave a note to say where she'd be. She's not answering her phone. Can you tell your people to keep an eye out? Send more people to help?'

'As many as I can. She can't be out there alone in this – and with some lunatic on the loose.'

'Did you get my message about the whole blackmail business?'

'I did. But I was just leaving Will's place – no luck there, by the way.'

'Trotter confirms what Judith was saying. But never mind now. I'm starting with the harbour and working my way up the cliff path to the church. It's not like Portia not to answer her mobile for this long.'

'Remember where you are. Spotty Coverage is our watchword. In fact, it's a selling point to lure in over-stressed yuppies. She may just not be reachable. No worries.'

THIRTY

The Lady Vanishes

Judith turned from the altar at his entrance. In her hand was an electric candle lighter.

'Isn't this something?' she greeted him. 'Landlines and the internet are both down, and mobile reception requires divine intervention. We just now lost power.' She set the lighter down on the altar.

The church was ablaze in candlelight. St. Just peered round the nave and the aisles, as if he might find Portia hiding in a pew. Having again scoured the tourist spots along the waterfront and popped into every restaurant or bar he'd found open and looked into every shop window on the high street, he still felt the church was the least likely place he might find her. But sometimes, as with missing keys or sunglasses, the last place you look . . .

Portia, caught out in the storm – might she not seek refuge here?

'Fortunately, the police have access to satellite phones and two-way radios,' he told Judith.

Mousse had told him the coat and basket retrieved by Whitelaw were on their way to forensics. He'd also filled him in a bit more on the backgrounds of several of the people they'd been interviewing.

'So take care,' Mousse had cautioned before they'd rung off. 'Suspects are sometimes miles ahead of us. We can only make educated guesses at the truth, while they sit wasting our time and knowing it all. Only *some* of it relevant.'

'That's good,' Judith was saying now. 'I don't like feeling cut off. It reminds me that the village is really only an unstable pile of rocks jutting out into the sea.'

She was cleaning again in the flickering candlelight, buffing a silver chalice and its matching paten until they gleamed. She held the paten up to her face to use as a mirror as she smoothed back her hair. The pieces looked antique and probably were worth a tidy sum.

'I was able to get a signal at the Fourteen Maidens earlier,' she told him, resuming her polishing. The paten had apparently not reached the desired standard. Why did he always think in cinematic terms when he was around Judith? Now he was put in mind of the *Stepford Wives*, endlessly cleaning, cleaning. 'Of course, I had to get special permission to be there from Sybil.' She used the sleeve of her robe to give the platen a final rub before setting it down among an array of silver and gold altar goods. It looked like an exhibit of treasures excavated from a Viking burial ship.

Turning to him, she smiled. Her teeth gleamed very white in the flames from the candles.

'She thinks she owns the place, does Sybil,' she said. 'I think she may be . . .' Judith traced a spinning motion with one finger against the side of her head. 'You know.'

'She may be alone too much,' said St. Just. 'It can affect one's perception.'

'I'm alone all the time, but you don't find me on the night of a full moon parading among the dolmens, chanting and banging on a drum. Of course, none of us are truly alone, for God is always with us. Didn't you find that to be so, during the Plague Time?'

St. Just reflected on some of the beliefs of the Christian tradi- tion – the bells and the chanting and the blessing of the wine and bread. The observance of the seasons and the calls to morning and evening prayer. Was it all so much different? Sybil had fewer followers in her 'church'; that was all. It may even have been a church of one. What he'd heard that night was likely a recording. He didn't, on reflection, believe Sybil had many friends. Perhaps, people having let her down so badly, she preferred things that way.

He ignored Judith's question, not only because he didn't want a theological debate. He had come very close to abandoning any belief in a higher power during the Plague Time. The devastation was too horrific to be explained to his satisfaction by any existing creed.

He asked, 'Was there a husband or partner? Was Sybil always alone?'

Judith shook her head mournfully. 'We don't ask; we don't speak of it. There was a daughter, I believe, but we don't think there was a husband.'

Was it to be credited that Judith didn't know the story of Sybil's loss? He supposed she might know more than she would say about some of the villagers. Will Ivey in particular.

Conversationally, he asked, 'Didn't you say you were a nurse before you got the calling to the priesthood?'

'No. I don't recall ever saying that. I was a care assistant. But one with nursing responsibilities.' This he knew from the background done by Mousse's team. He also knew from Mousse it wasn't the entire story.

He'd become so preoccupied with finding Portia that the case had only skirted his vision. But could the solution to the murders – the Maidsfell Murders, as the press had taken to calling them – be somehow staring him in the face?

'A fine distinction,' he said mildly. 'It's not easy work, whatever the job title. Often low-paid, too. It takes a special person to do that sort of job well.'

'Yes,' she agreed. 'Yes, it does.' Her expression had grown rigid with apprehension, eyes wide and unblinking as she concentrated on his words. As when they'd first met at the Lighthouse Café, he thought she might be hard of hearing.

'And where did you work?'

'It was a labour of love, not work.'

'I asked where.'

'St. Mary's. London. When I became a priest, I continued to serve there, doing pastoral care. Quite fulfilling.'

'There must be more than one St. Mary's in London. A hospital, was it?'

'Of sorts.' She busied herself brushing dust from her cassock.

'What sorts?'

'It was a nursing home. Run by the Church. St. Mary's Church.' Her tone was both puzzled – Where was he going with this? – and annoyed. She seemed to just be biting back a snarky *If you must know.*

'Let me hazard a guess,' he said. 'Was it by any chance an EMI nursing home? A facility for the elderly mentally infirm?' He knew full well from Mousse it had been.

'Something like that.'

'Something like that,' he repeated. 'In actual fact, you worked at St. Margaret's Care Home. Not St. Mary's.'

She said nothing. Her posture grew so still she might have stopped breathing. Her eyes wouldn't meet his.

'Judith, look at me. Isn't that right?'

'I got the names mixed up. St. Mary's, St. Margaret's. All these saints' names! It's hard to keep them all straight. There are hundreds of saints. Hundreds! From the time Christ walked the earth!'

He'd had enough. He needed to find Portia, and it wasn't at all clear if this woman's lies about her background had anything to do with the case. It wouldn't be the first time the Church had found a dodgy priest in its ranks. The crimes generally involved either embezzlement or sexual misbehaviour, though, rather than murder.

'You worked as an assistant at St. Margaret's Care Home for about six months. But you were never a trained nurse with any credentials.'

'It's something you learn on the job,' she said. 'I never said I was a nurse.'

'No, you didn't. Not to me, at any rate.'

'I mixed up the names. What's this really about?'

He was watching closely for her reactions, but he suspected she was so schooled in the art of deception that she would give little away.

'The funny thing is,' he went on, 'they had a patient with the same name as yours. Judith Abernathy. Sadly, she was one of their younger patients when she died. Early-onset Alzheimer's. She was about your age.'

'It's nothing to do with me. I don't remember her. It's a common name.'

'Not really that common. Anyway, we asked at what you said was your old parish of St. Mary's – so-called before it merged. Because of that merger, it took a while to track down the relevant party. They'd never heard of Judith Abernathy.'

'Well, you asked the wrong people, don.' She tried belligerence, her expression turning petulant. Like any liar, she did not like being confronted with her lies.

St. Just mused, 'If someone were a con artist, say, trying to steal another person's identity, the first place they might try is wherever Alzheimer's patients are gathered. A clinic or care facility of some sort. The patients of such establishments are unlikely to notice their things have gone missing or to complain if they do notice. They might not be believed if they say anything. They'd be called delusional, and a little note would be made on their chart, and that would be the end of it.'

She played along now. 'Dear God, yes. It's frightful. But you're right, of course. That's what might happen.'

She wouldn't go down without a fight, thought St. Just. He was reminded of the case of a clinic where the 'blood trail', as cyber-crime experts called it, led straight from the accounts office of a doctor specializing in mental diseases of the elderly to his receptionist, a woman who suddenly had the wherewithal to buy expensive cars and clothes and a getaway villa on the Costa del Sol. 'You have to wonder at the depravity of someone who would exploit the most vulnerable members of our population, don't you?'

She nodded sagely. Holding up one palm, probably in conscious imitation of some religious icon or other, she said, 'But Christ taught us to forgive thieves. Perhaps the person badly needed money.'

'Perhaps.'

'As Christ said, it—'

'Is that it, Judith?' he cut in, not unkindly. 'You needed money? Or did you just enjoy the game?'

'I don't understand what you're on about,' she said. 'This is a mistake. A horrible . . .' She looked down, seeming to notice for the first time that she held in her hands the paten she'd been polishing with such frenetic energy. 'A mistake,' she repeated, stepping back towards the altar, and suddenly, in the moment before St. Just had time to duck, the paten was spinning through the candlelit air like a frisbee.

The heavy metal clipped him on the forehead, hard enough to cause him to lose his footing but not enough to knock him out. He stumbled badly, however, falling off the bottom step of the altar and hitting his head – he could hear the *crack* of bone against stone. Trying to prop himself on both elbows, through blurred vision he watched Judith run through the open door leading to the vestry, black robes flying out behind, slamming the door.

He heard the click of a key being turned in the lock.

Fumbling for his phone, he rang Mousse.

'Send backup to St. Cuthbert's *now*,' he told him. 'Judith, or whoever she is, just left. Yes, I know you told me to wait. I ended up confronting her and I frightened her off. She must be headed downhill. And try the vicarage, too.'

He attempted to pull himself to his feet, marvelling at how his legs refused to recognize any connection to his knees, but it was just as well – he'd be dizzy if he stood too quickly. His brain telegraphed only one thought: *Portia*. He had a horrible suspicion the one person who might know where she was had just fled the interview.

Navigating his way in the uneven light wouldn't be difficult, as many English churches had been built to a pattern. The vestry room to the left of the altar would likely have its own exit, in this case through the graveyard to the vicarage. Once outside, even in the storm, Judith might go anywhere. He had the slightly hysterical thought she would be caught out without a raincoat.

He put a hand to his forehead and it came away red with blood. He tried using his handkerchief to apply pressure, but all it seemed to do was trigger what he knew would be a massive headache.

He berated himself for closing in hard on Judith before she could tell him when she had last seen Portia.

What she had *done* with Portia.

Gripping the back of a pew, he managed to pull himself upright and walk unsteadily, hand over hand, to the vestry door.

A key hung beside the door, a shiny modern key to replace the rusty ironworks of an earlier century. She must have carried a spare to lock the door from inside.

She'd be well gone by now. Nonetheless he unlocked the door and looked round the vestry using the torch on his mobile. Nothing. The door to the outside was closed.

He was just turning to leave when he noticed a floor rug askew – a rug partly covering a trapdoor. This was not unusual in an old church; it might be an entry to the crypt.

He pulled back the rug to reveal an iron ring attached to a wooden section of floor perhaps three feet square. He remembered the dust on Judith's robes. Maybe she'd been doing more than housework. Perhaps she'd been exploring beneath the church.

He pulled the ring. He'd expected resistance but it lifted easily, the segment of floor coming with it. Squatting on his haunches, using his hands for balance, he peered into utter blackness.

He pointed the mobile torch into the yawning space. He could just make out steps carved into the stone, leading into a womb-like vault. From that chamber the area narrowed into a tunnel perhaps six feet long – quite an elaborate tunnel of corbelled stone walls and roof. Whoever had built this had built it to last.

The steps had eroded with the centuries, and the way down looked treacherous. He weighed his options, scanning the space in the spotty light.

He could see a wooden door inside the tunnel, tightly shut with elaborate old ironworks, forged metal with a thumb latch. The mate to the latch would likely be on the other side of the door. If she had come this way, she'd probably have slid the lock home behind her.

Damn. This time there would not be easy access with a key. He'd practically need a battering ram.

What if Portia were on the other side of that door?

He thought the cavernous area might be a relic of mining days, like the smugglers' tunnel Portia had described running down from a pub to the cliffs of Sennen. Perhaps this was some vestige of a long-ago enterprise like that.

The air in the chamber was unexpectedly fresh, as if frequently in use or ventilated, the wooden door opening into . . . what? He could smell a sweet perfume, perhaps from scented candle wax or incense.

Along with a faint underlying scent of decay.

Whatever this space was used for, perhaps some esoteric private ritual, perhaps just extra storage, he wouldn't get far creeping about with a probable concussion and a mini-light. His first priority was to make sure Portia was out of harm's way, and for that he'd need help.

Again he rang Mousse. Connectivity, at least within the confines of the church, didn't seem to be as tricky as Judith had suggested.

'Any sign of Portia?'

'I was just going to call,' said Mousse. 'Yes, I've some good news there. Someone saw her making for the Fourteen Maidens. We've got a man headed there now.'

St. Just sighed. Sparks flew in front of his eyes from even that slight effort. 'What on earth was she doing out in a storm like this?'

'She may just have got caught out in it.'

'She's not here at the church, thank God.' There must be a good reason why she couldn't call or text. There *had* to be.

'We'll not stop looking until we find her, never you fear. Listen, something interesting just came in. Callum Page. It turns out that is not his birth name. He changed it by deed poll years ago.'

'Not an unusual thing for an actor to do, I suppose.'

'It is when you learn his birth name was Mermen Wells.'

'Wells? He's not—'

'Related to Morwenna? As it turns out, he is. He was born one of a set of twins, boy and girl. The girl, as we know, died. Gwithian.'

St. Just remembered the tattoo on Morwenna's wrist. The initials G and M. Gwithian and Mermen. Good Cornish names.

'Why didn't he tell us?'

'Perhaps because his father, named on the birth certificate, was Titus Bodwally. And with Titus murdered, he didn't want to drag his mother into it. Nor would anyone in the village want to, even assuming they knew the connection, which is doubtful. It all happened decades ago and Morwenna's life was in London until recent years. Callum went into the army and from there, all over the globe, so he wasn't around Maidsfell, either.'

'But Gwithian's accident, or whatever it was, happened here?'

'She was here with a school group from London. Maidsfell wasn't her home, either.'

St. Just took a moment for his mind to spin through all the

options suggested by this information. The one that alarmed him most was that Callum was somehow in cahoots with Judith. Or with his mother, in some scheme for revenge against Bodwally.

'Trees are down everywhere – the storm has blocked the way to the Maidens,' Mousse was telling him. 'It might take a while for searchers to clear a path.'

'I'm on my way to the Fourteen Maidens, regardless,' said St. Just. 'I first want to eliminate one possibility here. You're not going to believe what I've found in the church.'

'Try me. I'll believe anything at this point.'

Briefly, St. Just explained.

'I need to at least try that door, on the off chance, but you'll probably have to send a team to break it down.'

'I can't spare any more people right now, Arthur.'

'Could you at least have someone guard the exits to the church?'

'I wouldn't count on it if I were you. We're stretched so thin with this case I had to send Whitelaw to interview Callum or whatever his name is. Mermen.'

St. Just was torn. Was it wasting time to try the door, or should he prioritize getting around the obstacles to the Fourteen Maidens? He decided there was too much to risk in haring off immediately when trying the door would take mere minutes.

'If I can, I'm going to have a look in that tunnel or whatever it is, see what it leads to,' he told Mousse. 'I would say, "Call me," but I doubt I'll be able to get a signal once inside.'

'All right. It's what we can do for now. Let me know.'

He rang off.

It was a cave. Of all things, it was a cave. It had been built into the rocks – or rather, a natural cave had been widened and buttressed and strengthened here and there by human effort, leaving the original largely untouched. It was impossible to say how long ago this was done – the stone was worn smooth with time and seeping water.

She'd left the door unbolted on the other side, no doubt thinking the latch would fall shut automatically as she slammed the door closed, and that it was unlikely he'd find the steps concealed by the rug, anyway. She'd so nearly been right.

He decided to go in.

And so he spent half an hour tripping about, skidding on wet patches of stone where water dripped from the ceiling, his balance off from the blow to his head. The light from his mobile wasn't nearly enough.

The stone-lined passage led down and away from the church. It was on a steep decline, perhaps half a mile in length. The thing was a miracle of engineering. Here and there shelves and shallow chambers had been carved from the stone.

And here and there rats, big as kittens, scuttled out of his path.

A cloying smell assaulted his nostrils halfway through – no doubt a rat had expired. The odour receded as he reached fresh air wafting in from the tunnel's mouth.

Where he emerged into some sort of chapel. A pagan chapel, if that wasn't an oxymoron. A grotto, dedicated to some deity or deities working magic on their followers. Sybil had to have been aware of the space, and, indeed, he now saw ranged about the chapel several photos of a beautiful young girl, no doubt the daughter so cruelly taken from her.

He also felt certain he'd discovered the whereabouts of the fourteenth maiden. A tall narrow monolith rested against one wall.

What was stunning were the walls themselves – at first glance, some variety of Stone Age art that would not be out of place in one of today's living rooms. In fact, where had he seen such abstract designs not long ago? Of course, in Sepia's gallery. She had oil paintings for sale that were similar.

Someone had left rows of candles burning in the furthest reaches of the space, and he could see in the distance what looked like an illuminated stone altar. He stepped forward and nearly slipped on the uneven flooring. He knew he should go back, get reinforcements, get a lantern at least.

The walls shimmered with bright, variegated colours – every shade of blue and green and orange and yellow and red. Had he not read Horace Bude's exuberant description of the nearby Cave of Many Colours, he'd have been certain a human hand was at play here. This seemed too beautiful to exist by chance.

As with that famous Cornwall attraction, the oxidation of mineral deposits had stained the walls as water seeped down the rocks, leaving deposits behind to create this otherworldly dazzle for the human eye. It was like something out of a Disney World ride, this dizzying, kaleidoscopic array. The entire area shimmered in an otherworldly phosphorescent glow.

He pushed past the little altars holding votive candles and flowers and photos of the long dead and headed for the cave's exit, where stood the tree covered in clouties, hiding the entrance.

He heard a sound. Faint, muffled. He held his breath, waiting for the sound to come again. Now all he could hear was a steady drip, probably a constant sound as the cave continued to carve itself into the stone.

He called out for Portia, his voice echoing through the chapel and down the ancient passage behind him.

No reply.

Then a soft, shushing sound.

Sybil stood near the mouth of the cave, one finger to her lips, gesturing for him to be quiet.

She eyed him warily, like a woman who had spent a lifetime trusting all the wrong people. Her face, innocent of makeup, carried the expression of a frightened child. In the light from the candles burning in nooks round the cave, her eyes shone transparent as glass.

Where on earth had she come from? It was as if she'd dropped from the sky. She must have been there for some time, thought St. Just, pootling about with her herbs and candles and little altars.

She hadn't come by the path – not in recent hours, anyway, since a tree had blocked the way – and she certainly hadn't scaled the side of the cliff.

Alarmingly, she carried a sword, and looked prepared to wield it as an executioner would do. Not just any sword – what appeared to be a ceremonial blade, its pommel and cross-guard encrusted with jewels. Ceremonial or not, as it gleamed in the candlelight, he thought Sybil might do some serious damage with that.

The sudden transformation from mildly eccentric Wiccan to vengeful goddess was certainly impressive.

With her free hand she motioned to the cave's opening.

He nodded to let her know, message received, he'd be silent.

She'd been awaiting her moment, apparently, and her moment had arrived. She began inching toward the mouth of the cave.

THIRTY-ONE
Cliffhanger

Portia sensed a presence behind her. At the sound of a disturbance of dirt and gravel, she turned from the edge of the cliff of the Fourteen Maidens.

'Hello, Judith,' she tried tentatively. For Judith, erstwhile curate of St. Cuthbert's, looked to be past any pretence of politeness – or holiness, for that matter. She looked, in a word, crazed.

And frightened to see Portia.

'What are you doing here?' she demanded.

'Sorry to disturb you,' said Portia softly. 'I was just leaving, actually – I got stranded by the storm. And my phone seems to have called it quits.'

'Why are you here?' Judith demanded again.

'There was something I wanted to see for myself. Something Bodwally wrote about, some cave. Before he . . .'

Judith's 'What cave?' was unconvincing.

'It's just that I thought he'd . . . well, so, I'll leave you to it now.'

'Is there some problem?' said Judith, stepping into her path. The fake tone of concern, perhaps the tone she used in her pastoral care role, was more chilling than her anger.

'I'm fine,' Portia said, struggling to keep her voice light. 'It's nothing. I was imagining—'

'It's not nothing. Or do you always look like you've seen a ghost?'

'I'm just up here doing research. For my book, you know. But if I'm disturbing you, of course—'

'The cave,' said Judith flatly. 'How far in did you go?'

'I didn't go inside.'

Portia's reply – too quick, too soft – was met with an eloquent silence. Judith's impish expression had gone, her eyes and the hollows of her cheeks, seen now in shrouded moonlight, were sunk into a web of wrinkles.

'Even if I'd gone inside,' said Portia, keeping her voice even, 'who would I tell? For that matter, *what* would I tell? It's a cave, that's all. Pretty, but nothing spe—'

'Oh, come on. That cop you're engaged to. Do you really expect me to believe you wouldn't tell him?'

Portia looked straight at her, adopting her best confiding, woman-to-woman posture. 'We don't talk shop. In my work I've studied so many people wrongly convicted that I stay out of police matters. I simply can't remain impartial. But I tell myself it's nothing to do with me. I'm just an academic, a writer. An observer.'

Portia could see her wavering and was wondering if Judith could possibly swallow such a load of codswallop. Portia and St. Just did little but talk shop, swapping theories and trying to suss out the meanings of clues. But she had to keep her engaged, make Judith see her as a person, not an object standing between her and freedom.

'I'll be leaving the village soon,' said Judith suddenly.

'I am sorry to hear that. Do you have anywhere to go?'

'Not since my husband died.' The topic seemed to put her on the verge of tears. 'I have nothing.'

So that part of her story at least was true, thought Portia.

'Just leave now,' Portia said gently, 'and no one will be the wiser. Leave the way you came. You have a car, right? I'll send on your belongings; no need to shake your head – of course I will; it's the least I can do. You've been kind to me and Arthur during our stay here. I really think you would have made a wonderful priest for St. Cuthbert's, you know.'

'Oh, for God's sake, don't be so daft. I'm not a priest.'

'So it's . . . it's like a disguise, is it? Can you tell me why? You don't have to, I'm just curious. It's a wonderful cover, absolutely fooled me. Are you MI5 by any chance?'

Judith visibly swelled at this idea, tempted to own it, to be important at last.

'I might be,' she said. 'You do see why I have to remain, you know . . .'

'Undercover? Well, of course! You're trailing someone. You can't tell me who it is, I suppose – no matter.' Portia held up a hand, not wanting to push Judith into a corner. For she had hesitated, teetering between wanting to inflate her part as the derring-do secret agent, and realizing the pretence was too much work to keep straight – as well as unlikely to be believed.

'I'm sure it's classified information,' Portia said. 'Eyes only, right?'

With a regal nod, Judith acknowledged this was so.

Portia inched away from the cliff's edge, trying to judge the distance to the cliff path to her right, and the distance to the cave in front of her, and the time she'd need to reach either . . . and the chances either choice would offer a place of safety. The problem was, she had no idea what that cave led to. It could be a dead end and she'd be trapped like an animal inside.

The cliff path, while leaving her exposed, seemed the safer bet.

'I would bet it's Morwenna,' she said conversationally. 'I know you can't tell me, of course, but if there's anyone in the village with something to hide, it's Morwenna.'

The reaction was almost comic as Judith instantly dropped her guard. Nothing like a good juicy bit of gossip to get someone's attention, thought Portia. Apparently, even serial killers weren't immune to this universal truth.

'Did St. Just say so?'

'Well, no – again, we don't talk shop. It was my own observation. I'm a criminologist, you know, and I am called in to consult occasionally with MI5.' She paused – was this *slight* exaggeration too much? After all, there was every chance she might be consulted in future. From Judith's avid expression, no – nothing was too much. 'And there was something going on with Morwenna. Didn't you notice at the meeting over the fishers' plans, she suddenly changed her stance? I think she was being blackmailed – threatened by someone.'

'Not by me, she wasn't.'

'No, of course not! You're no blackmailer. Anyone can see that.' *A cold-blooded killer perhaps but . . .*

'Anyway, I think someone got to her. Told her to back down.'

'Oh, that. That was Bodwally.'

'Really?' In spite of herself, Portia was intrigued. Apparently, her best guess, her theory, turned out to have some teeth to it, after all. Her reaction was everything Judith might have hoped for.

Judith leaned in. Now they were two seasoned MI5 operatives discussing a case.

'Oh, yes. He told me, you know. The night I cooked him the fish dinner. He told me.' She stopped to straighten the sleeve of her priestly garb.

'Told you what?' Portia prodded. Softly, softly. Her natural gifts as a peacemaker were kicking in – an ability to see all sides, all opposing views. Even in dealing with a sociopath, which Judith clearly was, it was useful.

Judith's eyes narrowed. They held a look of poison as she gazed out at the heavy sky, bruised in purples and blues. The moving clouds seemed to stir her to speech.

'During the Plague Time, Morwenna broke all the rules, all the laws. It's how she survived, how the Maiden's Arms survived. There are big penalties for scofflaws like Morwenna. She could go to jail.'

'Oh, surely, after all this time, she—'

'I'm telling you she could. I got it straight from Lord Bodwally.'

'My goodness. You know, I should tell St. Just all this.'

'I thought you and he didn't talk shop.' A look of cunning came into her eyes, as if she had scored a major point. Portia realized she was dealing with a case of full-blown paranoia.

'No, we don't, but this could be crucial information to solving the murder case.'

Too late, Portia saw the trap. No need to solve the case.

The solution was standing right in front of her.

And unless Portia missed her guess, it was hiding a knife somewhere under the folds of that cassock.

'Does he know where you are?' Judith demanded, edging towards her.

Portia was forced to take a step back, realizing she now stood only a foot from the cliff's edge. There was no room to manoeuvre to either side. Leaving nowhere to go but over the edge, a drop of three stories.

She knew she wouldn't be the first to meet such a fate here at the Fourteen Maidens, by accident or design.

'Arthur, you mean? No. I was waiting for the storm to die down a bit. I'm meeting him later.' Portia knew St. Just would be moving heaven and earth to find her right then.

'You seem worried, Judith,' she said. 'You needn't be, with me.' She held up her hands in the classic pose of surrender.

But Judith wouldn't meet her eyes now. 'People won't mind their own business.' Her shoulders sagged in sad resignation. 'So I have to mind it for them, I guess.'

'I'm only up here because Bodwally wrote something about a cave, and I became intrigued. A multicoloured cave before which the Maidens stood guard. He seemed to think there was a book in the story. In the entire history of the village, which apparently has never really been told.'

Portia had decided not to mention she was there at the invitation of Sybil. Much better not to bring her into it, talking to someone in Judith's state of mind. Sybil had invited her to attend a pagan ceremony, and Portia hadn't been able to resist the opportunity for first-hand research into ancient traditions.

'Bodwally was a fool,' Judith said. 'No, worse – he was a *liar*.' She ended the sentence in a shriek on the word 'liar'.

'People seem to agree on that at least. Is that why . . .?'

'Why I killed him?' The cunning look returned and with a complete lack of convincingness, she said, 'I don't know what you're talking about.'

Portia suddenly knew what she must do; it was remembering Bodwally's book in progress that gave her the inspiration. Another monumental ego, this one writing about the underground, dry-stone structure – the fogou – that he was certain existed somewhere in or near the village. His own personal El Dorado.

It turned out he was right. And Judith had been the one to find it, pootling about the old church, doing her constant deep cleaning.

Would Judith, with her even larger ego, be even more susceptible to flattery? Portia realized her best hope was to keep her talking. To buy time. Time for what, she wasn't sure. But Arthur surely would be looking for her. She had been trapped in the cave by the storm, with no chance of a signal from her mobile. She'd been testing the connectivity outside the cave when Judith had come up behind her.

'Do you know,' Portia said, as if stuck with a new thought, 'there's a story in all this. The Fourteen Maidens, the tunnel, the cave, the fogou – is that how you pronounce it? Foo-goo?'

Judith agreed, in the condescending way she had suddenly adopted, that it was. Gone was the friendly woman of God in her cheerful Hawaiian shirt. Portia realized how thoroughly she'd been taken in.

She longed to ask her the one key question – Why did you do this? – but it did not seem to be the best time to provoke her.

'I would love to be the one to write it,' Portia said, 'but obviously it should be *you*. I can connect you with the right people. Wait until I tell my agent!'

She had snared Judith's attention, flushing her ego out of barely concealed hiding, using the perfect bait to set the trap.

Encouraged, Portia went on. 'In fact, my agent asked me some time ago if I could write such a story. I told him no, but I'd ask among my writer friends. The project would be perfect for you.'

Seeing she had Judith where she lived, behind the gates of her own colossal ego, she added, 'The potential for Hollywood film interest would be enormous. Maybe they'd ask you to direct or produce. That often happens.' Portia paused a moment to marvel at her capacity for invention. Well, she *was* a writer.

'I don't have any experience with that,' said Judith.

'No one does,' said Portia breezily. 'Believe me, no one knows what they're doing. Don't worry about that. Let me put you together with my agent. *Please*. He does know what he's doing and he would be so interested. I could help you write the proposal. You'll need a chapter-by-chapter breakdown . . .'

No reply to this. Probably she'd made it all sound like too much work.

'Look, Judith,' she said. 'I want to show you something. You won't believe . . . too marvellous.' She began walking slowly towards her. It was a mistake.

'It's a shame, really,' said Judith. 'You're not like him, not like the rest. But you can't unsee what you've seen.'

No use. The thought dropped into Portia's head. *I pushed too hard.*

She was frantically searching her mind for another tack to try when St. Just emerged from behind the wishing tree and began creeping stealthily towards Judith's back.

Behind him was Sybil, brandishing a sword. Her mouth was pulled back almost into a square, like on a samurai face mask; her eyes were red-rimmed and filled with rage.

Portia struggled to keep a poker face, to hide the surge of relief that made her knees want to buckle.

'I'm sorry,' said Portia. 'What do you mean, Judith? I've seen nothing.'

'Really.' Judith had been hiding something in the folds of her cassock. With a snarl of anger, she stepped forward, knife in hand.

'Arthur!' Portia cried.

Just as he started to charge Judith, Sybil came from behind him, brandishing her sword and shouting, 'This land is *sacred*. How dare you defile it!'

Judith spun out of St. Just's path to charge at Sybil. In a nicely judged movement, Sybil sidestepped the attack, and began walking backwards in slow measured steps towards the cliff's edge, waving the sword in Judith's face.

A warning shout stuck in Portia's throat; something told her Sybil could gauge the distance. She had, after all, spent much of her life on this clifftop and knew its contours and dimensions intimately.

Again Judith charged, shrieking wildly.

Portia, shaking, thought she glimpsed two hands gripping the edge of the cliff to one side. Someone had climbed to the top? She thought she must be hallucinating.

Suddenly, she became aware of Judith running towards her like a footballer, her arm pulled back, ready to strike. St. Just aimed himself at her feet for a flying tackle.

As Portia, with a neat, last-minute sidestep of her own, let Judith's velocity carry her over the cliff, her feet pedalling madly in the air as they lost touch with the ground.

Judith's scream as she took her deadly tumble would stay with Portia for a very long time.

The Maidens looked on in silent witness.

THIRTY-TWO

Rescue Me

As Portia had been trying to talk Judith down, the scene was skylined in full view of an assemblage of villagers, who thought they were witnessing a tombstoning stunt. The police had been alerted earlier by Sybil on discovering her sacred space had been invaded. The call centre was ready to dismiss her rambling story of pagan rites until Sybil said the magic words: 'Lord Bodwally's killer.' She claimed Judith was about to commit another murder at the Fourteen Maidens.

And that she, Sybil, wouldn't be held accountable for her actions if rescue didn't get there right away.

Callum Page, alerted to the emergency by a surging mob of villagers, stood sweeping his torch up and down the face of the cliff. The rain was still coming down, shredding the light from the torch. Beside him stood DCI Mousse.

'I'm going for it,' Callum said. His voice in the wind was staticky, like a poor radio signal.

'Climb the cliff, you mean? Don't be a fool, man. It'll be suicide in this weather. And it's been soaking for hours.'

'I've done worse and survived. I'll fetch my kit.'

Mousse didn't stay to argue: he could see no other option and no way to stop him, besides. Rescue would have qualified men and equipment, but rescue wasn't here yet. Whoever Callum was, he was an experienced climber. They could sort out the name-change business uncovered by the investigation later.

Still, Mousse wished there was another way, one that didn't put a civilian in mortal danger. He looked about him, assessing his options for rescuing Portia, his mind glancing off the limited choices, from climbing up behind Callum (impossible at his age and probably dangerous for Callum), to running up the lane and scrambling over trees to the top of the cliff (barely possible, and it could take hours), to ringing for a rescue helicopter (which he had done, but would *it* be in time? Could it land up there in this weather?), to trying to throw a rope up to Portia (no).

Just what they needed now – another victim. His mind shied away from the 'V' word but this was the reality of where they were now. Portia was obviously in danger of some kind – all he could see from the bottom of the cliff was a sort of pantomime, but her gestures appeared to be placating or pleading, while Judith's stance was menacing. Meanwhile, all he could do was stand by, wringing his hands and trying his best to stay calm. It was maddening, quite literally. Every outcome he could imagine was more dire than the last.

He watched and waited, frantic with frustration, as minutes later

Callum began to rope up, moving with agonizing slowness, the footholds too precarious and slick for haste, the slip of a foot on mud a guarantee of disaster.

Just as he reached the top the scream came.

Good *God*, that scream.

And a figure came flying through the air, growing larger as it approached. It landed not six yards from where Mousse stood.

Constable Whitelaw, his voice a hoarse shout, nearly inaudible against the *whup whup whup* of arriving rescue blades, ran to his side.

'What is that? Who?'

Mousse shook his head – no idea.

Portia. Please not.

He walked towards the misshapen mass.

St. Just saw Callum's white-blond head emerge at the top of the cliff. It was complete madness, but the man had apparently climbed up the side.

'You're a moment too late,' St. Just told him, holding Portia more tightly in his arms. 'But thanks anyway.'

'Don't mention it,' said Callum.

A red-and-white Coastguard Search and Rescue helicopter thundered into view just as the inshore lifeboat crew set off para flares to light the area for the rescue teams. There wasn't enough space for even an expert pilot to land and St. Just waved them off. The wind and rain made it too dangerous to attempt and, thankfully, there was no need.

But as the Coastguard craft sheared off, another helicopter, this one red and yellow and stamped *Cornwall Air Ambulance*, boomed overhead, no doubt on its way to the nearest beach, looking for a spot to land. The craft was so close St. Just felt he could reach out to shake the hand of the pilot, who nodded and waved. He tried to shield Portia as best he could from the din, holding her tightly. He could feel her heart beating violently against his chest, nearly in time with the chuff of the whirring rotors of the helicopter.

He knew what the rescue crews would find. Far below on the exposed rocks lay the body of the woman who called herself Judith. She could not possibly have survived. The inshore lifeboats would also have responded, but St. Just doubted they'd be needed.

She was not going to be harming anyone, again.

Much later, he and Portia sat sipping brandy by the fireplace in Seaside Cottage. It had taken over an hour to climb down the path, crawling over fallen branches, occasionally slipping in the mud.

Portia sat bundled in her fluffy pink bathrobe, which she clutched tightly to her neck. Even after a long, hot shower, she was shivering.

'What on earth was Callum doing there?' she asked.

'Just so you know, that's not his real name. He changed it, presumably taking a stage name at the start of his career.'

'Oh! I sort of vaguely knew that. It's something I picked up from my students. But the world knows him as Callum Page, the way the world knows Michael Caine as Michael Caine, not as Maurice Micklewhite.'

'Mm-hmm. I rather wish you'd thought to mention it. He was briefly considered a suspect because of it.'

'You didn't seem to like talking about him.'

'Yes, well, anyway. He was the son of Morwenna Wells and Titus Bodwally. His given name was Mermen Wells – Bodwally having wanted nothing to do with him, at least at first.'

She snapped her fingers. 'I remember now. He needed to join Equity, and they already had a Mermen Wells on their list, believe it or not. Two actors with the same name aren't allowed, so he changed the name he used professionally to Callum Page. Liking the change – it brought him luck in landing acting roles – he later changed his name legally by deed poll.'

'It would seem he came here to establish a firmer connection with his birth father,' said St. Just, who had earlier been updated by Mousse. 'A young Callum, pre-fame, was working as a waiter in France when they met, apparently by chance.'

'So the play on words in the dedication is exactly that: a play on words. Bodwally was finally acknowledging Callum as his son, but in a way only Callum would understand.'

'It would have been nice if Callum or Morwenna had thought to tell us about their connection to Bodwally,' said St. Just.

'But it gave them a motive: he'd rejected them both. It's no wonder they didn't say.'

St. Just sighed. 'I wish the public wouldn't treat the police like natural enemies out to trick them into life sentences but they do and there you have it.'

'Morwenna's experiences in the Plague Time probably taught her caution in dealing with authority.'

'Hmm. Anyway, you were going to tell me about the cave.'

'Right.' She stretched out her feet before her. 'It was Bodwally who tried to put me on to it but I listened with only half an ear. This might teach me a lesson on paying better attention. I thought at first he was saying foo-goo – a nonsense word. A fogou is generally enclosed, but this one happened to lead into a tunnel. Sepia knew all about it. She told me the tunnel had been dug from the crypt of St. Cuthbert's down to what had been a smuggler's cave behind the Fourteen Maidens. The tunnel opened into the ceremonial chamber you saw, which Sybil had converted into a sort of shrine to her daughter.'

'With those colourful rainbow walls, it looks more like an infant school. You wouldn't think it was a place designed for worship.'

'I would think it was designed for nothing else.'

'Yes.' St. Just took a slow sip of his brandy. 'I do know what you mean. It's magnificent, isn't it? A spectacular accident of nature.'

'Sybil wanted it kept secret from the tourists. She thought they'd spoil the quiet.'

'She was right about that.'

'Anyway, Sepia told me the fogou had been expanded as an escape route. Cornwall at one time was rife with smugglers who left behind countless caves and tunnels. Most of the tunnels remain unexplored, because nearly all of them are too dangerous to enter. Bodwally had discovered this one by accident and wanted to write about it.'

She lifted her glass in a *More, please* gesture, and he complied.

'Bodwally seemed to think the whole thing was ripe for a landslide, by the way,' she said. 'That cliff face is fragile, and even though the church itself was built on bedrock, the tunnel beneath probably destabilized the area further. The contents of the graveyard, coffins and bodies and all, might one day tumble on to the Fourteen Maidens, or further down into the village itself. Something similar happened at Whitby.'

'What an appalling image.'

'Sybil won't be pleased.'

'I did wonder at some point if Sybil might resent the intrusion into "her" space enough to kill over it. Once I saw her brandishing that sword, I certainly was convinced she was capable.'

Unexpectedly – they were now into the wee hours – St. Just's mobile rang. He reached to retrieve it from the coffee table.

'We've found the vicar,' Mousse informed him.

'I didn't know we were looking for the vicar,' said St. Just.

'It's Peder Wolfe. He's in the tunnel you found. Quite dead, I'm afraid. Has been for some time.'

'Just lying there?'

'He was folded inside a big chest and tucked into a chamber carved out of one side. Although he'd been wrapped in plastic, he was beginning to decompose; someone had tried to conceal the fact by burning incense and spraying the area with deodorizer. If I had to guess, he's been dead since the Reverend Judith Abernathy first blew into the village. I'd say it's past time we looked into that more closely – exactly what she was doing here in Maidsfell. Apart from being a serial killer.'

'How did Wolfe die?'

'Preliminarily, it looks like another stabbing. It's a clean wound and no signs of a struggle so he may have been incapacitated first – most likely drugged. No sign of a weapon.'

'I think we know who had the weapon.'

THIRTY-THREE
All's Well

Saturday

The next day, St. Just and Portia were finally able to pick up the threads of what remained of their holiday. St. Just had made dinner reservations at Morwenna's for seven o'clock.

At six they were drinking an aperitif at Seaside Cottage, revisiting the events of the past few days.

They both would have preferred seeing Judith brought to justice. Had she avoided detection, she might one day have moved on to another position with no one the wiser. Having discovered how easy it was to take over a parish church as a temporary fill-in, she might have replayed the stunt all over the UK. Churches were often run by people who were too trusting for their own good. Peder Wolfe had learned this the hard way.

A file was being prepared for the coroner by DCI Mousse and an inquest into the deaths of the Reverend Wolfe, Lord Titus Bodwally, and Mr Will Ivey would soon be opened and adjourned at Cornwall Coroner's Court; hearings would be held later to establish the full circumstances. St. Just and Portia might have to return to Cornwall, this time to Truro, although they might be offered a video-link to testify, as had become more common since the Plague Time.

'I still have a lot of questions,' said Portia.

St. Just said, 'As do I. But here's how we think it played out – how Bodwally came to be poisoned and later stabbed, the poisoning attempt having failed to kill him.'

'Right. Do go on. From the start. More wine?'

'Might as well. Why be sensible? We leave tomorrow and we shouldn't travel with an open bottle in the car.'

'You are always sensible.'

He held out his glass for a refill and settled deeper into the cushions. 'On Tuesday evening, Will gave the poison fish to Judith. Her visit to his house appears on the bank's CCTV for that day. We nearly missed this bit of footage because at first the police were only interested in the boat fire.

'Even though she isn't recognizable on the tape at Will's, she carries a basket that is – but it's of a design common in these parts. As Will is on the St. Cuthbert's list for pastoral care, she doesn't really need a reason beyond that for being there, in case anyone sees her coming or going. She knew there was a chance she might appear on the bank's CCTV but she'd think it didn't matter, and she was right. Even once we knew or suspected it was Judith in the footage – because she had possession of that colourful basket that often passed between Morwenna and her – she might well have been bringing Will vegetables or something from St. Cuthbert's Delivers. She was in fact bringing Will his usual allotment and doing a welfare check on him. But she was collecting something, as well.'

'An exotic, poisonous fish. How did she know he had such a thing?'

'He had to have told her about the fish he caught, all excited by his find – he thinks it's a sort of miracle because a fish like that is very seldom seen in these waters. It's quite a beautiful thing, too, with the gold stripes. Will Ivey was a religious man – sober or not, he was one of the regulars at St. Cuthbert's. He was also part of the AA group that met there every week.'

'"They that go down to the sea in ships,"' she murmured.

'"That do business in great waters,"' he answered. 'Precisely. People in such risky professions must live their lives in heightened awareness of how quickly it can all end.'

'He never saw through Judith.'

'He never did. By all accounts, he was legless with drink half the time, so if she said she was a priest, why would he question it? Why would anyone? Only Sybil, who tends to focus on this sort of thing – the religious trappings, if you will – caught the discrepancies here and there. The bits of services that were sometimes out of order or forgotten altogether. The rest of the parishioners put it down to nervousness or forgetfulness. But there was one mistake no priest would ever make, and Sybil caught it. Judith was play-acting and, to her, all priestly garb was just costuming, so she chose one day to wear a gown or whatever it's called with the "pretty" ruffled sleeves. She had no clue, of course. Only a bishop is allowed to wear such a thing.

'As it happens, she officiated at a number of marriage ceremonies, all of which are now rendered invalid. Everyone will need a do-over.'

'Oh, my. So back to Judith at Will Ivey's cottage. She takes the fish from him, after ooh-ing and ahh-ing over the miraculous find. Wouldn't he go straight to the pub and show off pictures of his amazing catch?'

'I wondered that, too,' said St. Just. 'I think when he rang her she suggested he not tell anyone, as it might cause a panic in the fishing industry. Poison fish in these waters is all the fishers need to further upend their industry.'

'Ah. That would work.'

'Or she asked him to wait, because she'd be preparing it – safely – as a special surprise for someone. In fact, I think Judith probably told Bodwally that Morwenna had prepared the meal she shared with him Tuesday night – a lie, just in case he survived the poisoning. Remember him saying "She'll kill me next time"?'

'I do,' said Portia.

'It was always a matter of time before Judith would have to do away with Will, I'm afraid, even though the poison fish plot didn't work. Once Bodwally was murdered for real, with a knife, Will might have put two and two together, or at least may have found the coincidence too big to believe.

'Anyway, Judith knew that type of fish was dangerous unless carefully prepared. Even though the head of the fish contains most of the poison, it's not simply a matter of chopping off the head. And how does she know all this? She probably saw an article when a fisherman caught another *Sarpa salpa* the year before – it made the national news. Something about climate change affecting the currents that bring the fish to the UK. A bit of online searching would enhance her knowledge – the vicarage computer showed someone had done such a search.

'Also, there was the case of elderly Christopher Carew, a recipient of meals from St. Cuthbert's Delivers. He fell deathly ill after consuming the *Sarpa salpa* and began acting strangely – more strangely than before. He was already thought to be showing the first signs of dementia, but it was discovered he had eaten the fish also. This event, known round the village, probably gave Judith an idea for how to do away with Bodwally in a way that couldn't be brought to her door, since everyone knew Carew's poisoning was accidental.

'But if she was planning actually to murder Bodwally with it – perhaps lead him into foolish behaviour, like tombstoning or driving a car under the influence, or simply to kill him outright – she got the dosage wrong.'

'Perhaps she just wanted to torment him first, see him suffer, before going in for the kill.'

'Perhaps,' he agreed. 'She's also Cornish, so of course she knows something of fish.'

'I didn't realize she was Cornish. She'd lost much of the accent.'

'Yes, but she didn't lose the turn of phrase. Remember what she said about Christmas when we first met her in the coffee shop? "My husband died right in the Christmas," she said. That line gave away her origins. Only someone with roots in Cornwall would use those words in exactly that way. She also called Bodwally a "heller". Pure Cornish.'

'Anyway, she invites Bodwally for dinner on the pretext of discussing his gift to the church, and to thank him. He's just updated his will, leaving St. Cuthbert's a large bequest. When I spoke with her, she pretended not to know this because she was afraid of being asked *when* she was told of it – as it happened, at that meant-to-be-fatal dinner.'

'But he doesn't die; he simply feels a bit off.'

'And the next day he complains about what a terrible cook Morwenna was!'

'So, she takes the fish from Will. You know, perhaps she pretends with Will she's worried about how to cook it since it can be poison. He offers to prepare it for her.'

'Here we were thinking only a pro could handle a fish like this,' said St. Just. 'We were right, except we forgot that Will *was* a pro. He just wasn't called a "chef".'

'Right,' said Portia. 'So maybe she watched as Will did the prep, and when he wasn't looking, retrieved the discarded, deadly bits from the rubbish. Her plan may have been to set Will up to take a fall when Bodwally died. But Bodwally was only mildly affected and simply found the whole thing embarrassing. Hallucinating out of his mind is a bad look for a lord.'

'Not realizing he'd been deliberately poisoned. Do you know, for a while I was certain Morwenna was involved because of the themes of food and fish and knives and cooking. I thought perhaps he'd rejected the wrong woman – an unstable one. But what she actually said was, some people aren't cut out for double harness.'

'She might have been talking about herself – a successful businesswoman. Rejecting *him*.'

'You're quite right. My earlier thinking was a bit sexist, wasn't it?'

Portia shrugged. 'Assumptions die hard.'

'Must work on that. Sorry. If you and I broke up, the world would know it was your idea. They'd only have to look at me. Do keep giving me chances, will you?'

'Of course,' she said. 'Do keep earning them. So, Callum is Bodwally's son. His son with Morwenna. Bodwally disowned both his son *and* his daughter.'

'Right. But in a certain justice, Callum will almost certainly inherit Revellick House, there being no other blood relatives.'

'I can't picture Callum giving up a life of derring-do to plan spring borders and dig in rose gardens, can you?'

'Not really. Perhaps he'll sell it to the National Trust and they can use it to host events, like weddings. But I have a feeling – Callum reaching the age where climbing every mountain holds less appeal – he may indeed be thinking of settling down. At least for a while, he might find it fun to play lord of the manor.'

'What gives you this feeling?' she asked.

'I saw him having dinner with Ramona Raven last night. They looked like they were having a grand time.'

Portia was astonished. 'Callum and Ramona? But . . . she must have ten years on him.'

'So?'

'Oh. Well, you're right. So what? Talk about being sexist. And now I think of it, the romance writer and the man of romantic adventures – that's a match made in heaven. Nora Roberts could do something with that plot.'

'Plus, Ramona gets to be the mistress of Revellick House. Surely that is her dream come true.'

Portia sat back, wrangling a pillow into position against her spine. St. Just put down his glass to help.

'Wasn't Bodwally supposed to have a wife somewhere?'

St. Just shook his head. 'There's no record of it. It would appear he was lying to get rid of Ramona. Probably not the first time he used that lie, knowing what we know of him.'

'Speaking of which, why did Sybil lie?'

'About her alibi for Bodwally's death, you mean?'

'Yes. She told you she was at home at the time, right? But if that wasn't true, where was she?'

'She was at the cave where she often sleeps, guarding the place.'

'Ah, of course. I get it. She doesn't want anyone to know about that astonishing cave, especially the tourists.'

'She wants no one to see her shrine to her daughter.'

'The poor woman.'

'Technically, she was trespassing, and she may have thought she'd be in trouble for it. I only know I'll never tell a soul.'

'Neither will I.'

THIRTY-FOUR
Come Fly with Me

St. Just checked his watch. *Plenty of time.*

'Arthur, I still don't understand. What was Judith's motive?'

'Good old revenge, I'm afraid.'

'There was a lot of that to go round. Ex-girlfriends, ex-lovers, people with ruined wedding plans. But . . . revenge for what exactly?'

He hesitated. 'She couldn't forget. And she couldn't forgive. Beneath the appearance of a life of service to others, she was seething with rage.' He shook his head. 'I had no inkling. I feel I should have *known* something was off there.'

'If everyone were a mind reader, we wouldn't need police,' said Portia. 'Or . . . come to think of it, we'd need them even more. Imagine being able to read each other's thoughts? The fights that would break out? Anyway, you missed the signs of severe mental trauma and so did I.'

'It really was staring me in the face. But I was derailed, thinking the murder had something to do with the fishermen's fight with the council. In part because of Ivey's death, and also it was all anyone really talked about.'

'So, it was a sort of spontaneous killing, was it? In a fit of rage, she decided she couldn't take any more – maybe Bodwally rejected her?'

'Rejected her? If anything, he probably thought she'd be easy prey because of her evident religious leanings, which I think amounted to a mania. A heightened sense of retribution, of the need to set things right – by divine right. But this killing had nothing to do with her being a jilted lover. Or not.'

'No?'

'No. And it was anything but a spontaneous crime, although I'm sure a good solicitor would have convinced her to plead it out that way. No, this took planning and a degree of reckless courage. She followed Bodwally to the village, and once settled in at St. Cuthbert's, she simply bided her time.

'Just as she did when she stole her new identity from the nursing facility where she worked. And where, by the way, she picked up some rudimentary knowledge of medicine and anatomy. The knife attack on Bodwally was precise, the blade inserted exactly where it would do immediate and fatal damage.

'Anyway, most people involved in identity theft are anything but spontaneous. They plot, they plan, they wait. The only time Judith improvised was when I cornered her at the church, forcing her to flee. Her inability to think that through, the need to improvise, is what led to her failure. Improv was not her strength; she was more like a stage actress who dresses the part and gets her lines down pat through constant rehearsal. Probably she spent hours on her sermons and had to practise them over and over in front of a mirror. The same with the liturgy.'

'Well, she certainly fooled me. It's rather awful how we take people at face value, especially when they're wearing a uniform or, in this case, clerical garb.'

'She fooled you and the villagers just long enough. She fooled the nursing home for six months. She had an entire life story mapped out. Everyone believed her. Not one word was true. She knew her local curate had been admitted to the care facility so she applied for a job there, using fake credentials. When the time was ripe she stole the curate's identity.'

'What was her real name, anyway?'

'Jane Smith.'

'You're joking.'

'No middle name, either, just plain Jane Smith.'

'I suppose that sort of anonymity can be useful.'

'The media are having a field day. So much for our holiday.'

'It's a holiday to remember, Arthur. Many people would envy us.'

'Do you think?'

He peered over at the view from the patio – that view! – and fought the rising temptation to move to Cornwall and take up the job left by DCI Mousse. It would mean a career settling boundary disputes between villagers and weekenders and being the last word on parking violations. He could adapt, he thought, but despite what she'd said, he knew Portia's life work was in Cambridge.

But if there were children one day? A part of him wanted them to have the sort of upbringing only a village childhood could provide.

'We could buy a weekend cottage here,' he said.

Portia smiled. 'Don't even joke about being a weekender,' she said. 'Not after all this. Retirement will come soon enough.'

He persisted: 'We could buy a house on the water with a big kitchen made for long mornings lingering over the newspaper with coffee and bread and chocolate. We might go for a stroll, pack a picnic lunch. I'd bring my paints, you could bring your notebook.

'Think of a life like that. As opposed to what we do now. Always chasing about with the blare of traffic horns our background noise.'

'You're serious. About moving here.'

'At some point in the future? Yes, I think I am. Could you be happy here?'

'I don't see how anyone could fail to be happy here,' she said. 'They'd need their heads examined. But I will be unhappy now if you don't rather quickly tell me what Judith's motive was. Jane's, I mean. Let's just call her Judith for simplicity's sake. What did she have against Bodwally that would make her go to all this trouble? That would make her want to kill him?'

'You remember Judith's husband?'

'I assume he never existed.'

'No, that was the one truth she did tell. She was a widow. Her husband owned a small business in London. A men's clothing store he'd built from the ground up. During the Plague Time, he was forced to close. Loans he had taken out came due. He tried to get government assistance, but it wasn't nearly enough to cover a year and a half with no income. He asked the lender for an extension, for help of any kind. It was denied.'

'Don't tell me. Bodwally.'

'His company. Yes. His financial services, for which he became Lord Bodwally, shedding plain old Titus Bodwally the way a snake sheds its skin. His amorous incontinence among other things led us to ignore his business dealings, which surely were as corrupt as the man himself.

'To Judith, he came to personify all that was evil, all that was cruel, all that was unfair in the world. She began to unravel. Almost for something to do, to prevent herself following her husband in suicide, she came up with this elaborate scheme of revenge.'

'Oh my,' Portia said. 'To be left behind by the suicide of a loved one. Now I feel rather awful.'

'Don't. You were preserving your own life. You thought on your feet and you survived. Judith . . . well, we can say Judith was never going to make it, never be restored to the life she'd had. Don't ever blame yourself for her death.'

Portia did not reply. She took a sip of her wine, sadness deepening her dark-blue eyes.

'Here's one thing *I* don't understand,' said St. Just, to distract her.

'Only one?'

'The fourteenth maiden, as we now know, is inside the cave. The belief was always that the fourteenth standing stone had been shoved over the side of the cliff by long-ago pranksters. In fact, didn't Sybil tell us that? But instead, it had been moved into the cave. The gap in the horseshoe circle was replaced by the prayer tree.'

'There's no way Sybil could have managed to move that,' said Portia. 'It's massive.'

'No, no. I'm talking centuries ago. That cave with its missing maiden went undiscovered for who knows how long. Perhaps Sybil was the first in this century to notice and explore that narrow opening into the cave.'

'It was Sybil's private and sacred space – a memorial to her daughter,' agreed Portia. 'It was where Sybil worshipped, without the distraction of other people. She would have done pretty much anything to keep the place secret. Did Judith find out, do you think?'

'That the tunnel under the church led down to the cave of the Fourteen Maidens? That's what I'm wondering. I'm sure at first she had no idea – she'd not been here long, recall. And it's a creepy place to explore – dark and spidery, not to mention full of rats. Perhaps her predecessor knew the church and the cave were joined by that tunnel, and it seems Lord Bodwally heard the rumours – perhaps from the vicar. *Her* interest in the tunnel was that it made the perfect place to hide the body of the vicar she'd killed. She may even have hoped to take over his job permanently. She told Church officials he'd gone "on retreat", sent emails from the vicarage computer to that effect, and when he didn't come back, counted on them letting her keep the position.'

'Maidsfell being a perfect hideout, far from the world.' Portia nodded. 'No wonder she was on the side of the fishers, as she told us. She wanted to keep the village as hidden from the outside as possible.'

'It could have been a sinecure for life, I suppose. Rather in the way Sybil has a job for life, since no one can be bothered to see what she's up to, and she does such a good job keeping the Fourteen Maidens in order.'

'Clear up another minor mystery for me if you can,' said Portia, turning to him. 'Why did Morwenna do such a sudden about-turn at the village meeting? One minute she's waving the banner for the fishers, and the next minute she'll not say a word on the topic, at least not in public.'

'I did ask her. She said, seeing various faces in the audience, she remembered something about the wisdom of not casting the first stone. Although she didn't say explicitly – not to a policeman, she wouldn't – the way she ran her business during the Plague Time wasn't all it should have been, and she didn't want word to get back to the council, who could shut her down any time they wanted. At best, they'd inspect her to within an inch of her life.'

He glanced at his watch. Not for the first time that afternoon.

'Are you late for an appointment, Arthur? Should I be hurrying to get dressed for dinner?'

'No, no. Not yet. Everything's fine. Let me get you another drink.'

'I'll just get changed. Let's have a drink at the restaurant.'

On the advice of Ramona Raven, romance writer, St. Just had booked a banner plane to fly over the harbour at six forty-five, the banner to read *Portia Marry Me*.

It was completely out of character for him, which is why Ramona insisted he do it. 'Marriage is full of ups and downs but as long

as she can remember the time you gave your all for her, even at
the risk of looking foolish, she will fly at your side for life. Trust
me on this. If more men took such risks – well, I'd be out of
business. Their women wouldn't be reading my books and
dreaming of a better life with the pool boy, now, would they?'
This coming from a woman who was well on her way to attaining
her heart's desire: handsome and dashing Callum Wells for a
husband and a manor house to live in . . . *well*. Who was he,
St. Just, to doubt she knew what she was doing?

So he'd placed the order with Mercury's Flying Messengers.
It was not inexpensive and he'd baulked at the price, but now
he couldn't wait to see it for himself, and witness the look of
delight on Portia's face. From about five in the afternoon of
that day, the last day before their return to Cambridge, he kept
checking his watch.

'Do you have a bus to catch?' Portia emerged from the bedroom
in a sapphire-blue dress, the colour perfectly matching her eyes.
She had tied her hair in a heavy knot at her neck, threaded with
a matching piece of blue silk. Her earrings were a shimmering
cascade of gold falling to her shoulders, emphasizing her long
neck. They caught the light like glowing chandeliers.

'What? No, I just . . . wondered what time it was.'

'It's ten minutes later than the last time you looked. For a
policeman, you're a terrible liar, Arthur.'

'What do you mean, for a policeman? It's not an occupational
hazard. I may stretch the truth at times with a suspect but only
to imply I know more than I do, and only in the pursuit of
justice, and only when I'm quite sure I'm on the right track.'

'I see. And the first time your hunch is wrong – what then?'

'I wouldn't be able to live with myself. I'd make it right, no
matter what it took.'

'I know,' she said. 'And that is what I love about you, Arthur.'

Her studies as a criminologist had left her with a learned
scepticism of the police. When he'd asked once why she'd resisted
his overtures for so long, she'd said, 'I wasn't used to the idea
of a decent, hard-working, honest policeman. A policeman without
a lot of angsty baggage and a drinking problem and a snarky
teenager. I couldn't believe you were for real.'

His ears strained now for the sound of a plane's engine. *Just a few minutes to go.* He was confident the pilot would be on the dot of time. He'd seemed the type to be ruled by the clock and had seemed offended at the suggestion he might run late because of some unforeseen eventuality.

'I plan ahead,' Dieter had said in his heavily accented English. 'My plane runs with maximum efficiency always.'

So St. Just had said what he wanted, given the man his credit card information, and – pleased with the vision of himself as a hero of romance – sat back to await the look of stunned amazement on Portia's face.

'I almost forgot!' said St. Just. 'I bought you a present. Something to help you remember our visit.'

'I don't think I could forget our visit any time soon. Will it always be like this, do you think? Every holiday a busman's holiday?'

'I sincerely hope not,' he said over his shoulder, going to retrieve a package from the hall closet where he'd hidden it.

'I bought you a present as well. An engagement present.' She vanished into the kitchen, emerging with a package shaped almost identically to his, flat and rectangular, and wrapped in brown paper.

They sat together on the sofa and tore off the wrappings.

'Oh, Arthur,' she sighed, on seeing her gift. It was the painting she had admired at Sepia's gallery.

His turned out to be the marvellous painting of the cliff.

'It's perfect,' they said together, laughing.

At last, the sound of a small engine spluttered overhead. Taking her hand, he walked her quickly to the door and partway down the lane.

'Look up! Look up!' he cried, pointing at the small plane, its banner trailing behind.

Porsche Marry Me, read the banner.

Oh no! No!

'Portia! *Portia!*' he exclaimed. 'I told him clearly. Portia! Of all the knuckleheaded . . .'

'It's all right, Arthur,' she said, laughing. 'Maybe you can get your money back, or a third of it. He got the other two-thirds right. Was the pilot German, by any chance?'

'He was, as it happens. This is my fault; I should have spelled it out for him. He didn't ask, and of course I assumed. Who doesn't know the name of one of Shakespeare's most famous characters?

Who wouldn't think to ask if he didn't know? Why would anyone name their child after a car, for that matter?'

'Lots of people, as it happens. It's the thought that counts, Arthur. And of course I'll marry you. Haven't I said so already?'

'I thought . . . well, I actually . . . I thought for a minute you might be interested in Callum.'

'You are joking. Aren't you?'

'No, I mean, he is everything a woman could want. Brave, handsome, fit. Wealthy. Even *more* wealthy now.'

'And living a boy's own adventure tale. I could never see him as anything but a slightly deranged friend. Honestly, Arthur. What gets into you? Besides, I have it on good authority – *Women's Day* magazine – until just recently he was engaged to marry an adventure psychologist and polar explorer. Pauline something. Before he met Ramona, of course. She's a much better match, don't you think?'

'What on earth is an adventure psychologist?'

'God knows. Someone who analyzes adventurous people? It's a wonder she can get them to sit still.'

He gathered her to him. 'I should say you're the adventurous type. Being a writer should come with danger money if our time here is anything to go by.'

'Quite right. Even literary skirmishes in the safety of publishers' offices are not for the faint-hearted.'

'I just wanted to make sure all this hadn't changed your mind. Sorry about the plane. I still find it hard to believe any woman in her right mind would marry a policeman . . .'

Portia sought his eyes. 'Not that again! Arthur, look at me. Your job carries risks. But if you were a polar explorer or a bin man or a brain surgeon, it wouldn't matter. I fell in love with the man you are. The caring, compassionate soul who doesn't suffer fools and who only wants to set the world to rights. And is so disappointed it can't always be done. Fools prosper, scoundrels lie, villains get away with murder.

'I'm not sure you and I can change that, but we can try, and I know for certain we can do more together than apart.

'Marry you? I've never been so sure of anything in my life.'

Printed in the USA
CPSIA information can be obtained
at www.ICGtesting.com
JSHW022120060524
62644JS00001B/122